COINS
OF
CHAOS

Edited by
Jennifer Brozek

EDGE SCIENCE FICTION AND FANTASY PUBLISHING
AN IMPRINT OF HADES PUBLICATIONS, INC.

CALGARY

Coins of Chaos
Copyright © 2013
Release: Canada: Fall 2013 / USA: Winter 2014

Edge Science Fiction and Fantasy Publishing
An Imprint of Hades Publications Inc.
P.O. Box 1714, Calgary, Alberta, T2P 2L7, Canada

Edited by Jennifer Brozek

"Silver and Copper, Iron and Ash" ©2013 Nathaniel Lee, "The Price of Serenity" ©2013 Kelly Swails, "Vinegar Pie" ©2013 Andrew Penn Romine, "The Fall of Jolly Tannum" ©2013 Brandie Tarvin, "Spendthrift" ©2013 Joseph E. Lake, Jr., "Incubus Nickel" ©2013 Erik Scott de Bie, "In His Name" ©2013 Martin Livings, "Lies of the Flesh" ©2013 Nathan Crowder, "Train Yard Blues" ©2013 Seanan McGuire, "Skull of Snakes" ©2013 Glenn Rolfe, "Searching for a Hero" ©2013 Dylan Birtolo, "Something in the Blood" ©2013 Kelly Lagor, "The Value of a Year of Tears and Sorrow" ©2013 Jason Andrew, "Definitely Dvořák" ©2013 Mae Empson, "Justice in Five Cents" ©2013 Richard Dansky, "Tithes" ©2013 Peter M. Ball, "With One Coin for Fee: An Invocation of Sorts" ©2013 Gary A. Braunbeck. Interior design by Janice Blaine, Interior art ©2013 John Ward
Cover art ©2013 Amber Clark

ISBN: 978-1-77053-048-5

EDGE Science Fiction and Fantasy Publishing and Hades Publications, Inc. acknowledges the ongoing support of the Alberta Foundation for the Arts and the Canada Council for the Arts for our publishing programme.

Library and Archives Canada Cataloguing in Publication

Coins of chaos / Jennifer Brozek, editor.
ISBN: 978-1-77053-048-5   (e-Book ISBN: 978-1-77053-049-2)

1. Science fiction, American. 2. Short stories, American.
3. American fiction--21st century. I. Brozek, Jennifer, 1970-, editor of compilation

PS648.S3C63 2013   813'.087620806   C2013-903263-0
C2013-903264-9

FIRST EDITION
(J-20130820)
Printed in Canada
www.edgewebsite.com

TABLE OF CONTENTS

WHY WOULD SOMEONE LIKE ME — *a magician steeped in the mysteries of magic — turn to something as mundane as a coin to fuel a great spell? The answer is simple: no one ever believes a coin worth so little can carry so much power. The beauty in this ritual's design is the fact that, like children, once I set these coins upon the world, I no longer have control over them. They will succeed or fail upon their own merit.*

I chose the 1913 Buffalo nickel because of a homeless man. He showed me the power such a small bit of art could carry. I am not the only Carver. I am one of many. Yet, I believe I am the only Carver who has attempted such a ritual as this.

Which is why I carved each nickel with care. They carry with them the seeds of my life, my success, and should anyone discover them all, my destruction. Twenty coins in total. Each one different than the last. Each imbued with chaos, hate, pain, and desire for destruction. With each life destroyed, taken, maimed, ruined, lost ... my life goes on. These coins are my immortality.

With other magic, I follow these coins on their journey through time and space. I examine each life sacrificed so I may be eternal. I'm willing to share seventeen stories from across the ages with you. Just seventeen. It would not be in my best interest to let you see them all, now would it? Powerful though I am, unwary I am not.

But I will let you see. It is why you have paid my price after all. I always honor my debts.

— The Carver

SILVER AND COPPER, IRON AND ASH

NATHANIEL LEE

THE RABBIT'S BACK WAS BROKEN, clenched in the smooth jaws of the trap. Its blood speckled the snow around it like a poisonous mushroom. James grunted and knelt to the ground to laboriously pry the jaws apart and claim his prize; the first success in a long day of checking the trapline. The creature wasn't much — rice-wafer bones and wispy, patchy fur — but it would mean meat in the pot, another few days of life and warmth in the icy chill.

James pushed the spring-loaded black iron arc back until it clicked, the hammer lifting into place like a spider sensing vibrations on its web. He scuffed dirt and leaf-litter gently across the newly reset trap and stood to carry his kill away before cleaning it; no sense filling the whole clearing with the smell of blood and scaring away everything but sour-fleshed predators and scavenger birds.

"Nice rabbit you got there," came a sudden voice from the shadows under the trees.

James spun, his knife already in his gloved hands. A man stood a short distance away, clad in a ragged coat that was far too thin for the Colorado mountain winter that was fast upon them. The man raised his hands in supplication.

"No harm meant, sir, no harm meant. If I'd wanted to steal, I'd'a made off with that rabbit whilst a-waiting for you to come." The man's beard was as mangy as the rabbit's fur, his skin pasty gray and unwholesome. All the past year and more, James had seen far too many men like this on his infrequent trips to town;

1

hungry men questing toward the coast in search of food and work, their farms and their lives dried to dust and blown out from beneath them.

"I've got nothing to give," James said shortly, not lowering his knife. "If you head down the mountain into the Springs, there's a mission can give you a blanket and a bowl of soup, at least."

"Aye, there would be," the tramp said, "if they weren't full to bursting already. Please, sir, I wouldn't ask if I weren't in need. A warm place to sleep, a cup of something hot. Might be as how you've some work needs doing, repairs to a shed or hauling or some such?" The man's crooked teeth glistened as he bared them in what was likely meant to be an ingratiating grin.

"We've nothing to spare and no work needs doing." James' conscience bit at him, and under its goad he heaved a sigh. "But wait for a spell, and I'll carve you some of this rabbit, at least. What's left will do for stew, and that'll be more than we'd have had otherwise."

The tramp's eyes gleamed, and he nodded his approval. James dusted off a handy stump and set to work with practiced hands. In a few short moments, he'd stripped the carcass of skin and offal, lifting the thin haunches and the lion's share of the meat for the other.

"No wax paper, I'm afraid," James said, in a weak attempt at a joke. He folded the skin and the offal aside, intending to get every bit of use he could out of the unlucky creature. Something clinked when he did. "What's this?" With his knife, James slit the rabbit's stomach open, and after a moment's rooting, came out with a silver coin. The tramp made a gasping sound, quickly strangled. James' mouth twisted. "No wonder the dumb beast was so thin, if this was filling its stomach."

The coin was a nickel, an Indian-head. He wiped at it with his gore-smeared thumb. 1913. Not quite twenty years old. There was something off about it, though. James scrubbed it in the snow, leaving the metal mostly clean. Tool marks were clearly visible where someone had chipped and scraped at the metal, twisting the familiar image. The Indian's profile was misshapen, feral, almost lupine, and the figure's mouth stretched up and up the side of its face, reaching almost to the ears. It looked like it was smiling.

Not a very pleasant smile at all.

"Well, now, a good-luck rabbit indeed," said James. "Could buy a meal, or part of one." He held the coin out to the tramp, whose hands were greasy slick around his gift of rabbit meat. The man recoiled as though James had proffered a scorpion.

"Not for me," the tramp said. "I'm not that desperate. Not yet."

James shrugged. "Some soap, then, or a bit of ribbon." He dropped the coin into his pocket.

The tramp was backing away, heading downslope. "If I've nothing else to offer," he called out, "then let me give you some advice. That coin's a hungry coin. Throw it away and forget you ever saw it. Nothing it buys is anything you'd want." He was running, now, his ratty boots kicking up a spray of powder from the ground. His voice floated through the trees and the deepening shadows. "Throw it away!"

James shook his head and gathered up his rabbit. Delphina would be waiting.

By the time James arrived home, the sun had reached the tops of the mountains, the treelines visible in exquisite detail even in the gloaming, so clear and crisp was the air. James' house was nestled in a small vale on the northeast side of the peaks. Normally, the sight of lamplight peeking out between the cracks of the shutters — or, in the brief summers, the fluttering floral-pattern curtains — made James' heart swell with pride and satisfaction, picturing Delphina inside, singing to herself as she went about the business of managing their tiny household. But today, he felt only a flutter of unease. The dark and lowering mountainside gave the valley the appearance of an open and jagged-toothed maw, his house perched like an egg on the tongue of some incomprehensibly vast beast. How swiftly the dark jaws could close and snuff out that light…

Something was following him. He had enough woodcraft to know that, although he hadn't been able to catch sight of it. A rogue wolf, perhaps, or a mountain lion; something solitary and hungry, cautious but lured by the smell of blood on him. He'd have to sit up with the rifle for a night or two and make sure the goats didn't come to harm.

With a final glance at the darkened woods, James hefted his gunnysack and began the final climb down to the fragile safety of walls.

"James!" Delphina turned at the sound of his entrance. She darted to him, quick as a hummingbird to a flower, and he gathered her to himself, snow still melting on his boots. He let his hand drift down to her midsection, the new thickness barely perceptible, and she covered his chilled fingers with her hearth-warmed palms. She leaned in and tilted her head up, gliding her nose along the fringe of his jaw, where his bristling beard gave way to delicate skin, tissue thin over pulsing arteries. Her lips brushed against his neck, once and again, more firmly. Her arm tightened around his waist, and James laughed and pulled away.

"I'm all over dirt, Delly. Let me wash up before you drag me down."

Delphina blushed at his teasing, embarrassed still at her need for him. "I missed you," she said.

"And I you." James left the sack beside the cutting board. "There's a bit of rabbit meat to add to the stewpot, at least. Oh, and here's a piece of luck." He fished the carved nickel from his pocket. "Add it to your purse, Delly. We might need it before the winter's through."

"Oh," Delphina said. She plucked the coin and held it to the light. "What an odd design."

"It'll spend as well as a prettier coin," James grunted, filling the wash basin and grimacing at the cold touch of the water. Delphina said nothing. "Darling? I've been out all day; I could use that stew."

"Oh, yes. Yes, of course." Delphina shook her head and returned to the bubbling pot on the stove.

Conversation, normally so fluid between them as to be effort-less, seemed on this evening to dry up like the frozen creeks of the mountain winter. James blamed his lack of success at hunting and vowed to redouble his efforts. Delphina had made an effort to conceal it, but it was plain as the gathering night that the stew was a watery affair, vegetable stock eked out to its very limits. Lost in his personal recriminations, his failure to provide for his family, James barely noticed Delphina's growing distraction. He ceded most of his portion of stew to her without saying anything; he could tighten his belt and survive, but the child she carried had no such options. She ate mechanically, unseeing, with one hand clutching her coin purse to her breast.

That night, James' sleep was troubled. He found himself pursued through the woods by things that looked like wolves, for all that he'd only seen wolves on a handful of occasions, and they'd always been warily respectful and left him unmolested. But now he ran for his life through dark and frozen trees, his feet crunching on the hard-packed snow, the ice-tinged air searing his breath in his lungs, fire-cold and steaming, while black shadows lunged and darted on every side. He could smell their fur, wet and matted and sour, with a stench he recognized from his days on the trapline, blood and meat gone septic.

The dream shifted, as dreams do, and James realized he was running through his home, the three rooms stretching into an impossible, endless mansion, like the one he'd toured once as a child in Virginia. He slammed doors behind him, trying to conceal himself, but his pursuers had grown cunning, sniffing him out in each new hiding place. He cowered at last behind his bedroom door, hearing the heavy bodies shuffling on the other side. The wood was drafty, and he felt a cold and wet pressure on his bare heels. A puddle? A questing nose?

A tongue?

At once, James realized that Delphina was not in the bedroom with him. With a shout, he fell forward onto the bed...

...and woke up. He was curled around the emptiness that should have contained Delphina, his hand resting in the small depression her form left behind. The sheets were cold. Pale light filtered through the curtains and the cracks in the shutters.

James heard movement from the kitchen. He'd drawn breath to call out to Delphina, find what had driven her from their bed, when she shuffled into view, and something froze the sounds in his throat. She wore her bonnet and nightdress, as usual, but her posture was... wrong. Her back was toward him, her face in shadow. She was crouched over something she held in her hand, a predatory stance that curdled James' stomach. She bent her head low and *snuffled*, like an animal trying to catch a scent.

Sleepwalking, James thought. *She's having some sort of ... strange dream.*

Her shambling form moved away, toward the common room and the big central fireplace, and James bit his lip to keep from crying out in fear. As she left, he caught a glimpse of the thing she clutched in her hands. Something small and round that gleamed silver in the starlight.

James shuddered, and sleep failed to return to him that night, just as Delphina did.

In the morning, James took the coin purse with him when he left. Delphina was working on her canning, looking pale and fatigued in the watery morning sun.

"Feeling better, Delly?"

She turned, and James had to swallow an exclamation; her eyes looked nearly bruised, as though she hadn't slept all night. Her body appeared almost skeletal under her dress, the baby a bulge like a wasp-gall in a sapling oak. "I'm hungry," was all she said. Her hands kept drifting to her side, as if looking for the missing coin purse. James felt it pulsing in his pocket like a second heart.

James swallowed. "I'll go out this afternoon, find us some more game. We'll have stew and jerky for a month if I can bring down a big buck." He gave her his most confident smile, but her lips barely twitched in response.

James surreptitiously hurled the carved nickel and its disturbing image out into the woods before he went to work hauling wood and water. The simple physical labor absorbed him, and for a time he was able to forget all of his troubles in the repetition and the narrow focus of one more step, one more log, one more swing. By mid-morning, he was lathered in sweat despite the fragile chill of the air — a storm was coming soon, and no question about it — and he headed for the house for a cold drink and a slab of thick brown bread.

He shooed away from the stoop one of the half-feral cats Delphina coddled. They'd get a cat when they had a barn to protect from mice, James had told her, but Delphina loved to dangle strings for the tatty, ragged creatures and offer them tidbits of the kills James brought home. He'd shrugged and tried to ignore them; cats were shifty and untrustworthy by nature, in his experience. This one, a half-eared ginger tom, was standing almost at attention, its snake-yellow eyes fixed on James as though he were no more than an unusually large vole.

He aimed a half-hearted kick at it, and it dodged lightly backwards, eyes still staring. James' foot came down and squished unpleasantly. The little beast had left a "present" for Delphina, after the manner of its kind: a tidy collection of internal organs from some unlucky rodent. James scraped his boot off on the side of the stoop, and as he did, he caught a glint of silver from the tiny pile of anonymous reds and purples.

Slowly, unwilling to countenance what he felt in his gut must be true, he reached down and plucked a gore-smeared coin from amid the mouse guts. The cruel, jagged-toothed grin of the carved Indian head was striped with blood. It looked as though it had just fed.

James whirled to curse the cat, but the creature was already gone. He wanted to hurl the coin away from him, finding its touch loathsome beyond the tacky feel of drying blood, but he stopped himself. It had already come back once.

If I skip a meal, James thought, ignoring the protesting rumble of his stomach, *that just means more for Delly and the baby.* He turned and stalked off to the rocky field behind the house, snatching up his spade while he did.

After he'd buried the coin, James went to wash up, pulling icy water from the pump. Normally, he'd heat it over the fire, but he didn't feel he could face Delphina's sunken-eyed gaze after this morning. He told himself the cold was invigorating, and he sat on the wood-chopping stump to think things through.

That tramp had recognized the coin, had warned him against it. A hungry coin, he'd said. If James had thrown it away then, would it be haunting him now, giving him terrible dreams and making his Delphina look like death warmed over? If he found the tramp, could he learn more about it? But what were the chances of finding a single nameless man in the streets of the Springs, and that time better spent checking the trapline and looking for a late-season deer to bring down. The coin had to come from somewhere, hadn't it?

James resolved himself. He'd trek back up the trapline, but when he came to where he'd found the rabbit the other day, he'd track it back and find where it had picked up the cursed thing to begin with. Perhaps then he could make an end to whatever nightmare he'd been caught up in.

The day proved to be cold almost to the point of immobility, the sky a dark and lowering gray that only deepened as time went on. The threat of a blizzard was apparent in every abortive gust of wind, every ice-coated branch, every plugged fox den and silent stream. James checked his traps methodically but without hope, catching only a scarf-thin squirrel for all of his efforts.

When he reached the last trap in the line, he found everything preserved as if in a photograph. The red spots still dotted the snow like ersatz flowers, and the ground was trampled with his and the other man's comings and goings. Casting a short distance away, James quickly picked up the rabbit's distinctive two-and one pattern in the snow. The animal had run in a curiously straight line, as though running an errand. Or as though terrified beyond reason. James checked the time as best he could, with the sun invisible behind the brooding clouds. He should be able to make it home before dark, assuming the rabbit hadn't gone too far. It couldn't have maintained the speed indicated by its nearest tracks for long.

The rabbit's trail led through the woods toward the saddle-back between two peaks and the narrow horse trail that went over the pass, at least in the summer months. It veered aside only for trees or rocks too large to climb over, and James had no difficulty following it even over hard ground or across frozen streams; it always resumed on the other side.

After three miles, James began to worry about losing the light before he made it home. After another mile, he'd given up and had to hope that he'd at least get back to familiar territory before full dark hit. Spending a night lost in the woods might finish him, especially as he hadn't eaten since the previous morning. His stomach writhed inside him like a separate animal, and one none too pleased with its master, at that.

At last, James caught sight of hard angles and metal through the trees, welcome signs of human habitation in the deep mountain woods. He pushed through the final leafless bushes into a small clearing and gasped.

It had been a traveling party of some kind, once, long ago. The wagon's ribs showed through where cloth had rotted away. The wood was bleached and preserved, like in a desert; the high altitude, cold, and dryness had left it nearly fossilized. James could see a snapped axle that had punched up through the floor of the wagon; no force on Earth would have been able to get that rig moving again, especially not if it had been trapped in the pass by weather. The remnants of a campsite were visible, here and there, peeping from beneath the snow. James wondered how many years the charred embers of the tiny fire had sat nearly undisturbed beneath snow and melt and snow again.

The central piece that caught and held his attention, however, was the human corpse propped in a spread-legged sitting position against the unbroken wheel of the wagon. It was clad in the rags of a dress and bonnet, blown now to shreds in the constant wind. The flesh had rotted away, leaving tendons and skin tight against bone; no signs of being disturbed by wildlife, which was odd. Worse than odd: downright uncanny. The skeletal hands lay face up by its sides, and all around it were scattered a ruin of animal bones, a veritable graveyard of rabbits and squirrels and raccoons; to be visible above the snow, they'd have to have been piled several inches deep all around the sprawled body. James, caught somewhere between entrancement and revulsion, took a step forward only to hear something snap beneath his boot. He reached down and retrieved a long, thin leg-bone. Not deer. Not bear, either. James had a suspicion he knew what kind of bone it was. He peered closer; the end was cracked open, as wolves did when they sought the rich bone marrow from their prey. The bone bore marks all along its length.

Tooth marks.

Human tooth marks.

James looked up at the horrid, desiccated thing that lay half-crumpled against the wagon, the body that had lasted so much longer than all of its companions. How many others lay beneath the snow in that terrible clearing?

The rabbit tracks led through the snow quite clearly up to the open palm of the corpse, and then away in that odd straight line. Straight to James and his traps.

His traps that hadn't been there the year before. Hadn't been close enough. Hadn't been in reach of the coin's call.

James turned and fled into the growing night, while the storm hovered overhead.

At the cabin, James was almost unsurprised to see a fresh hole where only that morning he'd broken the frozen earth and dropped the baneful coin into the dark. He stopped and muttered an oath when he saw what was inside it, however.

A mole, perhaps? It was hard to say. It was stuffed halfway down the gullet of a rattlesnake, of all creatures, which itself had apparently choked the emaciated fox that was wedged, foreparts first, into the tiny mole's burrow. None of those animals should even be abroad at this stage of the year, save perhaps the fox, if it were in some dire extremity. James couldn't imagine what could stir a rattler to venture into ice and snow, but clear enough something had. James fetched his spade and pried the grisly trio apart; sure enough, clutched in the half-digested forepaws of the little rodent was the silver nickel, still somehow gleaming despite the hefty coating of filth it now bore. James shoved it in his pocket. He'd say nothing to Delphina.

That, as it turned out, wasn't a problem. Delly's usual cheerful burble was reduced to monosyllables. She looked more wan than ever, and she greeted James' poor news of hunting with no more reaction than if he'd announced the presence of snow in the mountains. For his part, James found he had no appetite. He couldn't bear the smell of the stew on this second evening; it tasted like bark and leaf-mould in his mouth. He found his hand creeping to his pocket, to touch the coin and run his fingertips along its gleeful, hungry smile. Delphina ate rapidly, hardly seeming to taste her meal, either. They exchanged perfunctory monosyllables and retired to bed, James clutching the coin in his fist so hard that it dug into his skin. He could smell Delphina beside him, not her unwashed hair or the sickness he could see in her eyes, but the rich, warm smell of the blood beneath her skin.

Sometime after midnight, lying still awake, James realized that the strange sensations in his midsection were *hunger pangs*. He bit his lip and slipped silently from the bed. He was unable to resist a final lingering sniff of Delphina's uneasily sleeping body before he went.

In the morning, James left a short note telling Delphina that he had gone to town to pick up some last-minute supplies before the storm hit and locked them in till spring. He took their meager stock of cash with him, including the coin. He was stiff and awkward as he began the brisk walk to the city; he'd spent an uncomfortable night crouched in the common room, wrapped in the thickest quilt they had, unwilling to risk building a fire and waking Delphina. He'd put the coin down and picked it up a dozen times an hour, unable to bear the feel of it against his skin, but equally unable to bear being without it. He wondered if he had a fever, something picked up from an animal or that hideous abandoned camp up in the mountains. Hallucinations would be a much more comforting explanation for the past two days.

James wasn't certain what his plan was. All he knew was that he had to get rid of the coin before it drove him mad— if it hadn't already. He'd found it and claimed it; surely that meant he could also *spend* it? He tried not to think about what the coin might do once he'd let it loose in the dense population of the Springs, but he reassured himself that he was surely imagining most of the effects, regardless. Surely. Once the coin was out of his possession, he'd be able to leave the distracting thoughts behind.

The streets were busy with cars, horses, and pedestrians. James forgot, sometimes, up in his and Delphina's cozy home, that the rest of the world was not as bound to the seasons as they were. Traffic on the great roads would continue even in the depths of winter, and commerce in the city would hardly slow. He meandered somewhat aimlessly through the outskirts of the city. Should he purchase canned goods, for all that they'd barely eke out their existing supplies? Traps or a better gun? A coil of rope? Rope was always useful; rope and twine seemed to disappear the moment his back was turned. Muffled, booted city-dwellers and travelers jostled past James on every side, a constant distraction. He couldn't seem to find his bearings. He was so very hungry.

A tug at his sleeve brought James up short. He turned and beheld a half-familiar face, gnarled features nearly lost amid a tangle of hair.

"It's you!" James said. "You were there when…"

"The coin, yes," the man said. "I knew you'd come down here soon enough. Done its work, has it?"

"Its work?"

"Hunger has a power that's hard to know until you've faced it down, don't it?" The man's face was haggard; he clearly hadn't eaten or slept since James had last seen him, and for goodness knew how long before that, as well. "You've been, what, two days in its grip? And already you're here to fob it off on the first unlucky sap you can find." He grinned, displaying his snaggle-tooth grin. His breath reeked. "It won't work, you know. It has to be willed. Can't just slip it in with the change for a shiny new hammer."

"Then I'm lost," James said. "And Delly and the baby with me."

"Never give up hope, friend," the tramp said. He held out one filthy hand.

"You… you want the coin? But you said—"

"I know what I said!" The man's face contorted as he visibly brought himself back under control. "A man can change his mind, once he's seen his prospects more clearly. I've looked it in the face good and hard these past two days; I reckon I can handle it now. I'll take whatever it can get for me." He extended his arm again, insistent. "Give me the coin, and I'll be on my way."

James pulled the silver disc from his pocket. It hovered over the callused palm of the dirty beggar. It was hard to let go; James felt as though the coin were exerting some magnetic influence on his fingertips.

"How much hungrier can you get?" the man asked. "And your… your wife, your little one? I know, Jimmy. I know."

James released the coin. It tumbled for what felt like long seconds, minutes, perhaps hours. Then it disappeared, snapped into the tramp's grip like a drop of water into sun-parched soil. James felt a sudden openness, a clarity of vision, as though a hood had been pulled from his head. He watched the expressions warring on the tramp's muddied face, anger and glee, fear, resignation, and something harder to name.

"Thank you," James started to say, the oddest thing a man ever said to a panhandler who just took his money, but the tramp's eyes snapped open, and James stopped dead. He was reminded of the eyes of the rabbit in his trap, white-rimmed and full of pain-mad terror so fine it coalesced into a kind of power. The man fled into the crowd, leaving James standing stupefied at the corner.

It wasn't until later that he remembered: He'd never told the man his name.

James dawdled in the city for a time. He'd made some purchases in a desultory fashion; mostly he wanted to give the tramp a good, long head start. He didn't want to meet those eyes coming toward him on the trail up the mountain, in the dark and the cold of the wilderness. When he judged it as late as he could let it before the storm trapped him in the valley, he started on his way, his meager purchases bumping in his leather satchel. The clouds overhead looked improbably soft and cheerful, like a warm feather bed; a cruel illusion, that.

The first flakes began to fall as he neared the cabin, tiny, rock-hard things almost more hail than snow. This storm was settling in for the long haul, it seemed.

The light was on in the cabin, a butter-yellow gleam as welcome as the first songs of the angels in Paradise. James found his pace increasing, his appetite surging again for the first time since that miserable rabbit had found him. Delly would be at the stove, perhaps, just putting the finishing touches on dinner. He could almost see the vision as he drew near the door, almost smell the roast beef.

He paused on the threshold. He *could* smell a roast, it seemed. Not a well-prepared one, either; had Delly let the meat burn?

Where would she have gotten a roast *from*?

James rushed into the house, noting almost distractedly that the door was unlatched and hanging open. Inside, the smell of burning meat was stronger, almost overpowering. The fire had been left to burn down; the chimney was clogged and smoke filled the room. The heat radiating from the room almost stopped James at the door. By the far wall, he saw by the far wall, Delly had set up her ironing board and the rack of irons near the fireplace.

On the floor beside them, Delly lay, the tramp's body half on top of hers. A formerly red-hot iron was smashed into the side of his face, caving in his skull and setting his flesh to burning and bubbling, still warm enough to feel through James' clothes.

The tramp's dirty teeth were locked together in Delphina's ivory-pale throat. Blood dribbled down and soaked both of their clothes, sizzling on the iron and filling the room with the smell of burning.

James knelt on the floor. The cans in his bag clattered as they hit the floor. His tears burned tracks down his face like acid. He reached a hesitant hand out to touch the gruesome tableau, as though it might not be real, as though he might prove it all a dream.

As his fingers touched the tramp's stiff shoulder, the man's jaw fell open. Something flashed in the firelight as it fell to the floor. *Clink, clink, clink.*

Behind James, there was a gust of wind, and the door slammed open. Slow footsteps, like wooden peg-legs, made a staccato rhythm on the cabin floor. The fire flared up, thick black smoke pouring out. James felt the soot sting his eyes. He reached forward and picked up the coin, then turned.

The skin-and-bones thing from the mountain camp grinned back at him, fleshless face blank, eyes sunken like white marbles deep in the bony sockets. Its bonnet flapped incongruously around its hollow cheeks.

It held out one hand, like a winter-bare branch.

Moving carefully, James placed the coin almost reverently into the thing's palm. It drew back, pointed to him, to the man and woman locked in their death embrace behind him.

James nodded. He understood. He opened his mouth like he was taking Communion at church, and watched the twig-like fingers lift the coin up to catch the light, and then down.

James tasted silver. Then copper.

And lastly ash.

 SUCH A HUNGRY COIN. LIKE A growing child. Only this one eats more than food. When it does, it becomes more of what it will be. I knew the thing from the mountain, once. A woman who wanted to live forever. She took the coin, knowing it would make her hungry. She lives still today. At least, I have heard rumors of such. The coin … ah, that fickle thing … it has abandoned her to feast on more succulent flesh.

—The Carver

THE PRICE OF SERENITY

KELLY SWAILS

TRAGEDIES ARE A SHOWER of small incidents that add up to a storm, such as a misunderstanding that blossoms into a disagreement that grows into an estrangement. Such tragedies aren't uncommon, which perhaps makes them even more grievous. They even occur in families like the Moores. This is how it happened.

Late one night in early 1928 Charles and Lillian had a fight. This was uncommon. It could have been about Charles drinking or perhaps it had started over how much money Lillian had spent at the market, but that has no significance. Their shouts woke their son Daniel — he was only four and had night terrors and so even on the best of nights didn't sleep deeply — and he cried out. His son's whimpers angered Charles. He said it was because boys didn't cry, but really it was because Charles had caused the boy's pain. He stormed out of the house and walked through the rain to the local pub.

The cold walk back was not enough to leach the whiskey from his mind or his body.

Lillian had left a candle going on the front table so that Charles wouldn't come home in the dark. The wavering flame brought tears to his eyes — Lillian loved him even when he was a drunk bastard — and he carried the candle to the bedroom. Halfway there he stumbled on one of Daniel's toy trains, sending the candle into a heavy set of curtains. He cursed the boy as fire licked at the fabric and spilled heat and light throughout the room. He tried to extinguish the flames, at one point even dousing them with a

15

bottle of milk, but soon it became apparent that it was a losing battle. He struggled through the smoky house to Daniel's room, roused him, and carried him to Charles's and Lillian's bedroom.

The smoke in their bedroom was thick and noxious. Charles yelled at Lillian and kicked the bed, but she wouldn't wake. He told Daniel to hold his coat and not let go as he put him down and grabbed his wife. Daniel obeyed — he really was a good boy — as Charles slung her over his shoulder and stumbled from the room. Once he got outside Charles ran a short distance away and lay Lillian down in the cool grass. Only when she coughed and opened her eyes did Charles dare look around. Their little house was engulfed in flames and Daniel was nowhere to be seen. After calling for him and getting no answer, Charles ran back into the house. He tossed aside the burning table and crawled around the hot floor, but he couldn't find his only son. He would have stayed until the house took him, too, but a fireman dragged him to safety.

When they found Daniel in the smoldering remains of the house, he was lying in the fetal position in the living room, his hands curled around a misshapen toy train.

Charles rubbed his hand over his stubbly cheeks and hiked up his grungy workpants onto his slim hips. The scent of grilled meat wafted over him and he ignored his rumbling stomach. He had two dollars in his pocket he shouldn't spend on overpriced food, let alone frivolities, but there he was. Wasting money on a fortunetelling kook.

Carnivals had just started coming around again. The papers said the Depression was lifting even though he hadn't seen any evidence of that himself. He hadn't been to a fair or carnival or circus of any kind since Daniel had died. He needed a little hope. Even if it was fake. Even if he had to pay for it.

He navigated the crowd as he crossed the wide dirt path and pushed aside the garish curtain-door of the fortuneteller's tent. A plump woman with dark curly hair sat on the other side of a round table, a cloth covering the wooden legs that were surely underneath. A milky crystal ball sat in the center, its surface gleaming in the candlelight. He paused at the door and rubbed the scars on his arms, the ridges and groves grotesque under his palms. This place was one sudden movement away from going up in a huge blaze. That would be one way to find peace.

"Come, come, my friend," the woman said in a thick European accent he couldn't place. "Sit and allow Clarissa to amaze you with your future."

"I don't think you'll be able to do that," Charles said. He didn't move.

Clarissa sat back in her chair and studied him. "You are frightened."

He shuffled his feet. "You have a lot of candles in here," he said.

She glanced at his arms. "And you've been in a fire."

He was still rubbing his arms. "How'd you know?"

Clarissa smirked as she gestured around the tent. "I don't need accoutrements to do my job." She stood and blew out all the candles in the metal stands, leaving only the one on the table. "Better?"

He answered by sitting in the rickety wooden folding chair. He reached for his wallet but the fortuneteller shook her head.

"You have a way about you," she said. "You need this. I won't accept payment."

Shame spiraled in him. He hadn't heard that sentiment much, especially since most needed to feed themselves as much as he did. Most provided to families, too. He hadn't had that burden for awhile.

"Then we're at an impasse," he said. "Because I won't accept charity."

Clarissa crinkled her generous brows. "Let's do this. I will do your reading, and if you find it satisfactory, we will negotiate a price. Deal?"

What if she wished to charge him more than he carried? If there was any hope Clarissa, the Amazing Seer of Futures, could show him the path to happiness, it was a risk he was willing to take. He nodded and she smiled.

"Wonderful." Without another word, she set the crystal ball onto the ground, leaned over the table, and pressed both hands onto his face. When he recoiled — more out of surprise than revulsion — she tightened her grip and closed her eyes.

"Don't fight it," she murmured.

Warmth infused his skin and sent odd tingles dancing through his body. Her palms were soft against his cheeks and he breathed in her scent. How long had it been since a woman had touched him? Since well before Lillian had left. The last several months with his former spouse had been distant. Six years, maybe closer to seven. Unbidden, his hand reached up and touched hers. It was soft and strong.

If Clarissa noticed she didn't show it. Instead she bowed her head and moaned. "So much anguish," she said. "Too much for one person." She dug her fingers into his cheeks. "Too much." She shivered so hard it could more properly be called a convulsion. She ripped her hands away from his face and brought them to her chest, breathing hard.

Charles fought against the sudden emptiness inside him. He licked his dry lips and rubbed his face. It still felt warm where she'd touched it. He mourned the loss of contact.

"You are a haunted individual," Clarissa said as she pushed damp curls off her forehead. "More than most."

"Yes," he said, his words harsh in the quiet tent.

"He doesn't blame you, you know," she said. "I feel it."

Charles couldn't answer for fear she was wrong.

She stared at the table for several moments before pulling a small box from underneath. She placed the box in front of Charles and said, "Place your hand on this."

"Why?"

She pressed her lips into a line. "Inside are several objects that might bring you peace. I need you to touch the box in order to find the one for you."

Charles shuffled in his seat. Ordinarily he'd think all this was nonsense, a sort of charade for the poor saps that ambled through her curtain on a whim. His face was still warm where she's touched it, though, and he'd never felt anything like the tingles that had run through his body. He placed one hand on top of the engraved wooden box.

"Both," she said.

He did and closed his eyes. He expected to feel warmth or vibrations, but nothing happened. Outside the tent children laughed as they ran through the midway. Charles rubbed the wood beneath his fingers. Solid walnut, if he had to guess, though it was hard to tell in the dim lighting.

Without a word Clarissa pulled the box towards her and opened it. She ran her fingers over several trinkets inside until she gasped. She untangled a leather string and took it from the box, palming the charm at the end. The box was beneath the table again before he could make any inquires regarding the contents.

"Are you familiar with Hobo nickels?" she said.

"Yes," he said. His father had carved a few of them but had never made one really beautiful. They had just looked like nickels with scratches on them.

She wrapped the thin leather strap around her fingers and opened her hand as though displaying a fine piece of jewelry. "This one is unique."

He leaned forward to get a better look in the candlelight. Where his father's attempt at artwork had been awkward and laughable, whoever had carved this nickel had been brilliant. The Indian head stood out in sharp relief to its surroundings, his face wrinkled and worn with age. His eyes were full of sorrow. The artist had blended the date — 1913 — so well into its surroundings he had to squint to see the numbers. A hole had been bored into the top so the leather could be threaded through. He shivered.

"That's wonderful work," he said.

"Yes," she said, "but you only see a small fraction of the craftsmanship. This charm is a portal to the after."

"Excuse me?" He had to have heard her wrong. This was so much more than he had dared hope for.

"The after. This thins the barrier between our world and the one that comes after. When you wear this, someone who has passed can talk with you." She smiled but there was no joy in it. "If they want or need to."

Daniel. "I'll take it," he said. "How much?" He didn't care if it cost him every last thing he owned.

Clarissa shook her head. "You don't understand. It chose you." She grabbed his hand and slipped the necklace into it. "Besides, I told you I wouldn't except payment."

He blinked at the nickel in his hand. Warmth radiated from it, much more than could be attributed to the fortuneteller holding it. "No," he said finally. "We agreed we'd negotiate payment after the reading."

She stood. "We have." She squeezed around the table and opened the curtain behind him. "I have others that would like to see me," she said.

Charles held the nickel in his hand so hard the metal cut into his flesh. "I can't just take this," he said. Even though his two dollars wouldn't be enough. Even though everything he owned wouldn't be enough to pay for the chance to talk with Daniel.

"We've been over this," she said, her tone harried and put-upon.

He glanced outside. "No one's in line."

Clarissa let the curtain fall as she crossed her arms. "Our business is done, sir. You will accept my gift or I will run out of here screaming that you tried to have your way with me. Roughly."

"You wouldn't," Charles said.

She raised an eyebrow in response.

Charles swallowed as he thought of the carnival full of strong men who would love to defend her honor. He could take one or two. He couldn't take twenty. Imprisoning him wouldn't be hard, either. He cleared his throat as he stood.

"You'll receive payment from me, one way or the other," he said. "You have my word."

Her stern features turned soft once again. "I already have."

When Charles got home — if you can call one room with a saggy bed and a hot plate instead of a stove home — he hung his hat on the hook by the door and settled into the lone chair in the corner. He turned the pendant over in his hands. Was it a portal? Would he be able to talk with Daniel? Beg his forgiveness? Say he was sorry, that he loved him, that he never meant to destroy everything? He rubbed the metal with this thumb. What did he have to lose? He slipped the leather strap over his head and let the coin fall to his chest.

Unnatural warmth spread through his body as his constant anguish fell away. He sat back in the chair and smiled. He was content for the first time in years. Truly he hadn't ever felt this way, as though nothing could touch him, nothing could harm him, nothing would ever worry him again. This sensation, this peacefulness of being, must be what newborn babies felt every day. The idea brought tears to his eyes even as he laughed.

"Hello?" A voice said inside him.

Charles sat up. "Daniel? Oh my God, it works. It really works. Daniel? Is that really you?"

"No," the voice said again, and now Charles heard the gravelly rumble of it. "The name's Oscar. Who are you?"

"You're not Daniel?" he said as he gripped the pendant and slumped in the chair. He should have known the woman at the carnival had been a fake. The coin must have been drugged, something that worked through his skin, and that would explain the rush of feelings and the hallucinations. At least he hadn't paid for it.

"I said I wasn't," the voice said. "But is this Daniel a little boy? About five? Dark hair?"

Charles paused. "Yes." This had to have been a vivid dream. That was the only explanation.

"I'm not, but suit yourself," the voice said. "I could've let you talk to him, but—"

Talking with Daniel through a hallucination was better than not talking to him at all. "But what?"

"You could do a little something for me," Oscar said, an oily edge to his words. "Then I'd let you talk to Daniel."

"Why would I do that?" Charles said. "I'm not sure you're not just in my imagination."

"Tell you what," Oscar said, now sounding very put out. "Look up my death. Oscar Gillen, Hyannisport, 1913. You'll find I was shot and they never found my killer. My wife Josephine said a robber did it, and the cops never found anything to suggest otherwise."

"And that'll prove I'm not drugged." Or insane.

"Right."

"And then you'll let me talk to Daniel."

"I'll let you do something for me," he said. "Then we'll talk about Daniel."

Charles shook his head. Maybe he really was insane. "You have a deal."

Then the feeling was gone. He shivered in the darkness of the living room as despair and sadness crept back into him. His tendons creaked as he opened his hands and let the coin drop to his chest. He placed the pendant on the rickety end table next to him. Already his belief in what had happened was fading, but that didn't mean he couldn't do a little research. At least he had something to do the next day other than wonder how he was going to pay the rent.

The next morning he drank some watered-down, day-old coffee before walking to the library. When he got there he asked for the reference room, and once there he asked for the Hyannisport files from 1913, the entire time feeling like the biggest fool in the entire world. The library bound their newspapers into month-long volumes, making an unwieldy book of sorts. Charles chose a table at the far end of the small room and delved into the papers, being careful not to rip the pages or fold the edges. He figured he wouldn't find anything and that would be that. Part of him wanted to prove the coin was fraudulent. The other part — the bigger, desperate, dead part — needed the coin to be a portal.

He found what he needed in the third volume. It didn't take long to learn everything he needed to know about Oscar Gillen.

He'd been shot, just like he said, while lying asleep in bed. Only a few pieces of his wife's jewelry had been taken, and his wife — Ruby — had been unscathed. Oscar had been a business-man that had made his money in Texas before moving north, and over the next several weeks the investigators theorized that an angry competitor had shot him for revenge. But Oscar had been a prominent man in the community; it would have been easy to shoot him at almost any time. Why wait until he's sleeping at home? Then there was the jewelry to think about. The pieces weren't significant in value; why had they been taken? A weapon was never recovered, no evidence at the scene, and there were no witnesses. Finally the police called it a burglary gone wrong and let the case grow cold.

Charles closed the books with shaking fingers as he searched the far corners of his memory. Had he read or heard about this case years ago? Had Lillian gossiped about it? Is that why his brain had conjured up his conversation with Oscar? He found nothing in his memory to indicate that.

The voice in his head who called himself Oscar was real. Which meant that somehow, some way, Daniel still existed. And Charles could talk to him. Apologize, even though there were no words for that. Hear his son forgive him. Maybe, just maybe, find peace.

He left the library and hurried home, and when he got there he headed straight for the pendant. He slipped it as he collapsed in the chair, the eternal warmth and serenity washing over him. He trembled as he called out for Oscar.

"So look who's back," he said. "You found me."

"Yes," Charles said. "I'm sorry I doubted you. Can I speak to Daniel?"

"Can't say that I blame you," he said, ignoring the request. "If some dead guy had talked to me when I was alive, I'd have assumed I had lost my mind."

"That had occurred to me," Charles said. "But it was just like you'd said. Murder case that got cold."

"Funny thing about that," he said. "When you're murdered you know who did it but of course you're dead so you can't point the finger. Plus there're rules about that sort of thing." He cleared his throat. "So you want to talk to Daniel."

Charles licked his lips as desire nibbled on the edge of his blissfulness. "More than anything," he said.

"You're going to have to do something for me," Oscar said.

"Of course."

"Don't you want to know the terms of the deal before you agree to it?"

"It doesn't matter," Charles said. "I want to talk with my son."

Oscar didn't hesitate. "I need you to kill my wife."

Charles blinked. He hadn't known what to expect, but it hadn't been that. "Excuse me?"

"I told you I knew who murdered me. My wife did it."

"Why'd she do that?"

"I was sleeping around on her," Oscar said. Charles heard the shrug in his tone. "You roll the dice, you take your chances. I told one too many lies and I got caught."

"And you want your revenge," he said.

"Something like that."

"Then why do you want me to kill her?" Charles said. "Wouldn't you rather torment her? Haunt her? Get your revenge that way?"

"My terms aren't negotiable," Oscar said.

Desperation danced at the edge of his perception. What if Oscar changed his mind? "I'm not negotiating anything," Charles said. "I'm just wondering why you want her dead."

"Let's just say I have a few favors to call in on this side," he said. "My dear wife isn't going to going to like what comes after so much."

Charles breathed deeply and pushed the insinuation from his mind. He swallowed and said, "I'll have to think about it."

"Take all the time you need," Oscar said in that confident way people had when they knew they'd already won.

For Charles it was never a question of would he or would he not murder Oscar's wife Ruby. As soon as Oscar had named his price Charles knew he'd pay it. He wanted to talk to Daniel, period. He didn't care how he had to make that happen. He also didn't care about getting caught. Of course, he'd rather be a free man, but spending the rest of his life incarcerated by the state couldn't be any worse than the last several years. Inside he'd have guaranteed food and shelter.

No, the question was more of how. After planning several scenarios and discarding them all, he finally settled on a simple, direct approach. Break in, shoot her, leave. Maybe take something to lead the police down the robbery angle. Charles appreciated the irony.

Getting the gun was easy, as was locating Ruby. She had never moved. Charles walked through the darkened streets of Hyannisport and waited for the lights to go out in Ruby's house. Once they did, he waited twenty minutes, unlatched the door in the wooden fence, and crept across the backyard. Moonlight shone through the neighborhood's mature trees and illuminated his journey. His heart hammered in his chest as he tiptoed to the window in the back corner and opened it a crack. When nothing stirred, he pushed the window open more. A breeze kicked up and ruffled the lacy curtains as he leaned in the window. Ruby lay on the bed, her delicate snores keeping time to her breath.

Charles hoisted himself up and snaked a leg into the window. He shifted his weight and leaned in, freezing as the wood floor creaked beneath his foot. Ruby's snores continued for several moments, and when his heartbeat had returned to something like normal, he ducked beneath the sash and entered the bedroom. He walked to the bed, readied his gun — his hands only shook a little — and watched her sleep until she stirred.

When she opened her eyes she didn't scream or look surprised. It could have been that she thought this was a dream, or maybe she assumed it was her destiny catching up with her.

"Ruby?" Charles said.

She rubbed an eye. "Yes."

She had none of that grogginess in her words, which unnerved him. Lillian had taken an hour to fully wake; Ruby had been asleep one second and alert the next.

"Formerly married to Oscar?" He had to be absolutely sure.

"Yes," she said, "until I had the cheating bastard shot."

"I'm sorry." He raised the gun and aimed at her head.

"Don't be. What goes around comes around."

He pulled the trigger. His shaking stopped as a few feathers from her pillow settled back down to the bed. It was then that he noticed the barking dog down the street and the rose-scented perfume in the air. Lillian had worn something like it. He slipped the gun into his pocket and retraced his steps, pausing at the vanity table. He left the small jewelry box unopened; he'd already taken Ruby's most valuable possession and didn't see the need to take an expensive trinket, motives be damned. Once he hit the street he walked home, just a man taking a nighttime stroll to clear his head in no particular hurry to get anywhere.

Warmth, serenity, at peace with the world.

"You son-of-a-bitch," Oscar said. "You actually did it."

"We had an agreement," Charles said.

"Sure," he said, "but you're the first man I've talked to who was willing to do it."

"Maybe I'm the first man you've talked to with nothing to lose," Charles said. Anxiousness crept into his tranquility and he loosened his grip on the arms of the chair. He could push Oscar to get past the pleasantries and the small talk, but even though he had done his part, Oscar still held the cards. Did Oscar mean for him exact revenge on more people? Not that it mattered. He would do it. But it would mean that he wouldn't talk to Daniel tonight, and the thought pierced his heart like an ice pick.

Oscar chuckled. "That's not the case, I assure you." He paused. "You love your son very much."

"Yes," he said. He didn't trust himself to say anything else.

"Well, I'll tell you what," Oscar said, "Ruby's had a rough transition."

"She didn't seem surprised to see me," he said.

"I didn't think she would be," Oscar said. "Ruby knew what sort of man I was. She knew it was just a matter of time before I made sure she paid for my death." When Charles didn't respond, he cleared his throat "I suppose it's time to hold up my end. A deal's a deal."

"It is," Charles said.

"I have to do a little hocus-pocus on this end," Oscar said, "but you don't need to know the particulars about that. Once the transition is made this will be Daniel's portal and he can do whatever he wants with it."

"I understand."

"Been nice doing business with you."

"Likewise."

The warmth left his body then, the coin growing first cold then frigid on his chest. Nausea ripped through him as sweat prickled his skin. He had just moved to take off the pendant when heat replaced the cold and the familiar tranquility replaced the sickness. The quality of warmth was different than before— now it felt like a warm spring day as opposed to a hot summer's evening.

Daniel had control of the portal now.

Charles cleared his throat but found he was speechless. How many times had he wanted to talk to Daniel just one more time? And now he had the chance but didn't know what to say to his son.

"Daddy?" Daniel said in his young voice.

"Yes, it's Daddy," Charles said as emotions overcame him. Tears washed over his face as he laughed.

"Is it really, truly, you?"

"Yes," Charles said. "My God, I can't believe I'm really speaking with you. Is this a dream? If it is I never want to wake up. How is heaven? Are you happy?"

"I'm not in heaven," Daniel said. He sounded sullen.

"Oh," Charles said as dread prickled his chest. "You're not... you're not in the other place, are you?"

"No," Daniel said. "I'm not supposed to tell you about where I'm at, but I guess I won't get in trouble if I say it's not hell."

Charles blinked at his son's usage of a curse word. Chastising Daniel didn't cross his mind, though. "I wish your mother were here right now. I know she'd love to talk with you." Maybe he could lure her back with the promise of talking with Daniel. Maybe they could be a family again.

"Where is she?" Daniel said.

"She's... losing you was very hard, Daniel. Every time she saw me she remembered she wouldn't ever see you again." His tone faltered. "So she left."

Daniel didn't respond.

"I'm so sorry, Daniel," he said. "I know it's not enough, that I will never be able to say the right words. It's my fault you're dead and I'm sorry." He inhaled. "If I know you're happy, if I know you've forgiven me, then maybe I can find a way to live with myself."

Silence stretched over the distance for so long that he wondered if the connection had been broken. When Daniel's voice sounded in his head, though, it was loud and precise and so clear he could have been in the same room.

"I'm not happy," he said. "This place isn't fun. There aren't any toys and I can't run or play or— but I can't talk about it. They told me I can move once I've done what I need to do."

"And that is?" Charles said, hoping in the bottom of his heart that it was something arduous and time-consuming so he'd have more time with Daniel.

"This," he said. His voice sounded older, as though he'd aged ten years in two seconds. "I don't forgive you," Daniel said, the words cutting through the connection like so many knives. "I'm angry that you got drunk and started a fire and left me to die."

"I didn't leave you," Charles said. His heart beat fast and his breath wouldn't come. "I didn't. I got you first and then got your momma."

"You didn't save me," Daniel said. "Like you always promised you would. You said you'd keep me safe, that as long as you were alive nothing would hurt me. You said," he finished, the last words once again sounding like a four-year-old.

"I tried, oh God, I tried," Daniel said. "If I could have traded places with you I would have—"

"I don't forgive you." Daniel said. He sighed with relief, as though he had dropped a heavy load he'd carried for far too long. His next words sounded lighter, almost joyous. "I can go on now."

With those final words still hanging in his head, the warmth and tranquility left his body, despair and agony taking their place. The portal was closed. Charles ripped the pendant from his neck and threw it across the room, his sobs echoing off the walls.

Daniel didn't forgive him. Wouldn't ever, now. Or if he did Charles would never know it, which amounted to the same. He should find comfort that Daniel had gone on, that he was in heaven now, or at least someplace where there were toy trains and laughter and singing. But he couldn't.

Charles would never find comfort again.

Later, he walked the midway of the carnival and stopped where Clarissa's tent had been. It was gone now, the sparse grass trampled and the dirt packed hard. He wasn't surprised. He tossed the hobo nickel on its leather strap into the dirt where the tent had stood. Maybe some poor sap would come across it and find the peace they sought. He left and didn't look back.

◇◈◇

***ONE OF MY FAVORITE STORIES** of getting what you asked for and not thinking things through. Such delicious pain. Especially since it really was his fault. My lovely coin had nothing to do but reap an easy reward. Poor Charles. Following his guilt at what he did not only earned him the painful truth, it earned him an eternity away from the ones he loved. Or perhaps not. Once touched by one of my coins, you are forever changed.*

—The Carver

Vinegar Pie

ANDREW PENN ROMINE

NEVER REALLY THOUGHT of myself as lucky or not. I just took life as it came along. Sometimes things were good and sometimes they weren't. What can you do about that, really? You just got to go along with what the world's got planned for you.

Even if it's sitting on the beach talking to a stranger while the shadows gather.

Need a little money, buddy? I got some to spare. Thirty whole cents. All yours. I don't got much use for it anyhow. They'll be here soon, those shadows that don't need no light to make 'em.

Oh no, you don't got to worry. They ain't after you, just me. Here, take this quarter. Ought to get you a cup of coffee and a nice piece of banana cream pie at that cafe near the boardwalk. I personally prefer blueberry pie, but the banana up at Ferguson's is pretty swell.

The nickel?

I figure you don't want that one. Might cost you a little more to take it. Oh no fella, I don't need nothing for it. I already paid my price. Hate to see you pay it, too.

Your clothes are still nice but you look hungry. All right, all right. Keep your shirt on. But before you take the coin from me, you gotta hear my side of the story. It's only fair.

See it? Regular old buffalo nickel. Been carved up by some fella. You ever seen 'em like this? Me neither, not until this one, and I've been around. You see how the Indian's all carved up to look like a hobo, yeah? Metal's soft, even a sharp rock will do the job.

Yeah, now that you mention it, the fella on the front kind of looks like me, don't he? Say, you got a light, mister?

That's mighty nice. Haven't had a decent smoke in quite a while. Just butts rerolled in newspapers. Never tastes right. Guess this one will be my last. Heh.

New to the life, huh, fella? Well, between me and you, best not to show off too much of what you got. Ration it. But I was supposed to be telling you my story, wasn't I? I guess the place to start is the War.

I did my time Over There like a lot of other boys. Found myself in 'Frisco in 1919. Got my discharge, had a little pocket money. Didn't want to go back to Kansas. So I decided to stick around the city. It worked out for me for awhile. Got me a sweet wife, and she was a fine girl. I didn't deserve so fine as her. She was pretty and smart, and her old man made a decent living as a bookkeeper for one of those big shipping companies. I sold a little real estate, some insurance, but it was really his dough saw me and the missus in good stead all through the twenties.

I can't say I always treated her right, though. Got no regrets in this world, mister, but that one. I don't even regret the last three weeks compared to that. Sometimes it's hard for a man to settle down, huh?

So then comes the Crash and her old man loses it all. I guess that's not too different from anybody else's story, is it? Well he had a head full of shadows, let me tell you, and right at Halloween he took a pistol and shot his wife, his daughter, and himself. Folks told me I was lucky not being there at the time, but I told you how I feel about luck, mister.

We never had any kids, so I guess it was just me that suffered. Those nights were cold on the streets in 'Frisco, so I hightailed it down to Los Angeles. First time I ever hopped the rails, too. Nearly lost my leg trying to jump on that freight. Railroad bulls weren't watching too closely in those days. I think they had enough problems of their own. I heard you can't barely hop a freight now without getting beat within an inch of your life. S'okay, though, I'm done with that life. Guess I'm done with it all, really.

Well you don't say much, and I appreciate you listening, fella. But your stomach's been chattering all through my speech. Got a little more to say then I'll show you to the diner.

I came down here during the summer of '32. Nights were balmy, and there's places down on the beach where no one would bother you. I once stayed in a jungle camp down by the dunes in Manhattan Beach for a whole month! Police rousted us out eventually. Some nob complained, no doubt. I had a good run there with my feet sticking in the ocean and my belly full of salty black mussels and even a little of that white lightning that got passed around. Isn't a bad life when you can get it, you know, being out on the road. At least you don't got to answer to no one most of the time.

Well, when they kicked us off the beach, I figured I had to earn some scratch, and I'd never stay at the Sallies. I never much liked handouts, you know. I took the old man's money as long as I was married to his daughter, but she made me happy, so having extra jack was just like having a scoop of ice cream on top of your apple pie. "A la mode."

Oh sorry. You must be real hungry.

So I hightailed it up to the valley where all them farms are. Papers were full of leaflets advertising good work, pay by the bushel. I figured a few months would see me in good stead, I'd save it all. I don't got many needs and I don't spend it all on liquor like some do.

I don't want you to think I'm telling you a story fueled by a crock of moonshine.

Well the valley was full of Okies and so forth willing to pick apples for five cents a box when a decent wage should have been at least ten. Even so, I tramped around picking apples, peaches, and walnuts and the like for about two years. Some of them outfits aren't too bad, even if they make you buy all your food at the company store on little slips of credit. Potatoes ten cents a pound! Hamburger steak twenty cents a pound! Highway robbery, you know. But I was a single man and not looking to feed any belly but my own, so most times I did all right.

You know all those freaky storms we had this winter out here? I'm from Kansas and I never saw winds like that, and that's saying something. Sure, there's no dust, but we saw thunder, lightning, and hail the size of my fist for days and days. One storm ruined this strawberry crop we was picking. All those strawberries pounded into pulp. Looked like some muddy battlefield afterwards. Believe me, I've seen plenty of those.

I don't think I made more than five cents the whole month after that storm. Somehow I got by on scraps and kindnesses... and a little stealing. Pride's a feeling for the brain and not the belly.

Eventually I got work at a place about twenty miles north of Riverside. Picking oranges this time. Perfect sweet globes of heaven, you know. I'd as soon eat oranges as anything ever again. But the owners had a strict policy against eating the fruit, some of the pickers told me about a man beaten to death for stealing an orange. Well, they had too many pickers working the orchards, and wages fell like a stone down a well. Hell, if they could have found a way to make us pay for the privilege of picking their fruit, they would have.

Wait. Did you hear that, mister? No I guess it's just the surf. They don't like the surf.

Well, things got ugly. We called a strike. Never saw myself being one of those agitators, but remember what I said about the stomach? The police got their noses bloodied and us strikers went to ground before there was any killing. I decided to head back to Los Angeles. That old ocean sang to me like some sweet siren from a fairy tale. Spent plenty of time at sea during the war, never quite shook her off. It was time to cool my heels in the sand for a bit until I figured out what to do next.

Are you sure you didn't hear that? Thought it was something over in the dunes. Lordy, I could sure use a cup of coffee.

So I lit out of Riverside along the back roads so as not to have any friction with the local constabulary. I hid out during the day and skulked around for two whole nights before I came to that railroad trestle out around Mission Grove.

It was getting near light, and I was eager to find someplace to hide out of sight of the police. I wasn't being too picky or too careful, and I tripped right over the dead man lying under there. He was sort of curled up on his side, his long arms wrapped around himself like he couldn't get warm. It was summertime, though, mister, and plenty of heat to go around even at night.

He stank a little, as the dead do, but there wasn't a mark on him.

They'll probably find me that way. Don't mean to scare you, buddy, but I figure you ought to know.

This fella under the bridge, he was a solid one, I'll say. Broad shoulders, big hands, skin browned and creased from long days in the sun. He'd been tramping awhile, I'd guess. Clothes were all loose at the stitches and the dust'd eaten away at his shoes.

You're nodding. I guess you seen a lot like him around, buddy? You see a lot like me, too. Look at my clothes, my shoes. Not so different, huh?

I don't mean to sound crass. I got plenty of respect for the dead, see, but it'd been a few months since I'd seen more than a dime. I went through his pockets and found three whole dollars.

Sure been a lot of hard times since we got this Depression on, but I'd never stolen from a dead man before. I don't mind saying while I had that money clutched in my hand, I wasn't real sorry the man had died under that trestle.

I'm plenty sorry now.

None of the dead man's scratch was folding money, just a lot of coins. I shoved jingling fistfuls into my pockets. Fat, sappy tears rolled down my face as I dreamed of turkey and mashed potatoes, endless cups of coffee, pork chops and slices of pie. Sky was the limit on what kind of pie, too.

That's when I spied this here buffalo nickel. It was in the last handful, glinting among some dull pennies. I'm not sure if the dead man carved it, but it was just as you see it now. Look at that grizzled hobo carved on the front. Kind of looks like him, doesn't it? It kind of looks like me, too.

Oh, and there's this hunchbacked thing on the other side. I didn't show you that before.

Pretty odd, huh? Never seen no buffalo like that. I should know— they still have a few in Kansas. This looks more like a dog to me, or a big cat, maybe. See the details on the flanks— they look like scales. And those teeth and slitted eyes. You get a real good look at this nickel before you take it from me, mister.

Hey! Hold your horses! I know you're hungry, but you can't have it until I finish my tale.

I spent the daylight hours under that trestle with the dead man, then tramped my way west when it got dark. Stopped at a little place down the road. They didn't like the look of me none, but I had three cups of coffee and two slices of blueberry pie. God damn me, it was the best thing I'd ever eaten in my life. I was only a little sad that all it cost was someone having to die.

Took a few weeks to make it back to Los Angeles on foot.

You ever get the sense someone's watching when there's no one there? This is a hard life and you got to grow eyes in the back of your skull to see trouble coming. Well that whole time I was hiking back to the city, I felt watched, if you know what I mean. I wasn't worried about the cops anymore, but the Wind's got a funny way of sounding like it's calling your name. Dead men appear in nightmares whether you've had one toot too many from the jug or not. And I wasn't drinking.

I stopped walking the roads at night. Always felt like someone was right on my heels. I'm not usually one for such talk, but I can see in your eyes, mister, you think I'm nuts.

Well, I got back to Los Angeles, still in mostly good spirits and ready for the good life. Before I hit the beach again, I stopped at this diner downtown where I knew they had a fine blackberry pie to slather my innards with. Well damn me, there was no blackberry pie, on account of them running out. All they had was a big slice of vinegar pie. Isn't that always the way?

Ever had vinegar pie, mister? It's easy to make when you don't got fancy ingredients. Eggs, sugar, flour. Cider vinegar. A little cinnamon if you got it. I grew up eating the stuff. Momma couldn't afford much better out there on the prairie. Eat enough of it, you never want to see it again when you leave home. Things have a way of circling back around again.

So I sat there, shoving pie in my face and across the counter, there was this big wall-length mirror over the coffee pots where they'd write the prices. I'm not a vain man, fella, and don't look into mirrors because I usually don't like what's looking back.

Well damn me, I nearly choked on a bite when I saw the dead man staring back at me. He was eating vinegar pie, too, frowning and shoveling it into his muscly face like he was starving in the afterlife. It was the middle of the day, but the shadows got a little darker and the color sort of drained away from the world like in an old picture.

Good Lord, I'd a died on the spot looking into that mug except he dropped his fork and started howling and banging the countertop just like me. Exactly like me, if you catch my meaning. We were one and the same, spitting up bites of sour pie and whooping like mad men. The waitress called out a couple of beefy cooks and they tossed me into the alley before I could do too much damage to the place.

So there I was flailing on the ground, screaming all the while, "That's not me! Lord Almighty, that's not me!"

Their eyes were soapy with this sort of angry pity. Oh, they're happy to take your money and happy to feed you a little food sometimes as long as you don't make trouble, but from the second you enter their shop they get that narrow look. First sign of anything wrong with your head, they don't care about your custom. I popped one of them cooks right in the pickets.

I don't know what got into me, honest. I ain't a violent man. Never even been in a fight except that striking stuff out in Riverside, and I was just protecting myself from them son-of-a-bitch police. You got nothing to worry about from me, fella.

I scooted down the alley and away from the cooks, still blubbering about the dead man. Well I know you want to ask it, so I'm going to tell you straight. I am he and he is me and so on. At least on the outside.

The strange part about it is I still got my own hands as far as I can tell. I look down and see the veins and spots and all those little cuts I've always had. Hell, sometimes I catch sight of my nose when I cross my eyes and I think it's the same old nose saw me through the War in Europe.

What color are my eyes, fella?

Blue as the summer sky over the open road. They should be brown. I always favored my momma that way.

So I bet you think I'm crazy now, just like all the rest. I'm surprised the other stiffs didn't warn you about me. Well even if you don't believe me, I can see you're still ready to take my money. I see those ribs poking though that shirt. You can have a piece of pie yourself tonight. Big cup of coffee with apple pie "a la mode." No vinegar pie for you.

Hey, the wind has shifted did you notice? From the east, that's odd. Dropped a few degrees, too. It can get cold here nights, but I'm sure you knew that. Last chance, fella. Still want to hear the rest? Still want my nickel? Well all right then.

So I found a trash heap with an old dresser in it, the mirror mostly broken but it was enough to prove what I already feared. I wore the dead man's face, sure enough. Later I broke into a service station toilet and saw the same. Hell, the dead man looked back at me even in the chrome of the pumps.

I tell you fella, it raises the hair on your neck, it does, to see a sight like that. I might have gone a little nuts for real after seeing that bleary-eyed mug looking back at me that last time.

I ran out of there like some frightened critter. A mouse away from a cat.

A deer away from the wolves.

That's the night I first heard them howling, friend. You ever hear the coyotes up in the hills around the city? It spooks the marrow right out of your bones. Those little yips and quavery cries don't sound like they quite belong to this world.

That's just the way of it, mister. And I never seen any coyotes come down into the city like that, neither.

I swear they were right on my heels when I got to the beach. Mind you, I couldn't see a damn thing, but I *knew* they were there, right? The air shimmered around me and the colors ran out of the world and drained into the cracks in the sidewalk. I stumbled past a few folks and even raced right by a policeman sitting on his motorcycle. He didn't even glance my way. I almost asked him for help, but what could he do, huh? What can anyone do against such shrieking and howling and gnashing teeth?

I scrambled over them dunes yonder, kind of rolled face-first into the sand. They backed off. Turns out they hate the sea.

Hear that? The regular tumble and boom and froth of the surf. They hate it. Too unpredictable for their ways. You ever been out to sea? You hear things when you're out there, too, little tricks of the wind that sound like voices, like screeching seabirds or moaning cries that vibrate out of the deep.

But the ocean's got this way of being, especially at the shore. It's this big calm vastness that hugs the land. An infinite horizon. Maybe that's why they don't like it much. Their purpose is too narrow, too single-minded.

Stay close to shore, buddy.

The man who carved this coin. Did he look like me? Look, I dug these scratches into the chin to make a longer beard. My own whiskers grew! I bet you could carve anything you want on the front and you'll be anyone you'd ever wanted to be.

It will buy you some time, if you look a little different. They won't pick up the scent right away.

See on the reverse here? That loping, hunchbacked thing with six legs? For goddamn sure it's no coyote. There's a mark where I tried to gouge its eyes out. Hard as diamond that side of the coin is, right? Set in stone with no changing it. Except it isn't just one I hear out in the shadows of the night, no sir. A pack of them. Coming for me, sweet Jesus, I don't know why.

Hm. Who am I kidding. I stole from a dead man. I guess I deserve it.

I'm not a bad man, though, mister. Most of us out here on the road are just good people in rotten straits. Some of us just like the open air. We lie, we cheat, we sometimes glom a little to get by, but we don't mean anything by it. Whoever carved this, though, wants us to die, that's what I think. He hates us tramps and every one of us that takes this coin is going to hear those hellish shrieks on the wind at some point. Gonna feel the shadows nipping at our heels.

Is that the fog rolling in? It seems a lot darker than it was.

Oh, sweet Jesus, I just thought about it. How many of these nickels are out there? Why carve up just one when you can make a bunch and get us all?

I bet you don't want it now, do you? What good's a cup of coffee if you get the hounds of hell on your scent?

Buy *me* a cup of coffee? That's a turnabout, but kind of you. Well, fella, it's like this. I don't want to leave the shore where it's safe. Lordy, I'm so weary of the sand and surf, though.

Yeah, I can see the diner from here. You're right, lots of folks around up there. Maybe it would be safe. I'm pretty hungry. Last thing I had was that vinegar pie.

Wait, mister! I'll come as far as the boardwalk. Maybe you can bring me a slice of pie? Finish my story when you get back.

Don't laugh! You're new to the life, so you haven't seen how cruel the world can be, or you wouldn't laugh at me. I'm not crazy! I bet you nev—

Wait a minute! What've you got in your hand? You got plenty of money, why you begging me for—

Nickels. A whole goddamn handful.

You son-of-a-bitch. It's *you*! You carved them all! I'll kill you! You heard them snickering shadows out here past the dunes the whole time.

Take your goddamn nickel. Give to some other poor son-of-a-bitch.

Oh Jesus, oh Christ, save me!

God Almighty, look at them pouring out of the cracks of the boardwalk. White fangs and glinting scales. Not wolves, not coyotes. What are they? Sweet Jesus what are they?

You knew. You knew the whole time. You just let me talk and talk while the pack gathered.

I hope you starve, mister. I hope one day you look around and there's no food and you gotta steal a loaf of bread just to eat. I hope your last meal's a slice of sour vinegar pie, too.

Then one day maybe *they'll* be starving and you're all out of bums to feed them.

Goddamn you.

WHAT CAN I SAY? I WAS STILL *young. Still impetuous. Still reveled in the power of my children. This particular one, the shadow creatures that bonded to it, was so new and different that I had to watch it make its kill. I particularly loved the way the coin marked its victim. Do you want to know how he died? What those creatures did to him? That would be telling.*

—The Carver

THE FALL OF JOLLY TANNUM

BRANDIE TARVIN

THE RUNABOUT HAD SEEN better days. The pitted running boards sagged under the weight of abuse and mud. The bed wore the weather in its rusting sidewalls after only three years of ownership. Frayed bits of the canvas roof treacherously allowed the morning's hot sun to roast the top of Jolly Tannum's head.

His sweet wife, Emily, sat in the passenger seat, oblivious to the heat and singing hymns as the light shined around, but not upon, her. She'd gotten dolled up in her Sunday best for the trip into town, wearing a paisley dress of light cotton, white gloves, a feathered hat that appeared as if it might take flight at a moment's notice, and the costume pearls Jolly had bought her for Christmas. Plump and happy, her angelic voice filling the air with righteous biblical glory, Emily's profile put Jolly in mind of his mother— dead of a heart attack these past five years. Despite the heat, cold wormed down his spine, and he quickly pushed Mama from his thoughts.

The day was hot, summer hanging onto the last days of September with the desperate grip of a child refusing to relinquish a sweet. But it had been a good morning. At Jolly's insistence, Emily went shopping while he attended to business at the bank. The loan officer seemed confident that oil stocks were all the rage, making more money than ever before, and assured Jolly that no one lost money in the stock market these days. So, Jolly had signed the margin papers, using his father's forty acres as the collateral. In a few months, he'd sell the stocks and be the richest man in Christian County, Illinois. No longer would Jolly

Tannum be the person asking favors and working twice as hard as everyone else to prove his worth. Everyone would be looking up to him, admiring him from a distance, asking him for favors.

"When I am a rich man," he muttered to himself.

Emily glanced over. "What was that, sweetheart?"

"Nothing, honey. I was just reflecting what a fine day it is."

She smiled. "It is a fine morning. Though you wouldn't know it to hear Mrs. Beard complaining. She's carrying around four fans, acting as if the heat is going to melt her straight into the sidewalk. I had to avert my eyes to keep from laughing at her bloated red face. Poor woman wouldn't last a moment in an Alabama summer."

Jolly chuckled at the image as he shifted gears and slowed for an upcoming crossroads.

Towering cornfields had a way of making rural Illinois feel deserted in a peaceful sort of way. Distant silos poked their tall, conical shapes above the detasseled stalks, silent sentries of their farmland kingdoms. Houses could be seen up on the hilltops, surrounded by carpets of lush green and yellow crops, yet the driveways and roads were all but hidden. On occasion, the top of a tractor could be spotted rumbling along behind the screen of plants, but trucks and cars were far too short to be seen.

The engine eased as the Runabout's nose drifted forward into the intersection. A quick look both left and right showed no signs of approaching traffic, so Jolly eased off the clutch, shifted back into gear, and accelerated down the road toward home. Emily continued to regale him with tales from the beauty parlor gossip she'd overheard while sitting in a back corner chair where no one could see her.

"...and Ethel insisted that Mr. Penwell is looking to sink another shaft somewhere east of town. It sounds crazy to me. There's no way the town can compete with the Pennsylvania mines."

I could open up a mine, Jolly thought. *Hell, I even could buy another forty acres of farmland.*

In the depths of memory, his mother whacked him with the back of a bristle brush for his blasphemy. Jolly bent his head over the steering wheel, muttering a silent prayer for forgiveness.

"Jolly, look out!"

His head snapped up to see a box truck roaring straight toward him in the middle of the road. Jolly cursed, wrenching the Runabout to his right just as the truck labeled "Willie's

Construction" heeled to its right. Cheers, whistles, and laughter echoed in the air.

Emily's face paled as she clutched her seat. "Those horrible boys!"

"Least they're not a lynch mob," Jolly muttered over his shoulder as he pulled into the drive.

"Oh my god." Emily grabbed his knee as Jolly pulled into the drive. "Jolly…"

He looked forward right before the Runabout plowed into the police car sitting in the drive. Two officers, Martin and Moore, stared at the pile dumped in front of the farmhouse. Jolly had left orders for it to be delivered in the back, behind the barn, so he could level out the old dried-up creek bed. Instead, Willie's boys had barely crossed the property line before they dumped the load, letting half of it spill across the driveway and the other half bury Emily's flowerbeds. The signpost bearing the farm's name, "Order 15," was buried up to the bottom of the name board. The farm name had been Papa's little joke.

The cops turned to face Jolly, Martin leaning against the car while Moore hooked a thumb in his belt. "What's this then?" Moore asked.

The couple stepped out of the vehicle, Jolly walking up and examining the mess. His answer when it came was short and curt. "Fill."

Jolly had spent fifty dollars on it. A whole month's worth of pay from his part time job at the local gravel yard exchanged for pile of junk. Instead of the clean fill Willie promised, Jolly had gotten a pile of dirt, roots, branches, broken plates, clay clumps, and other trash. The soil itself had the texture of ash, gray and fine, instead of the thick, deep brown of normal Illinois dirt. The dry stench of mold made Jolly's nose itch.

"Got a permit, boy?" Martin asked.

Emily clutched her purse against her belly, biting her bottom lip. She stayed close to the Runabout.

Jolly clenched his fists in an effort to control his temper. "What do I need a permit for?"

"'What do I need a permit for, Sir'," Moore corrected. He walked up putting his face in Jolly's. "Can't you read, boy? Law says you need a construction permit before you can do any building."

"Not doing any building, Sir. Just wanted some dirt so I could have some dirt."

Martin snorted. Moore stared at Jolly for one long moment before backing away. "Well, good. 'Cause if you were building, I'd have to cite you."

Jolly stared at the dirt, not answering. Martin and Moore waited for another few moments before getting back in their car.

"We'll be back to check on your dirt, farmer boy," Martin called as they drove away. When the pair was out of sight, Jolly growled and kicked at the ground.

Emily threaded her arm into her husband's and leaned her head against his shoulder. "What are you going to do?"

"Ignore them. They're just playing their little game. Sort through the fill by hand." Jolly hissed through clenched teeth. "It's no good complaining to that Southern-bred bastard. He'd just have his boys truck over something worse, and only after making me wait all autumn for it. Damn that man for a liar and a cheat. I wish he weren't the only game in town."

This time, he shoved aside the image of Mama with the bristle brush, trying to ignore the memory of her anger by feeding his own.

Emily winced at his coarse language. "You could have ordered from Taylorville."

"And paid twice the price for the load and twice more again for delivery." Jolly snorted.

Emily shook her head. "But it would have been clean fill."

Jolly didn't respond. A glint of metal had caught his attention.

Emily squeezed his arm and reached up to kiss his cheek, but he slipped out of her embrace and approached the mound. Wood rot wormed its way into his nostrils. Bugs — silverfish, termites, and tiny white worms — skittered and squirmed across the surface as Jolly reached into a clump of roots to free a heavy clod of dirt. Something sharp torn into his sleeve and scratched into his arm. He yelped and pulled away a bit of thorny vine that had caught in the roots. A section of shirt sleeve came away with it.

The clod dropped into Jolly's outstretched hand, leaving a slimy trail of moisture behind it. Breaking apart the clod bit by bit, he revealed a silver disk the size and shape of a coin. The dirt had worked into the surface and hardened, obscuring the disk's features. Jolly rubbed at it with the hem of his shirt, but only pushed the slimy dirt into the cleaner crevices.

"What is it, sweetheart?" Emily had come up behind him and he hadn't even noticed.

Jolly shook his head, a laugh bubbling in the back of his throat. "I think it's money. This fill has money in it."

He ran over to the well pump and gave the handle a few shoves. Cold, clean water sluiced over his hands and the disk. Using his thumbnail, Jolly managed to pry most of the dirt off the surface. It took several minutes and quite a few pumps before he finally got the disk clean. The recognizable form of a buffalo standing on flat ground with the words "five cents" underneath it confirmed his suspicions.

Jolly snorted again, holding it up for Emily to see. "It's a nickel. Now Willie only owes me forty-nine ninety-five. You think the rest of it is buried in the dirt?"

Emily laughed as she took the coin from him. Then her face paled. "Jolly..." Her voice trailed off as she flipped the coin to show the obverse side.

Carved into the surface was a leering skull covered by a shroud. To the side of it, where the word "Liberty" usually occupied the coin's surface, were the words "Above All Else, Honor." Beneath the skull, the stamped year 1913 showed some sign of wear. Scratches marred the numbers' surface, as if someone had tried to cut out the date.

Jolly ran his thumb across the skull. Warmth pricked his skin like a kitten's teeth. The scratch on his arm flared hot with pain.

"I don't like that coin. Get rid of it, Jolly. Please," Emily begged.

"Of course, dear." He patted her shoulder with his free hand. "Why don't you go back into the house and finish dinner while I decide what to do with this damned fill."

He kissed her then, to distract her as he slid the coin in his jeans' left pocket — as was proper with a found coin, while silently reciting an old children's rhyme to himself.

Find a penny,
pick it up,
and all day long you'll have good luck.

If a found penny was lucky, how much luckier would a nickel be? Piles of money danced in his imagination. Maybe he'd been too conservative in his investment this morning. Tomorrow he would ring up the bank and invest in some steel as well.

Emily reluctantly pulled away from him, her eyes dark with concern. After a moment, she nodded, unloaded her shopping from the truck, and left Jolly to his work.

The heat of the day bled away for a moment, leaving Jolly shivering. The scratched arm twitched, pain shooting up and down as he changed into his work clothes. When he came back outside, it felt as if both heat and humidity had doubled. He fetched the second-hand tractor he'd been forced to purchase on account of the salesmen at the tractor store being busy with every other customer but him. Resentment twinged inside him, along with a surge of sudden anger. He didn't remember feeling this way at the time. He'd just accepted it as part and parcel of life. According to Papa, Illinois wasn't nearly as bad a place to live as Mississippi had been.

By the time Jolly finished clearing the fill off the driveway, cold had replaced the heat of the September sun. His sweating hands slipped off the smooth metal of the steering wheel. He couldn't find the brake levers and kept opening the throttle. The tractor nearly went through the barn wall instead of the open door. He managed to get the damned machine parked, then staggered up to the house.

"Perfect timing," Emily called from the kitchen. "I'm just pulling the roast out of the oven. Make sure to wash your hands, sweetheart."

With a mouth full of grit and a throat too sore and tight to allow words to pass, Jolly grunted an acknowledgement as he left his boots on the front stoop. He teetered to the bedroom, using the wall for balance because the floor seemed to buck underfoot. His grandmother's quilt was the last thing to fill Jolly's vision as he pitched forward and fell into darkness.

Dreams of raging hot summers and freezing blizzards assaulted Jolly as he slept. Blankets wound themselves around him, trapping him under a weight that made breathing impossible at times. Voices murmured, sometimes at a distance, sometimes close up. His arm kept sending lightning bolts of agony into his brain.

"I love you," Emily whispered from somewhere in the darkness. Her soothing touched helped ease the fire inside him. Only briefly, though.

At one point, Jolly managed to swim to consciousness, his eyes fluttering open to a darkened room. The curtains had been drawn and something wet lay plastered against his forehead. Emily sat beside the bed, stroking his arm. When she noticed he was awake, she laughed in relief and helped him drink a glass of water.

Jolly tried to choke out a word, but all he could do was cough against the soreness of his tonsils.

"Shh," Emily cautioned. "You need to rest, sweetheart."

"W… what happened?"

"You're sick with fever. Doctor Givens says there's nothing to do but wait it out. I can get you some chicken broth if you'd like something to eat."

Jolly's stomach growled with hunger, so he nodded. But by the time Emily came back with the broth, he'd fallen asleep again.

On the fifth day, Jolly woke feeling weak, but with a clear head. His arm no longer ached, the scratch having faded to a bare, red remnant of an injury, and his throat once again allowed him to swallow. Against Emily's protests, he got up, ate breakfast, and prepared for work. Emily must have done his laundry because the clothes he'd been wearing the day he got sick were in his dresser drawer, minus his good luck charm. The skull nickel was gone. Not in his pockets, not in his wallet, not in the coin bowl he kept on his nightstand. As Jolly searched for the nickel, Emily came into the bedroom. "You need to rest," she said.

"I need to get back to the gravel yard." His words were as sharp as his irritation. "Harvest is coming soon and I'll need all my days off to take care of that."

At her stricken expression, he regretted his tone of voice. "Honey, every farmer has a bumper crop. The prices are already dropping and we haven't even hit harvest. I'll be lucky to get three cents to the bushel come market day. We need the money from the yard to afford next year's corn seed."

He didn't mention the stocks. He'd impress her with his cleverness at Christmas when he bought her a real set of pearls and a Sunday dress made of silk to go with them.

The hurt in her eyes faded, but her smile remained tight and small. "My poppa was a sharecropper in Alabama, Jolly. I know how this works."

"Then let me do what I need to do, Emily." He kissed her forehead. "Have you seen that nickel?"

Her eyes flickered away from his. "You promised to get rid of it."

Jolly heaved an aggravated sigh. "I didn't have time. Now where did you put it?"

"It was staring at me, Jolly. I was doing laundry and found it in your pocket and it was just staring at me. So I tossed it into the pond."

His stomach clenched, his lungs wheezed. All that good luck, just tossed away as if it meant nothing. He needed that luck. They needed that luck. Emily had no idea how much in debt he'd gone this year just to be able to afford the fertilizer and pesticides. He thundered out of the house. Emily chased after him.

"Jolly—"

"Don't, Emily. Just don't. I've got to go to work."

"But that's what I need to tell you," she shouted after him. "Mr. McKellan called while you were sick."

Jolly stopped on the porch. Mr. McKellan owned the gravel yard, but didn't touch the business. The man spent his days running his law firm and left the running of the gravel yard to his son-in-law. Seeing the pallor of Emily's face, Jolly felt his heart drop into his stomach. He swallowed hard, then swallowed again. "What— What did he say?"

She shuffled her slippers against the patio floor, stepping back to the door, her gaze resting anywhere but on her husband's face. "The yard is running up against hard times. Costs have to be cut, so…"

"So?" A rising tide of anger spilled into him. His ears pounded. His fists clenched.

"He said not to come back, Jolly. That there isn't a place for you at the yard anymore."

Jolly rocked back on his heels. He'd been fired. Let go. McKellan didn't even have the decency to do it to his face, just left a message with his wife. A growl worked its way out of his chest. "When?"

"Three days ago."

"And when did you toss my nickel in the pond?"

Emily caught her breath, her eyes widening as Jolly wrapped his hands around her shoulders. He didn't even remember approaching her, but now that he had, he wanted to shake her to see if the coin would fall out of her dress.

"When, Emily?"

"The day after you took sick," she squeaked.

Mama's mocking laugh filled his ears. He slapped her, but his open palm cracked against Emily's delicate skin, not Mama's. "That was my lucky nickel!"

Tears flooded Emily's eyes, spilling in silence down her cheeks as she sank against the inner doorframe. Her shoulders shook as she wrapped her arms around herself. Blood welled from a split on her lip and painted a streak along the doorframe.

In the depths of his memory, his mother leaned over him, the bristle brush in one hand, soap in the other, and a mean glint in her eyes. *Don't you sass me none, boy.*

Jolly closed his eyes, rocked back on his heels, trying not to cringe from the bristle brush.

You want that blasted nickel so bad, you go dredging with your own two hands.

"Yes, Mama," he whispered, hope filling the tiny spaces that fear chose to ignore.

A bird screamed out, an almost human sound that ended in a wet gurgle. A sudden warmth burned into his chest, sunlight scorching his skin as he grabbed a group of cattails and yanked. The packed ground refused to yield to his fists, but he continued to pound until it softened. Thick, warm mud splattered up, covering his face, plastering his clothes. Frustration screamed out of Jolly's throat.

"Where's my lucky nickel?"

When exhaustion finally drained his strength, he dropped the cattails and wandered back to the porch steps, burying his face in his mud-covered hands. "Why, Emily? Why did you have to throw it out?"

He glanced over his shoulder. Emily leaned against the inner door, no longer nursing her bruised lip and still not willing to meet his eyes either.

Horror twisted in Jolly's gut at the fear in her expression.

Guilt chased him off the porch.

A heavy buzz filled his ears. His vision doubled, blurred, then went black. He found himself staring at the dirty fill, heaving aside shovelful after shovelful, screaming at the sky. When his vision cleared, he was sitting in the Runabout, coaxing it into gear.

Jolly had barely reached the end of the drive when a wind gust heaved against the Runabout's side and lifted the back left wheel off the road. Fear crawled through Jolly's gut. He stopped driving and held on for dear life while the truck bounced up and tottered at a precarious angle.

It would serve me right, he thought while crying out, "Oh, God, help me, please. I ain't never hit a woman before."

The wind stopped, leaving behind an eerie calm as the truck dropped for a final time. The western horizon boiled with a line of thick black while scattered gray clouds scudded across overhead. Jolly waited for the next gust, giving his heart a chance to stop racing. Sweat beaded his forehead and the back of his neck, so he pulled a handkerchief from his shirt pocket.

A silver disk fell out of it onto the floorboard.

It was the nickel. The skull's empty eye socket winked up at him.

In that instant, he figured out what had happened. Poor Emily only thought she'd thrown the coin in the pond. Instead, it must have landed in the laundry basket. She hadn't even noticed it caught in his handkerchiefs.

Laughing in relief, Jolly picked up the coin and kissed it before shoving it back into his left pocket of his jeans. "I knew you were lucky!"

He had a brief urge to go back into the house, to tell Emily he'd found the coin, until he remembered she tried to hide it from him. A little shard of anger worked its way back inside him. "When I am a rich man," he muttered, dark thoughts flitting around in his head. Maybe he wouldn't buy her pretty things for Christmas. She betrayed him after all. It was her fault he'd gotten fired. Not that he needed to keep the job for much longer, but until his ship came in, the extra cash would have helped.

She was such a weakling, falling down and weeping after a petty little argument. His mother never would have acted so soft.

Instead of going back to the house, Jolly pointed the car toward town. He could use a drink, and Sam still served from a room behind the pool hall despite the Prohibition mandate. The majority of the county may have voted themselves saloon-free, but Sam took care of the few that disagreed with the sentiment. Sam didn't care who sat at his hidden bar, so long as the fella's money was the same color as everyone else's.

The rain started up as Jolly drove away from the farm, drizzling through the frayed canvas and down Jolly's shirt. The Runabout's engine coughed and sputtered, a sickly thing that threatened to stall every time Jolly slowed for the blind corners decorating every rural road during the pre-harvest weeks.

"God damned piece of junk," Jolly muttered as he shifted to take a sharp corner. "What is wrong with you? You worked just fine last week."

This particular intersection had the dark sheen of a mud puddle and as soon as Jolly hit it, he felt the road suck at the runabout's tires. He hit the accelerator and the engine bucked, swinging around the back end as the front twisted in place. A shriek caught Jolly's attention and his head snapped up to see a car bearing down on him. The couple inside seemed as startled as he at the impending collision, the other fellow jerking his steering wheel in one direction while Jolly tried pulling the truck off to the right.

The truck bounced as the car seemed to make contact, the barest kiss of rubber against rubber, the front left tires of both vehicles bouncing off each other. Another screech came from the car, the lady inside sounding thoroughly distressed, but the car continued on none the worse for wear so far as Jolly could tell as he glanced over his shoulder. His own vehicle continued its heavy bouncing for quite some distance, going all over the road as Jolly fought to control it. Until finally the engine gave one last wheeze before failing completely.

The truck coasted to a stop as lightning flashed overhead. Jolly cursed, and got out to look at the engine. In that moment, the heavens opened up and dumped a river of rain over him, the truck, and the neighboring fields.

Despite his efforts, he couldn't get the truck started again. The pouring rain made sight difficult, and the engine didn't like getting wet, it seemed. After thirty minutes of effort, Jolly decided to leave the truck where it was and walk the rest of the way to town. No one would drive around in this type of weather unless they had to, which made rescue an unlikely option. And he was closer to the bar than his farm. One of the boys would surely help Jolly out in exchange for a drink.

So Jolly trudged alongside the dirt road the rest of the distance, gathering mud in his boots and water in his socks as he went. Drenched and filthy, he arrived at the pool hall feeling as if the storm had followed him the entire way. The lights were on, dimly visible behind the curtains of the near-sideways downpour. A few cars were lined up along the gravel drive.

Jolly made it up to the entrance and stepped inside with care, tapping his boots against the mat. A hum of conversation came to a halt, as six other men, wreathed in smoke and playing poker at the back table, turned and stared. The sharp scent of cigars made Jolly's eyes water. Jolly pulled out his wallet as he stepped up to the bar, and grabbed a dollar.

Sam slipped the bill under the till, shaking his head at the state of Jolly's clothes. "Bad storm out there."

"Bad week," Jolly growled.

"I've got some medicine that will shake the chill out of your bones."

"Make it a double."

Sam grinned and poured a double-slug of amber heaven into a glass. Jolly snatched it up before the glass had finished ringing against the bar top. The whiskey had a harsh edge that tasted like rotten oranges mulled in cider. But the kick in the aftertaste had the added advantage of clearing his eyes. Jolly shoved the glass back.

"Shall I start a tab?" Sam asked.

"If you don't mind," Jolly sighed. "I think I'm going to be here a while. Least till the storm lets up."

Sam tilted his head toward the silent group of poker players. "In that case, care to join the game?"

As Jolly stepped to the table, one of the men lifted his cap. Lightning flashed outside, lighting up Martin's sneer.

"Hope you brought your money, boy. We don't take dirt as collateral."

Sunlight poured through the pool hall's windows and straight into Jolly's grit-filled eyes. His head throbbed and his vision blurred as he woke to the smells of stale tobacco and strong coffee. The mug clattered down before him, sending a chain of howling bells echoing through his sore skull.

"Ow."

"That's what you get for drinking all night, Jolly." Sam laughed. "Don't worry, the coffee's free. But once you're done, you need to leave. I don't want the local temperance committee reporting me to the chief of police."

Jolly sipped at the awful brew, forcing the scalding liquid down his throat. "Isn't the chief one of your customers?"

"Only so long as no one reports me. Here's your I.O.U."

The scrap of paper drifted in the air for a moment before settling down on the table before Jolly. It took him that long to realize his poker buddies had disappeared, leaving Sam and him alone in the hall. Smacking his lips together, Jolly lifted the paper to find his signature scrawled underneath an I.O.U. for one hundred dollars.

Jolly reeled in his chair as the floor dropped out from under him. He couldn't have drunk that much. "What the hell?"

"Don't try that too-drunk-to-remember excuse, Jolly. I don't lend money out to just anyone, and the only reason I did was because you were buying drinks for everyone on account of your new-found riches. Though why the hell you'd let Martin egg you on like that is beyond me. You swore on your lucky nickel that you would remember, and I'm holding you to it."

Memory sparked, fuzzy and full of alcoholic warmth. Martin bumping up the pot, Martin mocking Jolly's playing skills, Martin scoffing when Jolly crowed about his soon-to-be Christmas riches. Everyone else had fawned over Jolly, convincing him to buy the rounds, to show off his lucky nickel. Martin even tried to snatch it off the table last night. Not only because he was buying but because he'd spilled the beans on his recent investments. His throat still ached from the crowing he'd done on how rich he'd be by Christmas. Chagrin darkened Jolly's cheeks. He'd meant to keep his luck a secret. He patted his left pocket and relaxed when he felt the cold skull outline prick his fingers.

Sam stood by the table, a frown filling his face.

Jolly waived it away. "No, I remember. It just took me a minute. Sorry."

The frown faded and Sam nodded. "I get it. Happens to people all the time. So we're good?"

"We're good. I'll get the money to you before Christmas."

"Need a ride back to the farm?"

"No. I think I'll walk off the hangover."

Relieved, Sam opened the door and let Jolly out.

The long walk home gave Jolly plenty of time to think. He'd been a mess yesterday and treated Emily poorly. The closer he got to the farm, the guiltier he felt. He stopped to collect a handful of wildflowers, choosing colors Emily would love. He'd give her the bouquet, apologize, then take her to town for dinner and a film at the new movie palace. She'd enjoy that. Emily always wanted to take in a talkie.

The farm felt quiet in an awkward way. He hesitated outside the door, then removed not only his dirty boots, but the socks for good measure. Emily would be more gracious if he weren't tracking dirt all over her clean floors. The door opened under his touch.

"Emily? Emily, I'm home."

He sniffed for the comforting smell of bacon and eggs, then frowned when it didn't come. Jolly padded to the kitchen, finding it empty. "Emily. Honey, I've got a present for you."

No reply came.

Perhaps she was still angry. He put the flowers in a vase for her, arranged it on the table, then went to the sitting room. That too was empty. Worry nagged at him but he brushed it aside as he checked the laundry room, then the backyard, the garden, and the barn without bothering to put his boots back on. He froze at the state of the garden. The tips of the tomato plants poked above a trash-filled mound of the bad fill. Willie's boys had done it again. Emily would be inconsolable.

"Emily," he yelled. "I need you!"

The memory of his mother brandishing the bristle brush came on strong. *Stupid boy. You go ahead and break your toys. See if you get new ones.*

Panic dug claws into his heart. Jolly ran back to the house, checked the root cellar, then went inside and threw open the bedroom door. "Emily, please. This isn't funny."

The wardrobe door swung wide as he stepped into the room, showing its barren insides. Hangers lay piled on the floor beside it. Emily's dresser drawers had been yanked off their stays and every stitch of clothing was missing. Her jewelry box was also gone, though Emily's precious costume pearls had been scattered across the floor and left behind.

Jolly's gaze wandered the room, searching for a sign, any sign that this was some sort of joke. Then his eyes fell upon the corner of the room where he had kept the traveling suitcase. He'd bought it after the wedding, promising her they'd use it for the "someday" that Jolly would have enough money for a proper honeymoon.

The suitcase was nowhere to be seen.

His knees gave way underneath him as the import of the scene sunk in. Emily had left him.

Jolly pulled the nickel out of his pocket. "Bring her back to me," he begged.

The skull stared back at him. An icy sensation sizzled up through his arm.

After several hours spent wallowing in guilt, Jolly drifted off to an uneasy sleep, dreaming about how he could win her back.

When Jolly woke, it was with the realization that Emily would go back to her mother. And if not there, then she'd be staying with her older sister. Both places Jolly knew well. They'd spent every other Easter with Emily's family. Buoyed by this knowledge, Jolly got up to pack a bag and spotted a trail of mud across Emily's floor.

That wouldn't do. She'd never taken him back if he left her house a mess. So he pulled out the mop and bucket and applied himself to a late summer house cleaning. Jolly worked the way he remembered Emily working, from the outskirts of the house in toward the kitchen. He scrubbed all the way to the patio door, then stood to dump his bucket when he saw reddish streaks and blotches marring the white paint. Jolly rested the fingers of one hand against one streak while pulling out his nickel with the other. The cold metal pricked at his fingers and shot fire through his arm.

A knock came at the outside door, but Jolly barely noted it. The nickel held his attention. The knock became a pounding, and he ignored it. Dipping the brush into the bucket, he scrubbed at the dried stains while holding the coin tight against his palm. The pounding became a hammering. He heard his name drifting on the breeze, called by a male voice, not by Emily.

The door squeaked open and footsteps clattered against the floor. Shoes. Someone had entered the house wearing shoes, spreading dirt all over Emily's nice clean floor no doubt. She'd pitch a fit for sure.

"Emily," he whispered.

"Jolly Tannum, what the hell are you doing, boy?" came an answering voice.

Jolly glanced over his shoulder. Martin and Moore flanked the door, Moore easing his pistol out of its holster while Martin gaped at the soapy scene.

"Hello, Mr. Moore," Jolly said, not quite comprehending their expressions. "Can I help you?"

Martin leaned toward his partner. "I don't think this sick bastard has the permit."

"Drop the brush and get to your feet, Tannum," Moore cracked, his sunburned face paling to a pinkish-gray. "Don't try anything funny."

"I've gotta clean the house before Emily gets back. "

53

Martin grabbed Jolly and yanked him upright. "He told everyone last night he was coming into money. Claimed it was from the stock market. Wanna bet it's an insurance payout?"

"Sounds like motive for murder," Moore commented. "Kill wife, hide the body, live the good life."

"No!" Jolly struggled in Martin's grip. The brush and nickel dropped to the floor. "I didn't kill anyone. Emily's at her mama's house."

"Sure she is," Martin said, slamming his fist into Jolly's stomach. "When did you first plot the death of your wife?"

"I didn't kill anyone!" Jolly shrieked, staring at his nickel, so close and so far away.

Moore kept the pistol pointed at Jolly as he eased forward. "Well, well. This looks valuable. Who'd you steal it from?"

"Give that back! It's mine! I found it and it's mine!" Jolly ripped out of Martin's grip and lunged at Moore.

Pain exploded in Jolly's temple as the pistol cracked across it. He sank to the floor, blood filling his sight. "I didn't do anything wrong," he whimpered.

"We believe you," said Martin. "And on the way to the jailhouse, you can tell us all about the bloody streaks you were trying to wash off that door."

GREED AND PRIDE ARE TWO *of my favorite vices. Add envy, and you get the perfect trifecta of sin to attract one of my coins. In this case, it blinded Jolly to his own folly — as well as everything else around him. He had what most men dream of: a loving wife, a sturdy home, a job he could be proud of. He should have been satisfied. Yet, he wasn't and that let my coin go to work. Too easy.*

— The Carver

SPENDTHRIFT

JAY LAKE

ALL OF MERAUKE whispered with the rumors. *The Japs are coming.* Springfield McKenna didn't place much faith in rumors. She'd traded in them far too long to lend credence to someone else's social munitions.

The Hotel Hindia-Belanda had stood above the port town's waterfront for two centuries, insofar as she knew. Springfield could believe that story, based on the eccentric interior fittings. The parlor seemed to have been constructed of lumber salvaged from a dozen wrecks. Parts of the walls were paneled in teak that would have fetched a fortune at auction in Honolulu or San Francisco. Other sections were raw, faded ash; gone to splinters and mottled with mysterious stains that could just as easily have been rotten durians burst in the heat or the lifeblood of a hapless crew overrun by Sea Dayaks.

The piebald interior suited the Hotel Hindia-Belanda, a piebald place in a piebald city at the edge of the Dutch East Indies. Which was insofar as Springfield was concerned precisely the ass end of nowhere.

She liked it that way.

Or had, until the war came creeping down the sea lanes and stepping across the islands, scaring the Dutch and the Aussies who ran most of the guns and money in these parts. Though she wouldn't have cared to be a *huisvrouw* in Merauke, the fat old traders and their lean factors were happy enough to do business with an American woman who could match them drink for drink

55

and joke for joke until the dawn came back around the curve of the world to light up another day.

Except for the damned Japanese and their damned Greater East Asia Co-Prosperity Sphere.

That, she thought, *and a certain American bastard who'd traded away almost every bit of my wealth, all for a nickel.*

The coin lay now on the tabletop. The familiar Indian head had been cut to a grinning skull, still wearing his braids and feathers. The old bastard looked positively happy. Which was strange, because the hobo nickel bore a patina that Springfield was barely able put words to. Speckled with time and hate, she could swear she heard it vibrating in her bureau drawer at night, mixing with her costume jewelry gold and her real silver.

First Ferris Roubicek had come into her life. Then he was gone again, leaving her with a broken heart, a failed business, a Japanese invasion, and a coin.

She wasn't sure the coin wasn't the worst of the whole business.

The scrape of chair legs prodded Springfield McKenna out of her reverie. "You still here?" asked a rough Aussie voice. Which was good, because her Dutch was crap; mostly useful for talking to bartenders and sailors.

Springfield peered up to discover to her surprise she was mildly drunk. Otherwise Captain Waldo Innerarity, Royal Australian Air Force, wouldn't have looked so good to her.

No way.

Not even for a moment.

He wasn't all that bad a view to take in, she had to admit. Tall for a pilot, with the shoulders of a shore patrolman and pale blue eyes like the Andaman Sea. Ruddy from sun and drinking, brown hair with enough of a kink to argue about where all his ancestors might have come from. All of that just made him more interesting to think about.

But looking good? Waldo? She'd have sooner kissed her brother.

"You're out of uniform," Springfield said. Which was true but pointless. Waldo wore canvas trousers and a short sleeved linen *barong Tagalog*. The embroidery looked a little queer on him.

"Uniforms might be pretty unpopular around here soon." Waldo threw himself down in the chair with reckless disregard for the stresses involved and signaled the bartender for a drink. The Hotel Hindia-Belanda knew how all its regulars took their booze.

Springfield was pretty sure that the Indonesians and New Guineans in Merauke hated their white masters with an indiscriminate abandon, but at least around the hotel they smiled and kept their opinions behind the kitchen doors. She was careful never to order any food that could easily be spat in on the way to the table.

Sometimes one just had to trust the cook.

"Not all of 'em," Springfield finally said, realizing she hadn't been holding up her end of the conversation. "Jap yellow could be all the rage for the next season's fashion."

Waldo nodded and reached for the coin on the table. She snatched it away before his big, oddly delicate fingers could close on it.

"What you got there, lass?" he asked. Innerarity's voice went oddly soft, as it did so often when he spoke to her. She knew what *that* meant, coming from a man like him.

"Nothing anyone here cares about." That, at least, was true.

"Been taking payoffs?"

She had to laugh. "In American nickels? One at a time? You're out of your mind, flyboy."

He leaned forward as a sweating glass of gin garnished with a sliver of mango tapped on the table. Springfield avoided the waiter's eye. Waldo bit his upper lip, then asked, "So if you ain't being paid, why are you still here?"

She met his stare with a level gaze of her own. "Everybody's got to be somewhere." The verbal equivalent of a shrug.

"Not every somewhere is in fear of Jap bombings. Or patrols. The boys had a shoot-up two nights ago in the hills not forty miles east of here."

"So I heard." Rumors, rumors. *The Japs are coming.* "They've got a lot better things to do than knock over one-horse towns where the horse died."

He smiled like moonlight on the Torres Strait. "You've got a lot better things to do than sit around waiting for one-horse towns to be knocked over."

Springfield thought that one through for a moment. "Are you propositioning me, Leftenant Innerarity?"

His smile blossomed to a grin. "Hell no, Sheila. A man ain't that daft. But I am trying to save your damned fool life. If you want a seat out of town, I'm flying over to Darwin in two days. Hitch a ride, see what comes next."

The name slipped unbidden from her lips. "Ferris Roubicek."

Waldo frowned. "*Mr.* Ferris is gone from these parts three months and more. Last seen on a Chinese steamer heading for Ceylon. And well understood not to be coming back."

"I'm tapped out," Springfield admitted. "Ferris took me good. I was running a pretty solid business in spice and batik, even with the war coming. Maybe especially because of the war. But he... promised..." *Confidences whispered under starlight as the insects whined against the netting.* She tried again, her head growing hot and tight under Innerarity's infuriatingly sympathetic gaze. "I made a bad deal, Waldo. I'm living on the last of my credit now." She turned the hobo nickel over in her hand, felt its patina through her skin even under the table and out of sight.

Somehow it all came down to the damned coin. Yet she hadn't been able to get rid of it. Not so far.

The words 'until death do us part' sprang unbidden and unwelcome into her mind.

"All the more reason to leave, eh? Seat's yours, no need to pay."

"Not in coin," she replied.

With those words, his face closed and his frown drew tight. Springfield knew she hadn't been fair, but damn it, this was *Waldo*. Not someone who had any right to have an interest in her.

"Besides," she added. "The Japs might never get here."

He stood up, tossed back his gin in one huge gulp that must have burned all the way down. The mango slice tumbled into his mouth with the booze. "You just keep telling yourself that, Spring. Who knows? Might even be true."

With that, the lieutenant left, taking his big shoulders and his manly ways with him.

After a while, Springfield signed her chitty and trudged up to her room. Doubtless the waiter would report what he'd heard to Inigo van Damme, the manager. Then the manager would ask, again, about her bringing her bill up to date.

She was fairly certain they wouldn't take a lone skull-faced nickel in payment.

That night Springfield McKenna had the dream again. Japs in their mustard yellow uniforms and peaked hats walked the muddy streets of Merauke. The city was under occupation, the Dutch and Australian defenders vanished as surely as if they'd never been here. There weren't even blood spatters or bullet holes. Just Japanese soldiers everywhere. Stolid. Silent. Shuffling. Staring at her with empty eyes.

They all marched to the beat of some distant tin drum. A rattle that carried from the hills outside of town all the way down to the portside slums along the banks of the Maro River. Even the endless nightly concerto of insect and bird and jungle screech had quieted in the face of that beat.

She heard that noise. Metallic. Small. Sly. It carried everywhere. It informed her heart and doused her hearing and set her thoughts to smoldering.

With a sweaty, fetid start, Springfield realized she was awake. But the beat which had carried through her dream of invasion still echoed.

It was the nickel. In her bureau drawer. The coin was rattling. Marching like a tiny army of its own through her dreams and through her life.

She slid from her bed and tugged on a pair of airman's coveralls. In the sticky heat of the New Guinea night, Springfield didn't even bother with foundation garments or makeup. She just dressed swiftly and angrily, then took a discarded cigarette tin in hand and stood before the bureau.

Inside, the skull-faced nickel rattled on its own. Counting time. As if it were one of those deathwatch beetles.

"You bastard," she hissed, though Springfield couldn't have said whether she was talking to Roubicek or Innerarity or her father or who. She yanked the drawer open with a savage tug and captured the dancing nickel in an empty tin. It rattled a moment, then fell quiet.

"You bastard," she repeated, and stalked out into the night.

It wasn't far from the Hotel Hindia-Belanda to the waterfront. Though in truth, nothing was far from anything else in Merauke. She scuttled the few blocks, keeping to the deepest shadows where possible.

As she approached the dockside, a single shot echoed. Springfield froze. She wasn't especially afraid of men with guns, but she had a lot of respect for what they could do in a careless moment. The only thing stupider than being shot in a war zone would be being shot by accident.

59

"Damn it all." Springfield froze next to a stack of fish traps that reeked of rot and creaked slightly in the wind questing off the night's water.

A voice called out nearby, indistinct but with the overtones of Dutch.

Someone answered cautiously from further down the docks.

A short laugh, barked with the clipped nervousness of a man under pressure.

Then another shot.

Her nerve broke. She ran back toward the Hotel Hindia-Belanda, cigarette tin clutched so tightly in one hand that the metal was being crushed. When Springfield reached her room, she dumped the coin out on the scarred marble top of the bureau amid the grimy doilies and empty atomizers. The skull grinned up at her.

"I should have known it wouldn't be that easy," she told it with a glare.

Waldo's offer of a seat on his flight was looking better and better. She absolutely hated that.

Rumors the next day were of Japanese spies on the waterfront, and graves being violated at the cathedral. Springfield was hard pressed to see how those two could be connected. That didn't stop people from speculating.

She used her copious free time to pack one small valise. It wouldn't do for van Damme to think she was leaving with her bill unpaid, after all. And nothing a woman wanted or needed in Merauke was going to be too hard to replace in Darwin, or wherever she wound up.

Lieutenant Innerarity wouldn't be footing her bills, Springfield promised herself.

She packed her last pair of silk stockings, a few necessaries, and one nice red dress. Just in case. With her dark hair and pale complexion, the color was striking, setting off her green eyes to great advantage. At least, that's what her mother had always said. Springfield figured she'd need all the advantages she could get.

Her gulden were pointless outside of the Dutch East Indies. Let the hotel staff squabble over the small stack of coins. She still had two hundred American dollars, the last of her working capital remaining from Ferris Roubicek's taking of her wealth and pride. *That* was what she couldn't give to the manager. What she couldn't afford to lose.

A few clothes, a little money, a nail file, and the nickel.

That was it.

Half a decade working here in the islands, a place where being a woman wasn't an automatic disqualification from business, by virtue of her being an American. All she had to show for five years was a valise that could have carried half a dozen newspapers. A little money and a red dress.

Even the rest of the clothes she'd leave behind. She'd meet Waldo at dawn in her coveralls.

That dealt with, Springfield decided to go out. She couldn't stand spending the day under the suspicious eyes of the waiters and the bartender. Everyone knew the white people were one panic away from leaving.

That night, she dreamt again of Japs in the streets. They shuffled as they walked, dragging their feet and staring downward as if afraid to say anything that might compromise their fealty to their Emperor. They were everywhere in Merauke, filling the streets as if division after division had landed and overrun the place. Shoulder to shoulder, chest to back, the soldiers moved in eerie silence except for the beat of their one tin drum.

She refused to wake up for that damned coin.

Absolutely refused.

In the end, Springfield awoke for Waldo Innerarity. Or at least his knock.

"We've got to get moving, love." His voice through the door was low almost to the point of being indistinct.

Her ride out. The dreams, the shots. It was over here in Merauke, her whole party done for. Ferris Roubicek had blown out the candles, but even the cake was nothing but crumbs now.

Springfield had slept in her flight overalls. She tugged on a pair of men's low quarter boots, ran her hands through her hair twice, grabbed her valise, unlocked the door, and threw it open.

"I—" Waldo swallowed his words as he stared at her.

"Ain't seen a woman before, flyboy?" She chucked him under the chin. "Let's go before the manager busts me."

"Too late, I am afraid." Van Damme stepped up behind the lieutenant. "You cannot be leaving us without a settlement?"

"Not at all," she began sweetly, but Waldo elbowed Inigo in the gut, effectively ending the discussion. Springfield shot him a wild look of thanks. She reached into her valise for the skull-faced nickel, intending to leave it for a tip, but all she could think of in that moment was the marching Japanese in their endless, mindless numbers.

"Get out while you can, van Damme," she whispered, the best tip she knew to give him. But Innerarity was already tugging her arm away, away, away.

The RAAF flying boat looked like a real beast as it floated at the dock. Beyond, over the hills east of town, the sun pearled the eastern sky the color of the inside of a compact. "Short Sunderland," Waldo said, as if that meant anything to her. "The boys are aboard already. Don't say nothing you don't have to, it'll go easier on us all."

Springfield felt a sudden and unexpected attack of cold feet. She stood on the dock, looking up at the looming side of the aircraft. Something whirred— bilge pump, starter motor, she had no idea.

She felt as if she were being invited to climb into her coffin.

"Waldo..." Springfield whispered.

"Come on, Sheila." He tugged at her arm. "We've got to be away before the sun comes up."

Before anyone sees me getting on the airplane, she thought. Then she remembered Inigo van Damme gasping on the floral carpet in the hotel's upstairs corridor.

She was committed now.

"I'm ready," Springfield whispered, mortified at the squeak in her voice.

Innerarity helped her aboard. As she stepped up the gangplank, she could swear she heard the skull-faced nickel rattling in her valise.

Takeoff was an agonizing bounce and drag over the waters offshore. The Short Sunderland was a roaring, stuttering monster that clearly had no affinity for the air. It coughed around her, reeking of electricity and fuel and exhaust and the sweat of nervous men. Cigarettes, too, though no one was smoking right then.

Perversely, Springfield wished she had a Lucky Strike. She didn't smoke, never had, but she'd always envied the easy way people who did could handle their nerves. Light up, take a draw, strike a pose. It was much more elegant than wringing one's hands and hoping for better.

The airplane lurched and banked. She looked out the porthole at the Arafura Sea gleaming in dawn's light. Sharks lurked in the waters along shore, visible in their silhouettes. The muddy beaches were littered with storm debris, the swamps thick with trees. Shadows still lay across the land in contrast to the ocean's morning glow.

The Japanese were down there somewhere.

Springfield glanced around the upper cabin. The rest of seats were empty. Which was strange. Surely other people had wanted to leave Merauke as badly as she. Though the RAAF wasn't in the habit of giving rides to anyone who just happened along.

It occurred to her to wonder once more what Waldo wanted. But then, that was obvious enough. *Not him*, she told herself. *Though in truth, not anyone.*

Not since Ferris Roubicek. Nor since long before him.

She found the nickel in her hand then. It lay cold and heavy, like a bullet. Heavier than a coin should ever have been. Springfield could feel it vibrating against her palm. Not in time with the overwhelming drone of the engines. Rather, the coin set its own rhythm. The rhythm of a thousand shambling Japanese.

Then one of the engines coughed harder. It emitted a blatting noise. Springfield shot a look out the window to see a haze of smoke coming from her side. Left. Port. Whatever they called it on an airplane.

The engine coughed again, stuttering before it settled into the slower rhythm of the nickel.

The little metal door leading forward banged open and Waldo leaned into the passenger cabin. "What the bloody hell happened?" he demanded.

Springfield closed her fist on the coin, feeling guilty for no reason she could name. "Something's wrong with your, um, port engine."

"I fewking know *that*." He stalked over to stare out her port. "Damn it, we can't just turn back."

The airplane bucked then. A series of thumps echoed from the outside.

"Japs," shouted Waldo, and rushed back to the flight deck.

Japs? But they walked in slow silence, taking over the world by numbers and rhythm. Not through violence in the air.

Outside her porthole, a slim aircraft slid by. She could see the big red circle on the side, painted over the jungle camouflage. *Why paint an airplane like a tree? Who would it hide from in the blue, blue sky?*

Three more of its fellows followed.

Zeroes. Even she knew that word, knew what those planes looked like.

One waggled his wings in salute, as if they were just friends sharing a pleasant morning's flying.

The flying boat banked hard to the right, tilting her view toward the clouds still colored salmon and rose. Springfield McKenna watched the heavens glare as around her Lieutenant Waldo Innerarity's airplane began to die. In her hand, the nickel pulsed like a beating heart.

The shoreline came rushing upward, a green fist folded over the troubled rim of the ocean. Waldo, or whoever was up on the flight deck with him, brought the Short Sunderland in hard, skimming the wave-tops. Springfield supposed they were aiming for a welcoming stretch of beach. All she saw was the end.

Smoke curled through the cabin, and both engines were ragged and stuttering. The flying boat wallowed like a puppet with half its strings cut. The Japanese were surely out there, following their prey to earth. Sharks on a dying swimmer.

Then the great fist of the land grabbed Springfield and punched her in the chest, took the air from her lungs and the fire from her belly and handed her only pain and pressure in return.

She was not so lucky as to pass out. Rather, she was thrown back and forth in her seat, somehow held in place by the flimsy safety harness, as the world outside the porthole dissolved into a mass of spray and sand and smoke.

"Out, out, out," someone was shouting. Springfield didn't know who. It might have been her. She still couldn't breathe, couldn't talk, but she could unclip her belt and tumble from the chair and slide across the carpeted wall and see nothing but sand out of the opposite porthole on set into the floor.

A man was screaming as well, the kind of scream someone lets out when their arm is ripped off. She ignored that, ignored the smoke and flames and reek of fuel and the irregular chatter of gunfire outside, to claw her way toward the portholes where the world still peered through. New Guinea was briefly surprised by her latest invader before the jungle would come to claim them all.

A few panicked moments later, Springfield found herself hidden away among great, tall roots. She watched the RAAF flying boat burn while one of the Japanese Zeroes lazed overhead, laying down gunfire on the beach every second or third pass. In case any of the Aussie airmen inside had notions of surviving their crash.

She stared impassive, tears streaming down her face, unfeeling, grief-stricken, the coin clutched in her hand like a beating heart, waiting for the fire to die and all of Innerarity's crewmates with it.

Springfield McKenna knew then that her life had been bought too cheaply.

Night brought wakefulness once more amid the reek of smoke and jungle rot. She didn't even realize she'd fallen asleep. The snarl of the last loitering Zero had been in her ears, until replaced by the chatter and howl of New Guinea's moonlit jungles.

The tree she'd wedged herself into still protected her. Sure, there were some bugs crawling down the leg of her coveralls, but they seemed to be using her as a throughway, not as a meal ticket.

At least someone is getting some good out of this.

The coin was quiescent in Springfield's hand. She slid from the tree's embrace and step aching onto the sand. Her body was bruised in places she didn't even know she had. The skin on the side of her head felt sticky and tight in a way that suggested she really didn't want to look into a mirror. The surf rolled in before her, foaming wave-tops glowing slightly in the light of the three quarter moon.

"Now I give you back to the ocean," she whispered into her clenched fist, then cocked her arm to throw the skull-faced nickel far out to sea. She might have been a girl, but Springfield McKenna could throw. Two seasons playing left field for the Jax Maids down in the Crescent City had proven that. Before she'd had to leave the country.

"Ferris," screamed Springfield, her eyes filling with tears for Waldo and the men she didn't even know, "you bastard."

A voice groaned out of the darkness. "Sheila..."

She aborted her throw, spinning in place to face the sound. "What?"

65

Someone was crawling toward her across the muddy beach. He *creaked* as he came, moving no faster than the shambling Japs of her dreams. "Spring…"

Dropping to her knees, Springfield peered at him. "Waldo?"

He made another three or four crawling steps, then collapsed to roll over on his side. "I…"

She looked close, trying to peer into those Andaman blue eyes. All she saw was rippled, bubbled skin. The smell of crisped pork filled her nostrils. His teeth gleamed unnaturally large, lips burned away and gums drawn back with the heat.

His breath… He had no breath at all. Lieutenant Waldo Innerarity had exhaled his last trying to reach her.

Springfield jumped to her feet and swallowed the urge to scream. This was another dream. All of it. The flight. The Zeroes. The crash. *This*. Waldo.

She backed away from him, slowly, her heels kicking at the slimy mud. Stumbling into a tree root, Springfield turned to catch herself on a branch.

Except it was no branch.

She had bumped into the leg of another burnt corpse. He hadn't been there a minute earlier, when she hopped out of the tree.

The nickel twisted in her hand. It vibrated, tapping out its rhythms as if preparing to sing.

The sea brought the odors of watery death and seaweed. Infinitely preferable to fuel fires and roasted pork. Behind her, the jungle breathed. Springfield stared at the two dead men at her feet. Then she opened her hand to drop the nickel.

"N'a do 'at," said another voice in her ear.

This time she did shriek. Springfield twisted to find another Aussie airman, crisped by fire, half his skull shattered from a Japanese bullet.

This was Waldo, she realized with horror. Not the corpse behind her. She spun again and he was gone. So was the other airman.

A dream, a dream, she told herself. *Like the shambling Japs. Wake up now, damn it.*

But there was no waking up. There were only burnt, bloody hands tugging at the sleeve of her coveralls, clumsily brushing through her hair which had come flyaway loose, stroking at her feet.

Springfield screamed again. She really put her lungs into it this time. She kicked, too, with what had once been deadly accuracy. But these men... creatures ... whatever they were... they didn't care.

She grabbed a piece of driftwood and swung it as hard as any Louisville Slugger. Teeth sprayed in the moonlight, a puff of ash flying with them. A broken skull shattered. Grasping hands were slapped back.

There were only two of them. Or maybe three, or four. Not like the Japanese soldiers in her dreams who filled the streets of Merauke and came on in their blind, implacable, unstoppable numbers.

Just a handful of men. One of whom she'd actually kind of liked in his strange way. "Damn you, Waldo," she shouted at the twitching corpses. "Why the hell did you go and do this?"

She kicked and kicked again, then had to whack her own leg with the stick to force an independent, questing hand off her calf. *Just like a man.* Breath whooping, tears threatening, Springfield McKenna fought a nightmare on the moonlit beach at the mouth of the Torres Strait until eventually she was surrounded by only bones and pulped flesh and shattered teeth and wispy shreds of scalp.

She stood over the corpse she thought might actually be Waldo. Like all of them, it was in several pieces. At the least, they'd come apart easily under the blows from her stick. Springfield resolutely ignored the fact that various severed body parts were moving and twitching. She ignored the yawning gap where her heart used to be, where her nerve used to live.

"It's yours now." She raised her clenched fist to drop the skull-faced nickel with the rest of her dead.

The click of a rifle bolt sliding home just behind her arrested Springfield's hand in mid-motion.

A small man, frowning, wearing horn rimmed glasses and a uniform pale gray by moonlight, stepped in front of her. A Jap officer.

"Some things are not meant to be thrown away."

Springfield blurted the first thing that came into her head. "You speak excellent English."

"For a Jap?" He nodded and smiled, a small, controlled expression that seemed more practiced than real. "Lieutenant Ginnosuke Sakamura. Stanford Law School, class of nineteen thirty-six." The officer glanced at her fist. "Do not let go of that."

What?, she wanted to ask, but it would have been a foolish question. She settled for, "How do you know?"

"Some things can be seen clearly enough." He shouted in Japanese over her shoulder, though she'd heard no noise behind her since the click of the rifle bolt sliding home.

Slowly, Springfield turned. Sakamura held his ground. She could feel his smile boring into her back like the first thrust of a knife.

An entire platoon of Japanese soldiers stood between her and the tree line. They were ranked in unbreathing silence, staring at not quite anything, moving no more than a line of stones might be expected to do.

Only one held his rifle trained on her. He was as unblinking, unmoving as the rest.

"I'm never going to wake up from this, am I?"

Sakamura chuckled lightly. "You already have woken up, Miss McKenna. That is the nature of your problem. You are no longer dreaming."

How did he know her name?

Ferris, she realized. Somehow, this Jap lieutenant had learned about her from Ferris Roubicek.

"You know what I hold, then," she said cautiously. Her heart shuddered. Waldo and the rest of the Aussies had died for, what? Ferris to play a revenge game against her? There was no justice in that.

Not that there was much justice anywhere else, either.

"You are a spendthrift, Miss McKenna." Sakamura sounded sympathetic. Almost loving, even. "You have sold your life cheaply and gained nothing in the bargain."

"Yet I am the one who has saved my nickel." *Thrift is a virtue, isn't it?*

Every time she'd tried to throw it away, things had gotten worse. Springfield seriously doubted that Lieutenant Sakamura would take the thing from her now. He knew too much already.

There was only one solution.

She slapped her hand over her mouth and swallowed the nickel, taking it down as hard and ugly as any emetic. Sakamura cried out, but he didn't wrestle her to the ground or try to stick his fingers down her throat.

"Good day, gentlemen," Springfield said, and began walking toward the water.

No shot rang out. No shouts called for her to halt or face the consequences.

She stepped into the surf. The water claimed first her feet, then her knees. Warm salt washed away the smoke and grime and blood and the last few stubborn beetles still clinging to her coveralls. The ocean slapped at her belly, at her bosom, took her hands like an eager lover.

Springfield McKenna allowed herself to be claimed, because she had come to understand that there was no escape. There had been none since her affair with Roubicek. All that was left to her was to deny him the fruits of his evil investment. No nickel, no gain from claiming her body or soul or spirit. Whatever it was he'd sought.

When the sea came for her mouth, she cried out in gladness and spent her life freely.

At least it isn't fire, she thought, choking on the water. The nickel thrummed in her gut. Already it sought a way back out into the world.

The sharks bumped her as they closed in.

OCCASIONALLY, PEOPLE CURSED by one of my coins fight back. Self sacrifice is always a good way to combat the power invested in them, but it is always a high cost; a Pyrrhic victory. One might think that a coin swallowed by a determined woman who throws herself into the ocean would be lost for a time. Those people don't know what real magic can do. The coin called to the shark. The shark did what sharks do best then ended up in the net himself. Found by a fisherman, the nickel continued its journey.

—The Carver

Incubus Nickel

ERIK SCOTT DE BIE

DISTANTLY, ANNA REMEMBERS SLEEP.

It's not the sound of the bombs that fall at all hours. Nor is it the falling buildings, men and women wailing in pain and fear, or children crying unattended. After November, Anna had grown accustomed to all of that. Even the renewed offensive that destroyed the historical center of London two weeks ago on December 29th hadn't rattled her. A hardened woman watched the dawn of 1941, knowing it offered only bleak days of waiting and nights of constant hell. Day after day, night after night, Anna simply rises, pulls on her stained nurse's uniform, and goes about her job. There are so many who need help, and there will be more by the end.

It isn't even the fear of death that robs her of sleep. She expects to be killed. Tens of thousands of her countrymen have been. Millions of homes have been destroyed. Their country is crippled, but it will fight to the death. She knows this and accepts it. She no longer works to live. She lives to work, that others might live — that others might win. She has already seen men and women go mad, whether wounded or whole, their minds shattered by the German offensive.

It's the shaking that keeps her awake. She first felt it when the bombs began to fall, making the city tremble to its foundations. The first time a bomb burst within a hundred meters of her, her brain shut down at the shock and when she woke to her senses, the building shook around her. Now, after three months of nearly constant bombardment, she never felt everything around her *not* shaking. It's all coming apart. London. England. The world itself is trembling. The very ground that the city stands on may break before the people do.

She knows this is the end of all things.

She has been working an hour at the King's Cross shelter when she reaches for a spare blanket and slips. It startles her to fall, but it frightens her when strong hands catch her. She didn't sense anyone nearby. Doctor Stilson sneaked up on her, as he always does. The man moves silently between the makeshift beds, his face almost the same color as his ash-gray beard. He is a wraith among the dead and dying.

"All right, love?" He extends a flask in her direction. "Take a bit of this. Stiffen that lip."

Anna hesitates to reply. With his face built for joviality, Stilson has lost much of himself in the war. He looks haunted now, old before his time, but soldiering on. "Yes," she says, and takes the proffered flask. The cognac burns, but at least she feels something.

Stilson nods and wipes bloody hands across his stained coat. He looks more like a butcher than a doctor. "Clear some beds for a ragged lot from Picadilly," he says.

"Not your tenement?" Anna asks. "You've been going out to visit them every week for months."

"The same. Jerry bombed the tenement with a hundred people inside. Eighty killed, the rest of the lot waiting to die." Stilson shakes his head. "Bloody fools. Bloody fools."

The doctors don't understand how the citizens of London can stay in their homes rather than go to the inconvenient shelters. Some even ignore the air sirens, and you can see them wandering the streets at night, looking for missing family members or discarded supplies. Anna understands, though. After so many months on so little sleep, nerves run ragged as worn leather, they simply don't want to leave the places they know. If they're going to die, it might as well be there.

Anna runs through the routine of care, the same thing she has done every night for what feels like her whole life. The victims that come in are horrific, but nothing frightens her anymore. A delirious man tries to beat back the stretcher crew with his missing hands. His bandages come loose and he slaps at his captors with mops made of cloth and bloody flesh. Another man can't stop screaming; all the drugs on hand, or even in the world, won't stop him. "A blockage in his brain," Dr. Stilson says.

Anna nods. She didn't ask. Half of these men will die and many of the others will wish they had.

The radio crackles with a speech by Churchill as four o'clock rolls around. Tea time. Despite being fifty feet underground, Anna can dimly hear the sirens. The Germans have attacked what seems like every night for months, and they show no sign of stopping. People flood the shelter. The doctors and nurses have almost finished treating the previous night's casualties when new ones start showing up. She's so tired, and she feels a little dizzy. The world won't stop shaking, even if the bombs have yet to fall tonight.

That's when Anna sees her.

The medics bring in a woman shivering and babbling on an improvised gurney. With so many wounded, they've had to scrape together whatever resources they can, and this one used to be a library cart. Stilson follows, shaking his head. "She's been like this for weeks. Can't do a damn thing about her," he says. "Care to give it a go?"

The woman thrashes in the grip of a nightmare, though she is quite awake. She screams words in a language Anna doesn't know— something that sounds vaguely Italian or perhaps French.

"Sedative?" Anna asks.

Stilson looks offended. "The next shipment was scheduled for Monday, but the blackguards haven't got here. Sold it on the black, no doubt," he says. "See what you can do to calm her. I have other patients."

The orderlies restrain the thrashing, moaning woman as Anna considers what to do. The thin creature's not dangerous — she looks like she might weigh seven stone, if that — but she could hurt herself if left to it. She wears dark clothes, sweat-plastered to her skin, but there's no sign of fever. She has no obvious wounds— no burns, bruises, or broken bones. Anna's seen many cases like this in the last months: a mind pushed past the breaking point.

"Hold her." Anna reaches for the patient's forehead. "I—"

The woman stops at Anna's touch, so suddenly she might have been shot. Her blue eyes open and regard Anna. It's not exactly fear in her eyes. Not pain or madness, either. Something like it, but not the same.

Hunger.

"Steady on, it'll be all right," Anna says to the woman. "You'll see."

The orderlies look at Anna, but she waves them away. The woman seems calm. She's beautiful, with a face made for the moving pictures or the stage. Seeing that everything's all right, the orderlies leave Anna with the woman and other patients. Even the screaming man has stopped carrying on. He just stares at Anna.

For the next half hour, Anna goes about her work, conscious of the woman watching her at all times. When she looks back, the woman lies there watching her— eyes consuming her every move.

"Ready to talk, love?" she asks. "What happened to you?"

The woman smiles at her but says nothing. Anna realizes she's clutching something in her hand, the fingers closed so tightly around it they've gone white. The tips are turning a dull purple color. Frost-bitten without frost. Anna touches her hand, but the woman pulls it away.

"You've got to let go," Anna says. "You're hurting—"

"He's coming," the woman says in a distinctively American accent. "You can't stop him."

Anna's skin prickles and she is sure that someone just came into the room behind her. "Dr. Stilson?" She turns, but no one is there. She is alone for the moment with the wounded and dying.

A hand closes tight on her wrist, and she jumps. The woman is looking at her very directly. "Of course you won't see him," she says. "Not until he wants you."

Anna is startled, but she composes herself again. "Well, our lads are doing their tip-top to stop him. So you can just—"

"Not Fritz. *Him.*"

Anna frowns. "Who?"

The woman's smile widens. "God."

The first bomb of the night hits what feels like directly above them, and Anna collapses to one knee from the shock. The shelter shakes and dust rains down from the ceiling. Screams rise throughout the tunnels— men and women strapped to gurneys, trying to pull themselves loose to flee. Anna summons the air to shout for Stilson, but the woman tightens her grip hard enough to bruise. Her other hand clenches hard enough to draw blood.

"He's here," she says. "He wants me."

Anna grits her teeth as she bends the fingers off her. She feels one break, but the woman still holds on. Finally Anna gets free, shakes herself, and goes to restrain one of the wounded: a soldier who's trying to get free. The man roars at her and tears his left hand free of the strap to box her ear. The world explodes into fireworks and her vision swims. She staggers aside, tries to stay standing, and slumps down next to the gurney.

The soldier gets off the gurney and starts working on his other hand when a falling chunk of rock smashes his head open. Blood boils up and instantly congeals in the dust. Suddenly nerveless, his corpse slumps forward and hangs over her from his still bound hand. Blood spills out his unsealed head and bits of brain slop onto her face. The stuff goes into her eyes, her nose, her mouth.

Stones are falling around the half-blinded Anna as she struggles to pull herself together, spit out gore, and stand. On the library cart gurney, the woman makes no attempt to move, but something is happening to her. She lies flat on her back, pressed out to her full height, and her chest rises rapidly and shallowly. At first, Anna thinks she is hysterical, but her expression has no panic in it. Instead, she looks pleased— *ecstatic*. Her eyes are shut and her mouth is open and moaning. Her hands, unbound, caress her breasts and body. She groans, loud and long, and pants for air that will not come.

Anna's skin prickles, and her stomach squirms. The taste of blood is in her mouth, but it becomes sweet and bitter at once. She wants...

The woman screams, but the sound is cut off. She is strangling.

A falling pipe hits Anna in the head, and she collapses to the ground. Blood trickles down her face.

There is a shape on top of the woman, Anna thinks. She sees two glowing red eyes.

The woman shudders one last time, and her clenched hand opens. A silver coin rolls through her limp, bloody fingers. It rolls, wheeling in a diminishing circle, until it ends up within Anna's reach. Dimly, she sees herself take it between her fingers, and she turns it over to look at the surface. On one side, it is just a coin: an American nickel, dated 1913. She turns it over, to where some president should be...

A demon stares at her.

She wakes thrashing, unable to breathe. The thick smell of blood and human filth mixes with stagnant air, threatening to choke her. They've moved deeper into the Underground, she realizes.

"Anna?"

A bright light is shining in one of her eyes. She claws her way back and finds herself lying on a gurney. She reaches up toward her face, but her hand won't move. Her whole body refuses to move.

She's seen men paralyzed by head and neck wounds. Suddenly terrified, she looks down at her body. Her hands are straining against the thick leather straps. She's relieved she can still move those, at least. Her legs, though are heavily splinted and don't move at all. She can't feel them.

Stilson sighs. "Glad you're still with us."

"Umm." Her voice slurs.

"Terribly sorry. Have some of this." He puts his flask of cognac to her lips. "Sorry it's not ether, but it'll have to do."

"Thank you," she manages, and chokes down a swallow. "What happened?"

"Bit of a collapse, but we managed to evacuate most of the patients in time. Some of them didn't make it. That woman— the American. She died in the collapse. Never even asked her name." He shakes his head.

Dimly, Anna feels a tremor of unease about that, but a different anxiety grows in her, overriding it. She speaks softly, afraid her voice will break. "My legs?"

"We don't know yet." Stilson pats her hand, his expression sympathetic. "You'll be all right. You just need to rest."

She smiles weakly as he holds her hand a little longer, looking deep into her eyes. There's something there, she realizes. There has been, for a long time, but she never realized it until now. Somehow, Anna knows he can't fill the hollow inside her.

At some point, Stilson apologizes and heads away, leaving Anna to herself. She lies there, willing her legs to wake up— to start moving again.

"Oi," says a man's voice, so suddenly Anna shivers. "Sorry, didna' mean to scare ye." He sits on the makeshift hospital bed next to hers, and she recognizes him as the screaming man. Peace has transfigured his face into that of a good-looking Irishman, as much as a red-haired man can ever be called good-looking. He holds up Stilson's flask. "Care for another go?"

"You stole that from Dr. Stilson."

"Too right. Eh?"

She nods at length. He steps to her side and tips the flask to her lips to give her a drink. She sputters a little, but the cognac is good.

"Sorry." He takes a swig himself. "I'm Percy."

"Anna." She goes to shake his hand before she remembers she's secured to the gurney.

"Bloody impressive that was, with the ceiling collapsing." He sits at the end of her gurney. "You stayed to help. Most blokes would have run screaming."

"Not... a bloke," she says.

"Heh, so I see." He takes a long swig, then the flask disappears.

Anna turns and shivers at Stilson's sudden appearance. How does he do that? In his hands, the doctor carries some of her personal effects, including a few yellowing photographs. "Hullo," he says. "Have you seen my flask? Damnedest thing, I know I left it here somewhere..."

Percy winks at Anna and she just shakes her head.

"Oh well." Stilson hands her the photographs. "Thought these might be a comfort. Cheers."

The first month of the war, Anna fell asleep looking at pictures of her life before, remembering and praying. Her smile on her wedding day was so vivid, and she could remember being there. She remembered feeling her husband's hand on her cheek. In those first months, when she closed her eyes, she could still feel him, even if he was hundreds of miles away, shivering alone on a lonely battlefield. She could sleep despite the bombs, dreaming of him.

Now she hardly recognizes the pictures. The smiling people depicted there are far from her life now. She's slim and pretty in the picture, but she thinks she looks like a fat, idiot girl with no idea what awaits her. She can't imagine being that clean.

Before she sleeps, she discards the pictures over the side of the gurney, for all the good they will do her.

Anna isn't sure what wakes her. The sickroom is still, all of the patients sound asleep or murmuring very softly to themselves. The air is warm, though it should be freezing in the depths of winter. So many huddled bodies keep the heat in. Bombs impact dully and very far away. Still, there is the relief of being unbound. She hears the faint crackle of the radio from the corridor outside the converted Underground assembly area.

All of these sounds are far below her perception, and none of them stand out.

But something woke her. Something is out of place.

She feels more than sees something move. Loose papers wave and dust swirls around medical equipment over at the work bench where the doctors left their supplies. Anna fully expects to see someone. Perhaps it will be Stilson, or at least an orderly. But the room stands empty.

"Hell-hello?" she asks. "Is someone there?"

Silence greets her, but it only increases her certainty that someone is there. She thinks she can almost see someone: a figure standing in the darkness, watching her. Her pulse picks up, and she can hear her heart beating.

A glint of light catches her eye, and she sees that there is a coin in her hand. It's the American woman's coin, with its ugly, defiled face leering up at her from the silver surface. Its eye burns bright red, like liquid flame in the darkness.

The thing moves closer. She can feel its closeness. The hairs on her neck and arms stand up, and her stomach churns. She wants it to come to her, but at the same time she is horrified that it might.

With all her half-asleep strength, she raises up the coin and hurls it at the darkness.

The presence vanishes on the instant, and she drifts back to sleep.

"Bad dream, eh?" Percy asks the next day.

"What?" Anna asks.

"Ye were thrashing and moaning something fierce." He toasts her with the mostly empty flask. "Didn't have the heart to wake ye."

He flicks something into the air. It sparkles in the flickering electric light: the woman's coin.

"That coin," Anna says. "Where did you get it?"

"This coin?" He dances the strange nickel across his knuckles. "Found it lying about. Devil, is it?" He looks at the etched face. "American, looks like. Leave it to a yank to deface his own riches."

Anna suddenly wants the coin with a burning need, as though it is the only thing that can soothe her.

"Probably from that woman they brought in. Shame: she was a looker, make no mistake."

Anna remembers the woman, and what happened to her. She remembers what the woman claimed to see. What Anna herself saw during the cave-in. "She died," she says. "It killed her."

"That much rock falling on a body will do right."

"No, she was dead before." She grasps for the coin as best she can. "Give me that."

He pulls the coin out of her reach. "Ah ah," he says. "Maybe when yer better. A dance fer the coin, eh?"

She licks her lips, which still feel dry. "Yes," she says. "Anything. I just... You need to give that to me."

His expression turns suspicious. "Well, I'd not be a gentleman if I denied a lady her e'ery need," he says. "But then, so I'm not." He sits back on his gurney and pours the last drop from the flask into his mouth. Then he tosses the empty husk aside. "Sleep, lassie. We'll talk more."

She knows, somehow, that they won't.

During the night, she wakes halfway to a hollow, rasping sound. She isn't sure what it is, but it sounds like the croak of a frog trapped and slowly suffocating beneath someone's boot. *Hurk*, it sounds like. *Hurk, hurk.* Something moves in the darkness near her, but her mind hardly registers it. The room feels uncomfortably warm again, almost sweltering, but maybe that's the German assault that shakes London to its foundations. She drifts back toward sleep.

Then she feels it: the same presence as before, huge and imposing and right next to her. Anna comes instantly awake, her eyes wide. She can barely see, with the little touch of light filtering from a lantern in the next chamber, where the doctors would be resting.

In the bed by her side, Percy thrashes, trying to get out from under something Anna can't see. His eyes are open but rolled up in his head. He courses up and down, rock-hard under his sweat-soiled blankets. A nightmare, maybe, but no. His expression, if anything, is enraptured. She's only seen the like on her husband's face, and then only on their wedding night.

Just faintly, in a flicker of light from the antechamber, she sees the indentations around his throat, as of invisible fingers. Something she can't see is choking him.

"Doctor." The word comes out in a broken whisper. Anna tries again. "Doctor!"

Her voice seems so tiny, no matter how hard she shouts. The dull roar of bombs and shuddering stone drowns her out. She can't get up. Her legs won't listen to her brain. She reaches for

Percy, but he's too far away. The devil coin is clutched tight in Percy's hand. She can see just a sliver between his fingers.

"Doctor!" This time, the word is loud, and it seems to echo all around the crumbling Underground station.

No one seems to hear her, except perhaps Percy. His eyes roll down and his expression becomes confused, then frightened. He tries to talk, but his throat is closed. He fights, punching and kicking, but to no avail. His face turns purple, then blue.

"Doctor!" she pleads with the darkness.

Hot tears sting Anna's eyes. She tries to reach for Percy, but he's too far. She can't move the gurney, with the brakes in place on the wheels and out of reach. She strains, overbalances, and falls to the floor, face first. Her stupid dead legs lie broken on the ground like kindling. She tries to roll over onto her back, fails, and pounds the floor in frustration. She can't do anything but lie there and call for help that won't come.

Above her, Percy stops thrashing, except for the occasional shudder. Then his body relaxes, and he lies back on the gurney, dead.

To Anna's horror, his body keeps moving for a few seconds, before that too ceases.

Then she feels the weight of its gaze on her, and words fail her in the face of the horror. She looks away, keeping her eyes fixed on her hands tightened into fists on the floor. It climbs down from the gurney and looms over her: a monstrous creature like a man but also an animal, a thing of pleasure and murder.

"I'm," she says, staring at the floor. "I'm not afraid. Not afraid of you."

There is nothing to hear, but she can feel its deep laughter.

Percy's hand opens, and the devil coin tumbles out. It bounces once and then stops, held aloft a foot off the ground by something Anna cannot see. It turns, so she can see both sides: both the human and the horrid devil.

The coin floats toward her of its own accord, and she flinches in spite of her courage. She tries to pull away as best she can from the coin, but the gurney is in the way. The best she can do is cringe against it.

The coin deposits itself on the floor inches from her face.

"Soon," a voice whispers in her ear. "Soon, my love."

She wakes again to Stilson and an orderly fussing over her. "How did you fall out of bed?" Stilson asks. "Are you all right? Are you hurt?"

Anna doesn't know what to say. Her leg is clearly broken. She can tell that at a look, but she can't feel it. That realization hurts worse than the memory of her horrible night.

Two men are worrying over Percy, having draped a sheet partly over his distorted face. His eyes hang half out of their sockets, and his tongue lolls, purple and very dead. One hand trails along the floor, the fingers clenched hard around something Anna recognizes without seeing it. That wasn't where the devil coin was, she thinks. Could she have dreamed that last part? Could she have dreamed the whole thing?

Stilson shakes his head over Percy's body. "Poor bloke."

"Doctor?" she asks. "What happened?"

"Sorry." He adjusts the sheet over Percy's face, which he doesn't need to do for Anna's benefit. She's seen her share of corpses. "Damnedest thing. Lungs must have failed during the night."

Anna nods, but she doesn't believe it. Even as the orderly is setting and splinting her broken leg, she ignores him. Rather, she watches Percy's hand as it scrapes along the broken paving tiles. It catches on a discarded hunk of stone and pops open. The coin rolls out. Anna catches her breath.

Stilson steps down on the coin, crushing it under his scuffed leather shoe. "Fancy," he says, and picks it up. "How dreadful. Who'd carve something like this into a coin?"

He turns it over, and Anna sees the full image clearly for the first time. The face is superficially like that of an American president but his features have hardened into something not quite human: handsome, but also alien. Tiny horns thrust out through his hair and fangs protrude over his lips. Anna expects to see a glowing red eye, but instead there's simply a hollow black gap where the coin has been gouged, repeatedly and violently.

Stilson sees her interest. "Here now, this yours? Did Mister… Blake, I think it was. Did he borrow it?" He extends it toward her, devil face first.

Anna can feel her heart beating in her throat. "Get rid of it. Throw it away. It's not safe."

Stilson looks taken aback. "All right, if it upsets you that much."

"Get it away!" Anna screams. She recoils and almost falls off the gurney, but the orderly catches her. "Get it away!"

Stilson pockets the coin. "Calm down, Anna, love. Everything will come out all right. You just rest."

Anna manages to calm herself a little when the coin disappears from sight, but her blood is still racing and she feels hot and filthy all over.

"I'm worried about you, Anna. After what you did to your leg, I don't want you falling out of bed again. I'm..." Stilson bites his lip. "I'll have to secure you again. Just for the night."

Anna flushes with anger and terror, but she manages to restrain herself. Having a hysterical fit will only harden Stilson's resolve. And if she starts shouting about devils attacking her, what will he do then? Dope her up on tranquilizers and make it even worse.

"That isn't necessary," she says. "I'm used to the gurney now. I can keep my balance."

"But what if you have a nightmare, or a bomb hits close by?" Stilson says. "You could damage yourself rather badly with another fall."

She stares at him, pleading with her eyes. "Doctor, I... I'll get scared," she says. "I need to be able to move."

"Steady on." He lays a hand beside her cheek. "You'll be just fine."

Anna nods, though she's practically shaking with fear. He can soothe her, though. Anna can trust in Stilson. He's been her friend ever since the war began, and he's always been there for her. Then, when the letter inevitably comes from the front that her husband has died in a battle, Anna might take their friendship farther. One must love in these dark times, or one is lost, and she has been lost for so long.

Finally, she nods, and the orderlies check the straps to secure her to the gurney. At least the coin won't be anywhere near her. The coin... She still feels a little confused, but at least she doesn't have the coin.

Stilson put the devil coin in his pocket. She has to warn him, somehow, without seeming insane.

"That... that coin," she says.

Stilson looks at her quizzically.

"It belonged to Percy. I mean, Mister Blake. It should really stay with his body."

Stilson purses his lips, then shrugs. "Quite right, quite right. Thank you. I wouldn't have had the slightest clue otherwise."

He heads away, following the gurney with Percy's body. Anna breathes out, knowing that maybe she can sleep tonight.

Sleep comes finally, and Anna only knows that she slept because she wakes from a vanishing dream. The room is dark and so hot she almost can't breathe. Her blankets are soaked with sweat and plastered to her broken, useless body. She tries to shift them off, but she can barely move her hands against the restraints. The best she can do is lie back and try to sleep. She does so, staring up at the ceiling and breathing deep.

Then it occurs to her to wonder why she woke up.

Someone moves past her gurney, and her heart freezes in her chest. She can hear breathing, she thinks, or maybe it's low, quiet laughter. She looks around, straining desperately for Stilson or one of the orderlies.

What she sees is the devil coin, resting marred face up, just out of reach next to her right hand.

Her mind can't make sense of it. Why would the coin be there? She'd seen Stilson carry it off, and thought it out of her life forever. Why would she have it again?

The devil stands beside her, blurry and indistinct in the darkness. She tries to see its face but cannot.

Something touches her face. It feels very much like a man's hand, but burning hot. Her flesh tingles under its touch and screams in pain as though she touched a hot iron. She flinches away and almost bites through her tongue. Undeterred, the devil trails its fingers down her face and neck, drawing down the wet blanket until only a thin layer of slip separates her skin from the putrid air. Her body convulses, thrilled and terrified both at once.

"No!" She reaches for the coin, but she can't get it. Her hands are too tightly bound. "Leave me alone!"

The gurney groans as the devil climbs onto it. She can feel its horrific presence looming over her— taste its breath like rotting flesh. Its hands roam over her body, igniting sparks of desire wherever they touch. It loves her and wants her, and her broken body wants it.

Anna makes a mad grab for the coin, but only succeeds in shaking the gurney, making the coin wobble. She shakes again, harder this time, and the coin wobbles more. One wheel comes entirely off the ground.

That's it.

She shakes. She's no longer trying to dislodge the coin, but instead pull the gurney over. The devil perches over her. She can feel its loathsome body suffocating her, lying on her chest so she can't breathe. Its awful breath burns her neck, and she feels its teeth on her ear. She doesn't bother to scream. No one will hear her.

She shakes, and the devil loses its balance for a moment. It swings wildly over her, holding itself in place only with an effort. She's doing it. She—

Then the creature strikes her. It punches her across the face so hard she can feel the muscles in her neck distend. Pain explodes through her, and she knows she has sprained her neck.

She can't stop, though. To stop is to die.

She shakes harder and harder, even as the devil presses down on top of her. Its hands go around her throat, now, and breath won't come. She gags, her vision melting into rivulets of light, but she keeps shaking. She moves back and forth, back and forth, until...

The gurney topples, and she is weightless for a split second. Then she crashes down to the floor in a heap of splintering wood and body. She crushes the thing underneath her, then rolls over it, taking part of the shattered gurney with her. A shard of wood protrudes from her leg, in the center of a growing pool of blood, but she can't feel it. Most important of all, her hand is free and around the devil coin.

She hurls it as far and as hard as it can go, until it plunks off the far wall.

Instantly, the devil is up and moving. It roars, a sound so loud and so close it makes Anna's ears ring. Then it lurches away, hobbling, and disappears into the darkness.

Anna lies still, panting and coughing and weeping. She feels weak. When she looks down, the blood is pooling on the floor. She must have struck an artery in her leg. Rotten luck.

But at least that monster would not kill her. She'd go to join her dead husband and...

A man's shape looms out of the darkness. This time, she can see him clearly. There's no blurry figure, no after-haze of sleep, no confusion born of narcotics slipped into cognac. She sees him, and knows him.

"Doctor," she says. "Dr. Stilson?"

He smiles, and the dim light gleams off his sharp teeth.

He puts the coin in her right hand and closes her fingers around it.

THE ONES WHO FIGHT THE *hardest taste the best. You don't know what a life is like until you feel it sliding inside you. This nickel was claimed by a demon that did not have form. We share its power. I don't know what It gets out of the bargain. Perhaps merely the ability to become corporeal. My end allows the taste of flesh and memory. It's a different taste than potential but just as sweet.*

—The Carver

In His Name

MARTIN LIVINGS

DAN BULOWSKI SITS WEARING everything he owns on the sodden steps of a run-down tenement building on 12th Street and watches people walking straight past him. Everyone seems to have somewhere to be, somewhere to go. Dan remembers feeling that way, once.

Someone tosses a penny into his hat, which is nestled between his feet. The man doesn't even look in his direction, just keeps on walking. Nobody else on the street notices Dan either. Or perhaps, they choose not to.

A movement across the street catches his eye. He looks over, and spies another hobo sprawled on the sidewalk, clearly drunk even at such an early hour. People walk around him as if he wasn't there, ignoring him.

Everyone, that is, except a small boy.

The boy kneels next to the ragged man. He speaks, but Dan can't make out the words from the other side of 12th. Then the boy reaches into a satchel on his shoulder, pulls out something blue and hands it to him. The drunk snatches it, tucks it inside his frayed jacket fast. The boy stands up and walks away, towards another hobo, this one huddled at the entrance of an alleyway.

"Mister?"

The voice startles Dan. He turns and sees a young girl standing beside him, no more than eight or nine years old. She's sensibly rugged up in winter clothes, a thick scarf around her neck, a black woolen hat covering her ears. A battered leather satchel hangs from one shoulder. He recognizes her; she lives in the neighborhood, he's seen her coming and going from the local bakery down the street.

He also notices the calipers on her legs, the crutches on her forearms. The crooked way she stands. His heart aches to see it.

"Yes?" he says.

She smiles, reaches into her satchel, and pulls out a small bag made of rough blue cloth, tied closed with a red ribbon. She offers it to Dan. "This is for you."

"For me?" He's confused, hesitates to take it. "What for?"

"Please take it. It's a gift. In His name." Her eyes plead even more than her words. God, even with her olive skin and dark eyes, she reminds Dan so much of Emily, his precious Emily. Or, worse, of...

Without thinking, he reaches out and takes the bag from the girl. He can't even feel it through his gloves.

"Thanks, mister," she says, and smiles that wide, guileless smile again. Perhaps that's the similarity, the echo that keeps coming back at him. "Thanks!" She turns and walks away, her metal calipers clanking quietly with each step, the tips of the crutches keeping time on the sidewalk.

"Wait!" he calls after her. "Who are you?"

She looks over her shoulder and smiles. "My name's Kilda," she says, then waves and continues on, soon lost in the crowd.

The girl's name rings in his head like a bell. Kilda. Kilda. Killed-a.

Killed her.

He takes a deep breath to steady himself. He looks at the bag in his hand; it fits in his palm and isn't very heavy. He wonders what might be inside it. Some sort of church thing, judging by what the kid said.

Dan isn't a religious man, not anymore. Not since France.

He removes his gloves with his teeth, carefully undoes the ribbon, and opens the bag.

He laughs in surprise. All that's there are a few walnuts, still in their shells. Then he notices something else in the bag. He reaches in, and pulls it out.

A nickel.

He looks closer at it. It's an original 1913 Buffalo nickel, he recognizes it from his childhood. But the Indian face has been carved into something else. A skull, but not a human skull, more like some sort of large cat, like a leopard or a jaguar. It's quite beautiful, if unnerving. Dan sits and looks at it for a long time, entranced. Then he puts it and the bag back in his pocket.

Another coin lands in his hat, from another anonymous suited stranger. Dan looks up at the back of the man already marching away, and smiles sadly. One gift; some nuts and a nickel. A drop in the goddamn ocean.

Still, a hell of a nice thing, which is a rarity in Dan's life. Or what's left of it.

Dan stands outside the soup kitchen and takes a sip from the steaming cracked old soup bowl he holds in his hands. The soup is thin and tasteless, but it's hot, and that's all that really matters. The sun's been down for hours and the temperature with it.

He glances over his shoulder, back into the kitchen. Inside, a dozen or so men sit at rough wooden tables and devour their soup greedily, grateful to be in the warm with a meal in front of them. As he watches through the grimy window, he sees two children amongst the ragged men. They're handing out blue bags tied up with red ribbon, just like the one Kilda...

...*killed her*...

...gave him. He squints, tries to see better.

"You get one?"

Dan is startled, and looks over to see a tattered man standing next to him. The man's beard is pure white, streaked with dirt and last night's soup. He grins around a crumpled cigarette, teeth brown or missing. He points into the soup kitchen, at the children there. "Did you get one?" he asks again, with a grin. "In 'His' name?"

Dan nods, dumb.

"Thought so," the old man chuckles. He takes a puff of his cigarette, breathes smoke like a destitute dragon. "Otherwise, they'd have been out here. They know, you see," he whispers conspiratorially.

Dan is confused. "Know what?"

"Who's got one already." He reaches into his pocket, and pulls out a blue bag, just like the one Dan still carries. The red ribbon is missing from it. "You can't get two," he says, with some disappointment. "Trust me. I've tried."

"What, for a nickel?"

The old man's rheumy eyes narrow a little. "You spent yours yet?"

Dan shakes his head.

A knife appears in the old man's other hand as if by magic. "Good," he growls around his cigarette. "Hand it over."

Dan sighs. "You don't want to do this, friend. Not for a nickel."

"A nickel's a nickel, pal. Hand it over, or I'll cut you."

Reflexes die hard and training can last a lifetime. Dan's hand shoots out and grasps the old man's wrist hard enough to make him squawk, his cigarette tumbling to the ground. Then a vicious twist outwards and the knife falls to the sidewalk with a muffled clatter. The old man's back arches as Dan continues to twist his wrist. His knees give out and he falls to the pavement, screaming. His eyes fill with fear and he desperately holds out his own blue bag towards Dan. He looks at it, considers his options.

Then he lets go of the man's wrist.

The old hobo collapses onto his back to the sidewalk, still screaming, a horrible high-pitched sound that makes Dan think of his wife, Susan, and that awful night over a year earlier, his last night in his own home, his first night on the street. Without thinking, he kicks out at the old man's head, a vicious blow to the temple. The screaming stops. Then he bends over and picks up the knife that the man dropped. It's a good knife; the steel clean, the hilt sturdy. He kneels and tucks it into his boot.

He leaves the man's bag, though. Something tells him to. It was a gift, a gift to him. He can no more steal it than the old man could steal his.

Dan Bulowski takes one last look back at the soup kitchen, at the human detritus sitting within, and then turns and walks away. The bag weighs heavy in his pocket, like an anchor, like a curse.

He knows what he should do. What he has to do.

He marches up 12th Street, more determination in each step than he's had for months. He knows exactly where he's going. As he walks, he sees a couple of local children handing out the blue bags to people sleeping on the streets. For some reason he can't quite articulate, this makes him more and more uncomfortable.

The bakery is on the corner of 5th Avenue, opposite the First Presbyterian Church. It's almost deserted, which is hardly surprising; in fact he's surprised to find it open at this time of the night at all, especially in the middle of winter. He climbs the four steps to its door and goes inside. The smell of freshly baked goods inside makes his mouth water.

"Hey!" The man behind the counter is about Dan's height but probably twice his weight, his bare arms covered with thick black hair. "You buyin' somethin'?"

Dan shakes his head.

"Then get the hell out, hobo!"

"No, wait..." Dan fumbles in his pocket. "I want to give something back."

"Give back?" The man's thick eyebrows shoot up. "You steal somethin'? You a thief?"

"No," Dan says quickly. "I have something to give back to a little girl. To..."

Killed her.

"...Kilda."

"Kilda?" The man frowns.

Dan nods.

The shopkeeper turns and yells at the door behind him. "Maria!"

After a few seconds a woman steps through the door at the back of the bakery, white flour dusting her olive cheeks. She looks about thirty, with those same large, dark eyes as the little girl. Dan knows who she is immediately.

She looks at him with some mistrust. "Yes?" she asks him. "Can I help you?"

"You're Kilda's mother, aren't you?" Dan asks her.

"Yes." She doesn't smile. "Who are you?"

"I'm Daniel Bulowski," he replies. "Dan."

"What do you want, Mister Bulowski?" the woman asks, still as cold as the winter's night outside.

He shoves his hand into his pocket, pulls out the blue bag. Holds it out to the woman.

She looks at it, then back at him. "Kilda gave you this?"

Dan nods.

"Then it's yours. In His name." Kilda's mother, Maria, still doesn't smile, but something warms deep in her eyes. No longer angry but grateful. And something else: just a hint of sadness.

"Please," Dan says, still holding the bag out to her. "She needs this more than me."

The woman shakes her head. "No, Mister Bulowski," she insists. "She needs you to have it."

"It's polio, isn't it?" he asks her.

"Yes." Such a simple word, short and sharp as a coffin nail.

"Then she needs all the money she can get. Your family does, I mean." Dan tries to give the bag back, but the woman refuses, shies back from it. "Why won't you take it?"

"Because it's yours." She looks at him in a new light. "You're not like the others."

Dan feels his heart harden at that, a frost spreading from its center. "Yes I am," he tells her. "We're all the same."

"No, Mister Bulowski," Maria says, her tone brooking no argument. "The others have already spent what they were given, on alcohol and drugs. They wasted the pure gifts of a child. You didn't. I wonder why that is."

"The night is young," Dan grunts. "There's still plenty of time to get loaded."

She shakes her head. "You *are* different, Daniel Bulowski." She turns, and walks back to the door behind the counter. Then she stops in the doorway, looks back over her shoulder. "Come on," she says, smiling at last, and gestures for him to follow her.

Dan hesitates for a moment. But the night outside is cold and harsh. He walks around the counter, ignoring the baleful glare of the man behind it, and follows the woman.

Behind the shop, the house is warm and dark, and still smells of the bakery. She turns on the light in the hallway, and leads Dan up some stairs. He follows like a sheep, like a sleepwalker. They come to the landing at the top, where there is another hallway with some doors along its length. She walks to the first one and opens it.

Inside is a small bedroom, just a narrow single. But that bed has blankets and pillows, and the room is warm and smells of the bakery. Dan looks at the bed, and is suddenly very, very tired. He can't remember the last time he slept in a bed. No, that's a lie, he *can* remember, he just chooses not to. Like so many things, he chooses not to remember. Like that day, his wife's face, her nose bloodied, her eyes wounded and afraid. Like the farmhouse in France, the glint of metal from a sniper, the grenade.

So many things to forget. Why can't he just forget?

"Sleep here, Mister Bulowski," the woman says. "Be warm and safe. The streets are dangerous, especially tonight."

"Why?" he mumbles. But the bed is already calling him, a siren song, irresistible. His feet carry him to its edge, and he topples onto it. It's soft and warm.

He tries to speak again, ask the woman what is going on, but he's asleep before he can even form the words.

It's five years ago, and Corporal Dan Bulowski is on patrol in occupied France, near Bordeaux. He and his men tramp down a muddy road, a light drizzle soaking them through to the skin. Then he sees it, a glint of metal, just a flash in a nearby farm-house's window.

"Sniper!" he barks. They all duck down as one, training and experience kicking in. Dan reaches to his belt and unhooks a gre-nade. He shoots another glance at the window, can't see anyone.

"Fire in the hole!"

He pulls the pin and hurls the grenade straight at the open window. It sails through and clatters on the wooden floor inside. Dan turns his back to the farmhouse, gets as low as he can. The rest of his squad does the same.

The explosion makes the ground shake and his ears ring. Shards of wood and brick patter on his helmet, like a sudden heavy rain. Then it stops.

Dan turns again, stands up straight. Black smoke billows from the window of the farmhouse. He signals his squad to move forward. They approach, rifles at the ready. Dan is lead-ing, reaches the door first. He kicks it open.

At first he can't see anything, the entire room filled with smoke. Then it slowly clears, and he sees that the farmhouse is empty.

No, not empty. There, in the corner...

Dan wakes screaming, completely disoriented. For a long moment, he thinks he's home, at home with Susan and Emily. Then he remembers where he is, and his heart sinks.

There's another scream, not his this time.

"What the hell?" He stumbles out of bed, caught for a moment in the heavy blankets. He moves to the door, tries the handle.

Locked.

Another scream. He spins towards it. It's coming from out-side. He moves to the window and tries to open it, but it's stuck, painted closed. The glass is fogged up. He wipes it, tries to see outside. The night is nearly ended, the sky turning that dark blue that comes just before the sun rises. He can see someone on the street outside, running through the middle of the road, dashing left and right in desperation. And behind that person, another, this one running straight and fast. He holds something in his hands, something with a long handle.

The screaming again. This time words vibrate through the glass. "Help me! Jesus Christ, someone help me!"

Dan doesn't think, just smashes the glass in the window with his elbow, then leans out and looks.

It's the old white-bearded hobo. He's dashing frantically down the street, looking over his shoulder. The man chasing him is a stranger, Dan doesn't know him. Dressed well enough, though. He's only a step or two behind the hobo.

"Look out!" Dan yells, then immediately regrets it. The hobo looks up, distracted, stumbling for a moment.

That's all the chance his pursuer needs. He swings the thing he holds in his hands. There's a flash of metal in the streetlights...

Sniper!

...and Dan realizes what the man is wielding an instant before it hits the old hobo.

A scythe.

The blade enters the old man's back, just behind his right shoulder. Dan can hear the meaty thud of it even from the window. Blood sprays from the old hobo's mouth, soaking his white beard. He collapses forwards, a puppet with its strings cut, all life gone in an instant.

The man with the scythe leans over and yanks it free. Its blade looks black in the twilight.

There's another shriek. Dan turns his attention to the other end of the street. There, a small man he knows from the soup kitchens is being slaughtered, a knife plunged into his chest over and over again by an old woman. And not far from them, another ragged man is held against a wall by two other men. A third wearing a black overcoat walks up calmly and buries an axe in his face.

Then more screams, and more, these from somewhere mercifully out of sight. Dan is frozen, watching.

The door handle behind him rattles.

He turns to face the door, crouches down and pulls the knife he took from the old man, the dead old man now, from his boot.

The door opens, and Dan lunges.

"Mister?" a small voice asks, and he comes to a halt, the knife falling from numb fingers.

It's the little girl, Kilda.

"What are you doing here?" he hisses. He leans past her, looks up and down the hall.

Kilda laughs at that. She's wearing a warm night-dress, her calipers left behind, leaning entirely on her crutches, her back crooked. "I live here, silly!"

"We have to get out of here, kid," he tells her, still looking down the hallway. "It's not safe."

From the window behind him, Dan hears a new noise now; the high, pure voices of dozens of children singing. He can't make out the words, but it's beautiful, and it chills his blood.

"Yes it is," Kilda murmurs. "I'm sorry."

Something jabs into his thigh, straight through his rough trousers. Dan cries out in pain and spins around, lashing out in pure reflex, but Kilda has already stepped back out of his reach. The empty hypodermic clatters to the wooden floor, its needle still coated with his blood.

"What...?" Dan looks at the girl, who is watching him with big sad eyes. So much like Emily. So much like... "What did you do?"

"Mommy says you're special," Kilda tells him, still smiling. "I knew that. I knew it was you. She says you can save me."

"Save you?" Dan's speech is slurred, his lips numb. The room lurches to one side, then the other. He shakes his head, looks for the knife, for a way out, anything. "I don't understand."

Hands grab his upper arms, strong hands. He tries to turn, to see who is holding him, but his neck is floppy and weak. He's half-carried from the bedroom, down the darkened hallway, back down the stairs. Kilda walks in front of him the whole way, crutches clunking on the floorboards. She looks back over her shoulder from time to time, her face filled with concern.

"It's all right, mister," she assures him. "It's all right."

Dan tries to respond, but he can't speak, can hardly keep his eyes open. The walls around him blur as he's shepherded into a back room. It's large, much larger than he'd have expected in such a small building, and almost bare, just a table in the middle. The only light is from dozens of candles lit and placed on the floor. There are other doors leading into it, and these doors are open too. Through them come men and women, white, black, every ethnicity. Neighborhood folks. Folks who'd drop a penny in his hat, folks who'd nod and smile on the street. Good folks.

Some are empty handed. Others drag the bloodied bodies of hobos. Or parts of them.

Dan is led to the middle of the room, and strong hands lift him up, lay him on the table. There is no malice here, no violence. They treat him like an infant, putting him to bed.

Kilda's mother leans into his view. "I told you, Mister Bulowski," she says with hushed reverence. "You're different. You're special." Her slim, warm hands slide into his pockets, a woman's touch he hasn't felt since Susan threw him out of their home over a year ago. His skin tingles beneath it. Then she pulls out the blue bag that Kilda gave him. She opens it, and takes out the carved nickel. Looks at it, and smiles.

"I knew it," she breathes. "You have the cougar skull." She holds the coin up for the others in the room to see. "Amen," she says.

Amen," the others in the room echo. So many voices. The whole neighborhood?

She's opening his jacket now, unbuttoning his shirt, baring his chest. Then something is placed upon it, something warm and soft. He can smell bread, and sugar, and walnuts.

"I..." Dan mumbles. "I..."

"Hush now," Kilda's mother says, and touches the coin to his lips. "The others, they were just a sacrifice, to appease Him. To grant us good fortune for the year. But you," she says, and leans close, "you will do what no doctor could. You will save my daughter."

Kilda. Killed her.

Save her?

The room seems to be full of smoke now, his eyes clouded. Then the smoke clears, and in one corner he can see a tiny figure slumped. It's a small girl, wearing the clothes of a French peasant, a colorful scarf around her head, striped dress rumpled across grazed knees. She looks like she's sleeping, but Dan knows better.

A trickle of blood runs down her chin from her left ear.

It wasn't the explosion from the grenade that killed her. She's untouched by shrapnel. No, it was the pressure it caused that burst her eardrums, sucked the oxygen from her lungs. It would have been quick, at least.

In her hands, her dead hands, she still clings to the model airplane she'd been playing with in the window. Its shiny silver fuselage is now smeared with black smoke residue, the American star still visible on its side.

"No," Dan slurs.

Her eyes open.

"It's alright," she says, and her voice sounds like Kilda's. "It's not your fault."

"Not..."

"You can't save me," she says. "It's too late."

A hand touches his shoulder. He turns his head slowly, and sees his wife, Susan, looking down at him. Her nose is bruised and bloody, from where he struck her over a year ago. So much anger brought back from the war, so much guilt, nowhere for it to go. Susan got in the way of his rage, God bless her, God forgive him.

"It's all right," Susan says, and smiles.

"It's all right," Emily says from beside her. His daughter, his beautiful blonde blue-eyed daughter, just an infant when he went away to war, a perfect little girl when he came back. Tears run down his cheeks, burning his skin. He's lost her. He's lost them both.

"You can't save me, daddy," she says. "You can't save mommy. It's too late."

Another touch, on his other shoulder. He doesn't want to look away from his wife and daughter; he doesn't know where they are now, they moved away to be with Susan's family upstate somewhere, refused to tell him where they'd gone. He doesn't want to look away, but his head moves of its own volition.

It's Kilda. She's dressed in a beautiful white summer dress now, but she seems happy and warm. She has no crutches now, no calipers; she stands tall and true, straight as a soldier at attention. She beams at him.

"You can save me, Dan," she whispers. "In His name, you can save me."

"Yes..." he gasps. His eyelids close with a flutter, a deep crimson darkness claiming him.

"Yes?" Kilda's mother's voice is close to his ear.

"Yes."

Something cold and straight rests against his throat. From somewhere in the distance, someone cries out.

"In His name!"

Then the cold becomes hot, so very hot, but only for an instant. Then wet. Then nothing at all.

Amen.

◇◈◇

ANY WHO SAY THAT CHAOS *is inherently evil does not know the world. This tale proves it. Fueled by the power of my coin, this cult has created a way to help those who need it the most within their families. Yes, sacrifice is required. It is always about blood. But, in the case of Dan — his flesh, his blood — it gave back a little girl's life. She will grow up strong and beautiful. It does my old mind good to see it.*

—The Carver

LIES OF THE FLESH

NATHAN CROWDER

THE RAZOR SLID PURPOSEFULLY across his scalp, revealing his true self one slow pass after another. Jimmy's fine hair drifted past his shoulders, soft as Minnesota's January snow, dark as coal. It dusted the gritty tiles of the gas station restroom floor off Hennepin, a testament to who he used to be. His hair would not define him any longer; not the color or the stupid haircut his mother had forced on him for class pictures. He had tried punking it out like Johnny Rotten, but his hair was too fine and his mom too diligent in combing it down. Just trying earned him another whipping with the yardstick.

Jimmy put down the disposable razor and passed a trembling hand over the bare skin. He could feel the ridges of his skull below his fingertips. He leaned in close, heard the buzzing of the overhead light like an angel's hum, like a warning purr. There would be a beating waiting for him at home. But at least she couldn't "fix" it with a trip to Hair Masters or a wet comb. At least he could finally show her. He wasn't going to let her define him.

Fingers explored the scalp to find the small patches the razor had missed. These he retouched dry with his grip high up, almost to the razor's head. He gingerly brushed fingertips over the sting where a surprise mole had been sliced off causing a several minute delay as he staunched the flow of blood. A pair of bloody paper towels sat crumpled on the back of the sink. He hadn't known such a small cut could produce so much blood. He had used some of the mess to write his new name on the mirror with his finger.

The meat was weak. If he hadn't known it before, the cut would have been yet one more indication.

The word "Skull" stared back at him from the fly-specked glass.

"Skull," he said aloud, liking the way the hard "k" exploded off the roof of his mouth.

He splashed handfuls of water onto his face. Delirious in the feel of the bare skin, Skull rinsed his head clean and dabbed it dry with a paper towel, looking for any telltale blood to point out a cut he had missed. The collar of his thermal shirt was soaked beneath the torn Suicide Commandos tee he bought out of the back of a van after their last show at the Longhorn. He was too young to get into the bar at the Longhorn. Thankfully the Commandos played loud enough that he stood shivering with a half-dozen other teens on the sidewalk to listen for several songs until the bull-necked bouncer chased them off. It was probably for the best. Even layered up, there was only so long a person should stand around on a sidewalk in Minneapolis in November.

His leather jacket hung from the bathroom door handle. He pulled it on. The latest issue of punk zine, *Your Flesh,* was sticking out of the pocket. He took it out and thumbed through crisp pages as he pushed out into the bitter January cold. The first blast of air caused a sharp snort of surprise and he felt the inside of his nostrils freeze together momentarily. The sun had gone down while Skull shaved his head. The temperature had dropped close to freezing in that time. It would be worse in the wind and he debated going to meet the other McPunks uptown or catching the bus back home to get the beating out of the way early.

The wind whipped a flurry of discarded newspaper up the street towards him and he kicked himself for not bringing a hat. Being punk rock was one thing. Freezing his brain solid in the Minnesota winter was something else entirely. Even the Sex Pistols must wear hats when it got this cold. While some of the McPunks might be hanging out at the bus stop near McDonalds, there wouldn't be many of them. Not in this cold. He could show them his new look tomorrow.

Hands jammed deep into his jeans pockets, Skull set his sights on the City Center skyway and 7th where just beyond a bus would take him close to home. He briefly considered going into the Lumber Exchange building to take the skyway most of the way to his stop. He fingered the bruise above his left elbow where a security guard had held him in a vise-like grip and marched him out of Baker Center earlier in the day. With the stolen shaving gear in his pockets, Skull had been too scared to put up much of a fight, even when he heard a couple of junior hockey thugs from his school laughing at his removal.

The skyways weren't public property, not like the streets. The individual buildings owned their own section of the two or three story high enclosed walkways, linked together to form a network that covered a significant part of downtown. Those were policed by their own security; hard-faced men who didn't have to answer to the same rules that normal police had to. Private property meant they got to decide who could use the skyways and who had to use the streets.

There were no bums in the skyways and precious few punks.

Go downtown, do your shopping, your banking, see your movies, and forget about the rest of the world beneath your feet.

Forget about the sixteen year old boys with mothers who beat them for wanting to spike their hair. Forget about the rest of us being forced to live a lie.

We don't need you, Skull thought, jaw set hard against the plunging temperatures. *We don't need any of you.*

As his fingers explored the pockets of his jeans, he realized what he did need was bus fare. He had enough money to get home earlier. He knew it. He might be able to use a phone somewhere to call his mom to pick him up, but if she saw his shaved head, there, on the street, he couldn't know how she'd react. Probably leave him there to freeze for a bit and think about what he did. There was no one else he could call except Callie, but she was working late, waiting tables at Mario's, where the customers were rude and the owner grabbed her ass at least once a shift.

Panic rising, Skull slowed his pace towards the bus stop. Shaking hands searched pants and jacket pockets, even the small coin pocket in his jeans. He found a dime and two pennies. Useless.

On the virtually deserted street ahead of him, Skull saw a huddled shape beneath the shelter of the skyway. The dark bulk was pushed back into a shallow depression in the concrete wall to shield against the wind. Old army blankets layered with packing blankets masked a form that was almost certainly human. He had a tin tomato can sitting in front of him. As Skull approached, he noticed the sign, scrawled on the cardboard scrap held down by a broken piece of brick. "Please help! God Bless!"

He couldn't tell how many coins were in the can. Not at a glance. But it was probably enough to bus him home and maybe a bit more beyond that.

The bum was huddled so deep that Skull couldn't see his face in the yellow streetlight hum. He didn't move. Maybe he was sleeping, or drunk, or so far gone on drugs he wouldn't miss a few coins. The smell was almost overpowering, bitter and sour all at once. Skull crouched as silently as possible to avoid alerting the still transient and wincing at the creak of his leather jacket.

No motion from beneath the blankets. That was good. Skull flexed his fingers like he saw stage magicians do on television. He glanced down at the can, inched his fingers forward, felt the inside rim. Victory all but assured, he held his breath and turned his attention to what he now assumed was the sleeping figure before him. Cold fingertips displaced shifting metal shapes. Accepting that yes, he was going to do this, he drove his fingers the rest of the way into the can to grab a few coins before he lost his nerve. Something deep within the can sliced through the tip of his index finger. He howled with pain, pulling his hand back so quickly he lost his balance.

Skull fell onto his ass with surprise as the can spilled its contents on the dirty cardboard sign. There among the scattered coins, he saw a razor blade, shining crimson with fresh blood. "What kind of sick fuck...?"

Hard, dark eyes stared at him from the folds of the blankets. They glistened like onyx, unblinking. "Take it," a thin voice sliced through the icy night air. "You need it more than me."

Like a statue, the figure sat, unmoving as Skull gathered up the handful of coins. But those unblinking eyes, the timeless voice, empty of fear— he both wanted to see what this person looked like, and was terrified with what that investigation might reveal. "Thanks?"

"Don't thank me, you little shit stain," the voice cracked like thawing ice. "I'm not doing you a favor. You've earned it."

Skull stood, jamming the coins down into his jeans pocket. His sliced finger stung. He could feel blood seep into his pocket. He was pretty sure he had some McDonalds napkins in his jacket to staunch the flow, but the injury, however slight, woke a rage that had been simmering beneath the surface for days.

"Earned it?" He skipped forward and kicked the blankets as hard as he could. He felt his toes connect with something leg-like inside the mysterious shape. "Earned it?" He skipped back and then in again, swinging his leg as hard as he could. "You earned this!"

The figure under the blankets did nothing to fight back. Didn't shift to avoid the kicks or raise a hand to try and stop the assault. The sidewalks were abandoned and the cars that raced by either didn't see the beating or didn't care. There weren't a lot of kindly souls ready to jump in when the temperature was so low. Problems when it was freezing were other people's problems.

Skull felt like he was watching the violence from somewhere outside of himself. It wasn't real and it wasn't his fault. He was just a channel through which the rage coursed like an electric current. He felt disconnected and sick to his stomach because he wanted it to stop. He wanted all of it to stop. But he didn't know how.

Instead, Skull stopped mid-kick disgusted with himself for letting anger take the reins and with this piece of human refuse that sat there and just took it. The bastard hadn't cried out, hadn't even curled up to try and defend himself. Skull might as well be kicking a big doll or a corpse. It felt ridiculous and barely took the edge from his anger. He staggered back, fists clenched, blood pooling in his palm and dripping onto the concrete. Skull realized belatedly that he had been crying and he rubbed the tears away with the ball of one hand, angry for that small humiliation as well.

Sparing a single glance over his shoulder, Skull jogged for the bus stop a few blocks away. The frozen air burned in his lungs. His injured finger throbbed. He wrapped it in napkins and leaned against the wall, closing his eyes against the pain and the cold.

When the bleeding stopped, he tossed the bloody napkin in the gutter and went about the business of counting the coins. There were more quarters in there than he had anticipated. He thought about going home and the landmines that were waiting for him there.

He considered his other options. He could go to Mario's. Soda refills were free, and he had enough money for a slice of pizza and a coke that he could nurse until Callie got off shift. She might even let him sleep on the floor next to her bed as long as he promised to be gone before her parents woke her up in the morning. He pushed the blood-smeared coins around in his palm, taking stock, and froze when he saw a skull staring up at him from the cold metal.

The world turned crystalline around him, dreamlike. The coin was the size of a nickel and the date was stamped as 1913. But it was no president, no Indian chief. It was a skull shown in profile, clearly defined, with cracks along the top where the plates fused, with vertebrae below outlined by drying blood.

A rumble and hiss snapped him back to awareness. He looked up to see the bus that would have taken him home pulling away from the curb. A stooped woman, layered in gray scarves and a purple coat, shuffled past Skull on the sidewalk, muttering "Junkie," under her breath.

He hadn't noticed the bus pull up. The hand which cupped the coins was numb from cold. *How long have I been standing here?* Skull glanced down at the coin which bore his namesake. On impulse, he plucked it from the others and tucked it down into the small coin pocket of his Levis. The decision had been made for him. The bus that would take him to Mario's was a few minutes away. He pulled out enough coins for his fare then slid the rest back into his jacket pocket to wait.

You earned this.

Goddamned right I did.

Minutes later, he sprawled over a sideways seat on a half-full bus, the air close and musty from the heaters and drying coats and mittens. The bus was a mixed load, mostly adults from stiffs in suits to thick-faced fast-food drones. There were some kids his age, but they weren't like him. No, they were sitting with family or friends, faces lit with animated conversations that filtered up to him. The crackle of overheard conversations was all nonsense, talking about this boy, or that stupid band, or how the Vikings got slaughtered by Jets and would Kramer be the quarterback next year or not. None of it mattered. Every smile, every casual sneer or roll of the eyes in his direction. Everything was bullshit. A pretense. An act. A hundred little lies and deceptions sparked in the brain, twitching and shaping the muscles beneath the skin, transmitting the illusion of sincerity, of interest, of honesty.

The strange nickel burned cold against Skull's hip the entire way to the greasy pizza place where Callie worked. It was a welcome distraction from the thought that his fellow passengers were judging him. Like they knew that he didn't belong, or what he had done to get his bus fare. The skull nickel felt more real somehow. More… honest. It was a relief when he reached his stop. Hands thrust deep into jacket pockets, he hunched his shoulders and sped off in the direction of Mario's three blocks away.

The neon OPEN sign hanging below "Mario's by the Slice" in the foggy restaurant window was a welcoming beacon. The heat from the ovens washed over him as he opened the door bearing the smells of Italian spices and tomatoes and pepperoni. Callie looked up from a table she was clearing, eyes wide behind the frizzy blonde bangs. Her gaze darted to the counter where her boss was busy making a pizza, oblivious to Skull's entrance. She looked back to Skull with a tight shake of her head.

Skull ignored Callie's unspoken warning and stepped to the counter. After a moment's hesitation, she hurried behind the register to take his order, alerting Mario that they had a customer.

Before she could open her mouth to ask how she could help, Mario slid up next to her and pointed a thick finger across the counter. "Callie's friend, yes? Timmy?" His voice challenged, daring Skull to correct him.

"Jimmy," Callie answered for him. "What can I get you?"

"No free food or drink," Mario said slowly, a sneer spreading upon his thick lips, exposing teeth that would have earned him braces in a family with money.

"It's Skull," he said. "And I have money. A slice of the pepperoni and a Coke." Skull looked pointedly at Mario who hadn't relinquished the sneer yet. "For here."

"New haircut doesn't earn you a new name, Jimmy," Mario said. "Ring him up, sweetie."

Skull couldn't see what Mario's hand did beneath the cover of the counter, but he had a pretty good idea. Mario never took his eyes off Skull, even tilted his head towards Callie as if to say, *You see what I did there? You want to do something about it?*

Callie flushed, swallowed, and wouldn't look up from the register. She rang in the slice of pizza and soda. With triumphant calm, Skull brought out the stack of quarters and dimes and paid the total.

"Where did you get the money, kid? Scraping through fountains?"

Skull leaned into the counter. He could feel the skull nickel pushing into his hip, trapped between flesh and the unyielding wood. Rather than being uncomfortable, it gave him confidence, and he felt his face fall slack, devoid of any emotion. Even without expression, the earlier rage still lay coiled in his gut, around the base of his spine. His voice was coldly sincere. "I kicked it out of a bum."

Mario's smile faltered, unsure if Skull was joking. He seemed to be aware that other than Callie, who had very little reason to like him, he was alone with this leather-jacketed and freshly bald punk after dark. He backed up and went back to making his pizza without another word.

Skull took the paper plate with his slice and the red plastic tumbler of soda. He chose the table next to the one Callie had been clearing when he came in. Before he sat, he took the nickel out of his pocket and set it down next to his drink. The barren socket stared up at him. He stared back and ran his fingers across his bare head, feeling for the bone beneath.

"You really did it," Callie said quietly behind his left shoulder. He hadn't heard her come back out to finish clearing the table. "Did you do it yourself or did Brodie help you?"

"Myself," Skull said. He traced the edge of the nickel with his cut forefinger. "It's good," he corrected himself, "It feels good. But…"

"But?"

"I don't know." He looked at the window and saw his newly unfamiliar reflection. What would his mom think? What would his dad have thought? *Dad would have understood*, he decided. *Dad would have known why*. "It doesn't feel like enough."

He tilted his head down a bit, causing his eyes to appear shadowed. It brought a smile to his face, and he broadened the smile, showing as many teeth as possible. *Not enough*, he thought. *I can still see it*. "Have you ever heard of Martin Delcove?"

"No. Why?"

"August, 1970, he snatched two hitchhikers, took them to a motel room over in Twin Falls, killed and skinned them. He was shot dead by the police in the parking lot after the motel manager got suspicious of the smell and called the cops."

After a few seconds, Callie started breathing again, her voice shaking with a note of suspicion. "I never heard about that."

"My dad went to school with him. He knew my folks." Skull kept his voice level. He had heard about Delcove once or twice growing up, usually when his mom was drunk. *The psycho friend of your dad who got what he deserved*.

Callie was quiet for a while as she wiped down the table, processing the new information. "Is it true?"

He shifted his gaze up just a bit to see his friend's reflection in the window. Her face was just a bit plump, that undeniable look of Minnesota dairy farm girl, no matter how much green eye shadow she wore or how she cut her hair. Concern was plastered on her face. The same face that had shown joy and fear and anger and, once in his presence, the ecstasy of sex, now held concern. Concern for whom? Him? Herself? Did it even matter?

"Everything is fake," he said slowly as realization crept in at the corners of his mind.

"What's fake? The story about your dad's friend?"

"Not that. But everything else. The skin is a mask we wear to cover our true selves. The meat lies. Bone," he said. "Bone is what's true."

"Jimmy, did you really beat up someone for that money?"

Skull blinked at Callie's bluntness and turned away from the reflection. He looked over his other shoulder. He knew her fear face, and she wore it now, eyes wide, lower lip trembling slightly. "I don't know. A little bit maybe. I lost my bus money, and…"

A silence settled between them.

"I'm sorry," Skull said quietly.

Callie neither accepted nor denied his apology, as if she never heard it to begin with. "Your mom is going to freak when she sees what you did to your hair."

He tensed involuntarily between the shoulders as he remembered the previous whippings. "It isn't going to be pretty, but I don't care."

She bit her lip and looked for Mario as if to make sure he wasn't listening in, but he was nowhere to be seen. "You can stay with me tonight. I'll sneak you in my window like last time."

"Thanks."

"And…" her round cheeks were pink, "you don't have to sleep on the floor if you don't want to."

He nodded. They had slept together for the first time two months ago, and while he had slept over several times since then, they had not had sex since that first night. For a while, he wasn't even sure if they were still considered to be dating anymore. They still spent time together, but something had shifted; imperceptible and undeniable. She still offered the comfort of her bed every time. And every time Skull diligently chose the floor. It was less confusing.

Callie had a car, an old beater 1070's Ford Falcon almost as old as her that used to belong to her big brother. He moved to California for college and left it behind, making her Skull's only friend who didn't have to rely on the bus to get around. It was a faded brick red and the inside smelled like burning oil and nacho cheese from a drive-in spill the summer before that never got cleaned up properly. She drove them back to her house with "Anarchy in the UK" playing on the tinny cassette deck and empty Pepsi bottles rattling around Skull's feet.

They barely talked. She asked about him shaving his head and robbing the bum. Skull countered by asking when she was going to slap Mario for groping her. That shut her up for most of the ride and left him sitting there feeling silently guilty for bringing it up.

Skull had to wait, shivering in the side yard while Callie went in and said good night to her parents. He wondered if he had made Callie angry enough to leave him out there to freeze, the skull nickel pinched between fingers like a talisman. He was deep enough in the suburbs that getting anywhere other than home would be a problem. His house was less than a mile away. A cold trip for sure, but he had walked it in reverse more than once. He stared at his reflection in her window. *Should have shaved the eyebrows. Too late for that now.*

The sudden light inside the room startled him, casting his shadow onto the high cedar fence behind. Callie was at the window in an instant, sliding it open with one hand, hushing him unnecessarily with a finger in front of the lips with the other. He tucked the coin back into its pocket and climbed in quickly.

Callie's room had last been decorated when she was in a Holly Hobbie phase at age twelve. The place was a pre-teen dream of blue gingham and patchwork. She had started covering the relentlessly cheerful wallpaper with fliers announcing all-ages shows at Goofy's/Upper Deck and 21+ shows at The Longhorn, including a battered poster for The Police from their first U.S. tour three years ago that she found at a yard sale.

She sat on the edge of the bed, lips pursed with a question she was biting back. Skull made a nest of sorts between her bed and the wall with some of the spare decorative pillows and the extra comforter from her closet. "Are we going to talk about it?"

His mind whirled. *Where to start?* "I'm kind of tired..."

"Bullshit, Jimmy," she said. He opened his mouth to correct her, but her sharp glare convinced him to keep quiet. "I don't care what you call yourself now or how you cut your hair. You've been Jimmy Wayne Lundquist since I met you in fourth grade. You can't hide from me. You're sleeping on my floor, so we're going to talk about it. Did you talk to your mom about the picture?"

Skull remembered the look of pain, the shock, in his mom's blue eyes. He remembered how quickly it turned to anger. "Yes." He took off his jacket and set it near his improvised bed. "She had been drinking."

"She's always drinking," Callie countered.

"She's always drinking," he agreed. He rolled up the sleeve of his thermal where his mother's grip was displayed in vivid purple on his pale arm. "The cop gave me a bruise above the elbow," he said. "But this was all her from when she threw me in my room."

Her voice was the barest whisper. Shaking fingers reached out to touch the bruise then retreated several inches short. "Jesus, Jimmy."

"It doesn't matter," he said. He felt the coin in his pocket and it gave his strength. "I'm leaving it all behind."

Callie narrowed her eyes. "You're running away?"

Skull shrugged. He didn't honestly know. He didn't even know why he'd said it to begin with. But having spoken the words, he knew they were true. His skin didn't feel like it belonged to him anymore— like it ever had. He had always felt uncomfortable, awkward and had never known why. His skin was just a canvas given him by others, by the circumstances of his birth, by every bruise and scar that he had been inflicted upon him. It had never been his, just something he rented. *Bone is what's true.* "I don't know. I'm sorry Callie. I just... I don't have any answers right now. Maybe I'll know tomorrow."

It seemed to be enough to ease her concern back a notch. They talked about the latest issue of *Your Flesh* and their review of the Loud Fast Rules show from last week that both of them had been at. After a while, she turned out the light and Skull lay there, staring at the shadows on the ceiling.

He couldn't sleep. Every time he closed his eyes, he saw his mom's face, shrieking at him. He remembered the bloodshot blue eyes, wide and defensive. He saw her mouth, lipstick smeared, twisted in a lazy snarl. He heard the name she hurled at him like a curse. Martin Delcove. He looked past her head to the family photo, little Jimmy Wayne Lundquist bracketed by two smiling Vikings— mom and dad, both so blonde, and him, thin face framed by fine, dark hair. He never realized before how fake and strained his parent's smiles were.

He never questioned it. But what does a kid know about genetics? And women dye their hair, don't they? There was a whole aisle of the stuff at the Cub Foods. It never occurred to him that he never once saw his mom buy any of it. If he hadn't found the old photo in the box of his dad's things, questioned the similarity of his own face with that of his father's childhood friend, he might have gone his whole life without knowing.

When Callie's breathing became slow and regular, Skull stood and slipped on his jacket. He left the way he had come in. At some point between Callie's home and his own, he realized that he had slipped the skull-faced nickel from his pocket. He had squeezed it so hard that it had sliced into his palm. *Don't worry,* the coin seemed to say when he opened his fingers to see metal and blood. *It's just meat... and meat lies.*

He didn't try the front door. The lights were all off, so his mom would be asleep or passed out by now. She would have locked the door, as always. But his window on the second floor was easy to reach from the porch, and he had jimmied the latch since he was ten. Skull crept into the room, careful not to alert his mom just in case. The room was partly lit from the streetlight shining through the bare tree branches outside, and in the half-light he saw a stranger in his bureau mirror. He tilted his head to shadow the eyes, smiled wide to display his teeth.

Close. Not quite. Soon, the coin whispered, reassuringly.

He opened the door to his room and saw the old photo, torn into scraps on the threadbare carpet where his mom had left it. He crouched and collected the pieces, tucking them into his jacket. It was, after all, the only photo he had of his real father.

Skull followed the sound of snoring to his mother's room. She was wearing the same floral housedress from earlier. A mostly empty bottle of vodka was propped against the pillows next to her head. *That won't do,* the coin said.

"It's alcohol, isn't it? Alcohol burns."

Trust me. Gasoline will do the trick.

The voice was familiar. Walking up the stairs with the can of gasoline from the garage, he remembered where he had heard it before. Thin and mean, just that evening that same voice had told him that he'd *earned it*.

"Goddamned right," Skull said again without missing a step.

It was the gasoline fumes that made his eyes water as he doused his mom's bed. He convinced himself it wasn't tears as he fought the thin voice urging him on. *You want the truth, don't you? Bones are truth. In a little while you'll understand.*

Skull found his mother's lighter, a cheap blue Bic tucked into her pack of Virginia Slims in the bedside table. Then he tied his feet securely to the heavy legs of the bed frame. "Will it hurt?"

Not a bit.

"Really?"

The hand holding both coin and lighter flicked it to life.

Would I lie to you?

 TRUST IS A HARD THING TO come by in one so jaded. In this case, I can tell you that the nickel did not lie— for one of them. You get to decide for whom. I particularly like this tale as it helped Skull figure out who he really was after years of being lied to. It's a shame his mother didn't see fit to tell him in clearer ways than the fist. Things might have been different.

—*The Carver*

Train Yard Blues

SEANAN MCGUIRE

A LOT OF WISE OLD ghosts have told me that once you've been dead long enough, the world loses the ability to shock you. Everything has been done before, according to them, sometimes more than once, and definitely better than it's being done now. When they were alive, the grass was greener, the sky was bluer, the ambulomancers were nicer, and the drivers were freer with their offers of rides and extra coats. Basically, if you listen to them, we all exist inside the greater ghost of a better world that died a long time before any of us did, and all we're doing now is watching its echoes as they slowly fade to gray. When those echoes have been laid to rest is when the *real* fun will start for those of us on the ghostroads.

I don't like to say that my elders are full of crap, but there are times when I really hope that they are. There are things that shouldn't have happened once, much less over and over again since the world began. Things that don't make enough sense to be recurring themes in the history of time.

This is one of them.

Albuquerque, New Mexico, 1985

It's a beautiful night in Albuquerque. My last ride was a cargo jockey for the railroad. That's what put me here, strolling down the street outside the yard with a borrowed coat on my back and nothing that needs my attention until the sun comes up and the ghostroads take me back. Nights like this would make me glad to be alive, if I hadn't been dead for more than forty years. As it is, they just make me glad that I'm the kind of dead girl who still gets the chance to come out and play every once in a while. The unquiet dead must spend a lot of time bored out of their fleshless skulls.

Someone is roasting pork in a little shack at the end of the block. The smell borders on orgasmic, promising satisfaction that is probably illegal in at least five counties. I shift direction, heading straight for it. I can't pay for my meal — there are rules that govern my interaction with the living — but I can beg, and if it's freely given, then it's truly mine. I can almost taste the charred meat and smoky sauce on my tongue, and that just makes me walk a little faster. Nothing motivates a ghost like the thought of food.

The sound of a train leaning on its horn pulls my attention away from the smell of pork, and just like that, the smell of ashes and burning heather fills my nose: there's about to be an accident. It would be lilies, not heather, if it was a car colliding with another car. I smell heather because a car is about to collide with a train. I break into a run, already knowing that I'm too late. The smell is too strong, and I'll never make it in time. That doesn't matter as much as the simple act of running, of knowing that even if I could never have done anything, I tried. I always try. Trying is what separates the dead from the lost. While I may be the first, I will fight forever to avoid becoming the second.

I'm not the fastest of runners. When I'm wearing a borrowed coat and the borrowed flesh to go with it, I'm still an out of shape sixteen-year-old. I'm fast enough to reach the intersection a split second before the train slams into the side of the old beater that someone has parked across the tracks. I see a man's pale, anxious face through the windscreen. Then the car is gone, taking his body with it. I stop running. There's no point in hurrying now; what needs to be done can wait until the end of the world if it has to.

The train is bleeding speed like a wound, and it rolls to a stop as I'm walking toward the pale, half-translucent man now standing in the road, his expression slowly relaxing as he begins to realize what has happened to him. He's wearing the clothes he died in. New ghosts always are. It takes time to learn how to change that, to turn bloodstained jackets or green silk gowns into whatever you want to wear. In a way, those bloody, ripped-up clothes make him seem like a newborn. Here on the ghostroads, that's essentially what it is. His eyes fix on me. The few others who witnessed the accident are shouting and running after the dragged-away car, but not me. I know there's nothing left to save... and somehow, he looks at me, and knows that I know.

"I'm dead," he says.

This isn't how these things are supposed to work. "Yes," I agree, and release my hold on the coat I got from my dreamy-eyed cargo boy. I hope someone gives it back to him. It won't be me. My flesh drops away with the fabric, replaced by the intangible substance of the dead. I keep the jeans and tank top. This isn't a good time for a prom dress, and that's what I died in. "I'm Rose."

He doesn't tell me his name. Instead, he smiles, all that half-glimpsed worry washed away on a wave of giddy relief. "I'm dead! The train hit me and I died!"

"That's usually what happens when you argue with a train. You lose. Look, I'm here because—"

"I'm *dead*!" He grabs my hand with both of his, spinning me around in a drunken whirl. I stumble to stay upright. I don't know why the dead don't drop through the earth when we walk on it, but we don't, and those of us who can't fly — like me — have to work to keep our balance just like the living do. It's one of the unexplained rules that govern our existence, and it's annoying as hell. "Oh, sugar, if I weren't a dead man, I'd kiss you."

"If you tried, I'd clock you one."

He laughs out loud and lets me go, fading right out of the world before I can explain to him about the twilight, or the ghostroads, or anything else. He doesn't even leave me time for my patented "moving on to your reward is a pail of crap, but you're welcome to try" speech. He's just *gone*, leaving me staring blankly into the air where he used to be. I wonder if this is what the living feel like after they've seen a ghost.

There's something in the hand that he grabbed. I open my fingers and stare, slack-jawed, at the silver coin winking back at me like the blind eye of a dead man. It was a nickel, once, before someone carved it into a grinning skull with spiders in its teeth. It looks like one of the loa. It looks like trouble.

"The fucker slipped me a hobo nickel," I say, horrified beyond words. The nickel, grinning, says nothing.

If that man weren't dead and gone, I'd kill him myself.

Hobo nickels are one more piece of proof that mankind, when sufficiently bored, will always find a way to stay amused. They're portable works of art and I understand that there are some swanky galleries run by idiots that will pay top dollar for the things. Those people don't understand the nature of sympathetic magic, or the power of the road. The further a thing travels, the more strength it has, accreting layers of distance like a pearl. Vehicles are usually the strongest, but money comes in a close second. You can also gain power through repeated handling. A thing that has had many owners, or been carried far enough by one owner, will be stronger than something that has kept still, kept safe at home.

And a thing which is crafted out of desperation and pain, midwifed by the road, raised by a hundred pairs of hands passing it from one to the next, will be stronger than it has any right to be. Hobo nickels aren't always bad things. It's just that they're more likely to be nasty than not. I'd been given this one by a dead man, who by all rights shouldn't have been able to give me anything at all. What you own on the ghostroads will vary from ghost to ghost, but as a rule, we don't have many knick-knacks to pass on to our nearest and dearest. That means the nickel I'm holding is a ghost in its own right and that doesn't make me the least bit comfortable.

Hoping that I was being overly-dramatic — I'm allowed to be overly-dramatic on occasion, I'm sixteen, and I will be until the stars burn out — I open my hand and let the nickel drop into the roadway dust. It hits with a faint "clink" that would be inaudible if I weren't standing on the ghostroads, one foot in the twilight, one foot in the daylight of the mortal world. I eye it warily, like a snake that might decide to strike at any moment. The nickel stays where it is, a small disk of gleaming metal.

I'm being paranoid. You'd think the dead wouldn't have much to be paranoid about, but when your existence is a shadow-thing, you're even more afraid of losing it. An afterlife is still a life, after all, and anything that lives can be destroyed.

Still the nickel doesn't move. I laugh a little in relief and turn to head back toward the train yard, where I can try to cadge a coat out of someone else. I'm not over the idea of pulled pork sandwiches just yet.

It really is a beautiful night. I stick my hands in the pockets of my jeans as I walk, and freeze when my fingers touch something that shouldn't be there. It's almost not a surprise when I pull my hand out and see the hobo nickel resting in my palm. *Miss me?*

I've been dead too long to enjoy being haunted by the ghost of a coin. I'd been dead too long for this shit before my funeral. "Fuck me," I mutter.

No one hears me. The people who rushed over to see the accident are too distracted to pay attention to one scrawny teenager and the ones who didn't are too far away. I shove the nickel back into my pocket and start walking again, faster this time. I need to get rid of this thing before it screws me over, and there's only way that's going to happen.

I've got a train to catch.

In the lands of the dead, if you want to talk to someone about the road, you find a routewitch; if you want to talk to someone about the places you walk when you walk alone, you find an ambulomancer; and if you want to deal with the great steel beasts that once roared their domination across the Earth, you find yourself a trainspotter. They hold dominion over the trains and the greedy hands of the rails, which clasp North America in a grip that will never be broken. Theirs are the hobos and the lost ones, the rail-riders, the runaways. Theirs are the steam and the coal and the broken piston. In the shadow of the train yard, hallowed be thine engines, amen.

The trouble is, trainspotters don't have much truck with road ghosts, especially not now, when the mortal railroads are in decline and the railroads of the twilight are forever ascending. There are too many of us. There was a time when most of us would have died on the rails, runaways and stowaways, and been one with the tracks forever. Since that didn't happen, there's a certain resentment when we come into their territory, like we're the ones changing the rules.

I approach the sleeping train with my hands visible and my head bowed as a sign of respect. It doesn't stir as I come closer. That's a good sign. I'm close enough to the daylight that I don't need to worry about the engine opening its jaws and taking me in, but it might still express its disapproval of my presence. This is a passenger train, set to depart soon for Ann Arbor, Michigan: a short enough trip that the train can't amass too much power, but long enough for my purposes. If I'm quick. If I'm clever. If the trainspotters will see me.

"I have no ticket," I say softly. "I have no passage. I have no pennies in my pocket, not a nickel to my name." The hobo nickel may cling to me like a burr, but it isn't mine; I refuse to claim it, refuse to let its story own me. "I beg the mercy of the rails. I beg the swift wind in my hair, the taste of smoke, the sound of wheels against the steel. I beg permission to come with you, and to see what might be seen."

There is a long silence between us, myself and the train, and in that silence, an answer grows. It is not spoken; some words need never to be said. *Yes,* says the stillness of the train. I clasp that permission to myself as the armor that it is and walk toward the first passenger car, past the porters who check tickets and hoist luggage, past the weary-eyed wanderers taking the midnight train to anywhere but here.

No one sees me board. No one ever does.

Trains are funny things. They're a moving liminal space once they pull out of their stations, neither here nor there, neither home nor their destination. Even the most well-lit trip takes place half in the twilight. I walk the length of the car, watching the shadows pulse and move around the travelers who are sometimes visible, sometimes not. They're passing in and out of the ghostroads, and I'm straddling the line. The hobo nickel is heavy in my pocket. I want this thing away from me as soon as possible, before it makes my unlife more difficult than it already is.

I walk through the passenger cars to the first luggage car. There's a burning sensation when I cross the threshold, making the tattoo of Persephone's blessing on my lower back twitch and ache. That's not a good sign. Persephone is Lady of the Dead, and while I may not follow Her teachings, I respect Her warnings. I turn back toward the door to the passenger section, intending to go back to where I was before the burning began—

—and stop as I see the sigils cut into the wall around the door. They're tiny things, barely chicken scratches on the daylight side, but in the twilight, they pulse and gleam with power, glowing silver-red from within. This is an old, old language, the language of Orpheus and Eurydice; older even than Greek, because the culture that claims a myth isn't always the culture where that myth was born. I can't read the words, but I don't need to. I know what they say. *No ghosts welcome here.* I was able to cross the threshold out. That doesn't mean the doorway will allow me to go back *in*.

My stomach suddenly churning, I turn and make my way through the luggage car as calmly as I can. There's another passenger car on the other side, lower-class riders here, lower-cost tickets. None of them see me walk through the door that connects them to the rest of the train; none of them look up as I half-walk, half-run down the length of the aisle to the next door. I'm picking up speed by the time I reach it, and I don't feel like slowing down, so I just keep going, and I slam into the wood with as much force as any girl made of flesh and blood and panic. Still no one looks up. I have no coat, I have no borrowed body for them to fuss over and worry about. And here, on the railroad, where being a hitchhiking ghost is just this side of useless, I can't get those things.

I was so worried about getting the nickel to the trainspotters and out of my hands that I didn't bother to stop and think about what would happen after I got onto the train. Now here I am, and someone has set a ghost trap on these two cars. There's no way out. The only real question is why anyone would do that, and pardon me for being a little self-absorbed here, but I don't give a fuck. You want to catch ghosts? More power to you. I don't care. I'll keep on not caring right up until one of your captive dead folks rips your soul out and eats it in front of you. Only this ghost trap caught *me*, and I'm not much of a soul-eater. I really prefer burgers.

"Think, Rose," I say, picking myself up from the train floor. A few people glance over — children and older people, usually, ones who stand closer to the twilight on a daily basis — but they look quickly away, expressions puzzled, like they're not sure what they were looking at. I run a hand back through my hair. At least it's still short. Most of the time, I can choose what my hair and clothes look like. When I'm in real danger, though, I wind up back in the green silk gown I was wearing when I died, with shoulder-length hair that I never treated well enough.

Who builds a ghost trap on a train? Answer: no one I wanted to meet, but probably someone who was hunting rail ghosts, not road ghosts. All I have to do is wait. Eventually, they'll come to see what their trap has caught. Then they'll see that I'm the wrong kind of prey and toss me back. I'll still need to find the trainspotters, but there are lots of trains riding the rails. I'll have another shot.

Satisfied that I've found the answer of least resistance, I move toward one of the open seats. I don't have to wait out this journey standing up.

All things considered, it's a good thing I moved, because it means that when the little rail ghost runs by, I'm not in his way. It's a little boy who was no more than eleven when he died, all rosy cheeks and signs of lingering frostbite on his fingers, carried over from the body he lost some time ago, if the cut of his clothes is anything to judge by. He doesn't seem to see me, or if he does, he doesn't care; I'm an obstacle, not an ally. He hits the same door I hit a few moments ago. Unlike me, he doesn't bounce off. He *clings*, fingers scrabbling against the wood like the claws of a desperate animal.

"Hey," I say, straightening up again. "Hey! Kid! What's going on here?"

His head whips around, and the fear in his eyes is enough to make me take a step back. "Who are you?" he demands. "Help me! We have to get this open. Oh, sweet Hel, we're on one of the tithing trains..." His words come out as a moan at the end, devoid of hope or strength.

"Tithing trains? What are you talking about?"

Now his eyes widen. "You're not a rail ghost. You're dead but you're not a rail ghost. What are you?"

"Hitcher. What are you?"

"Breezer." He says the word like it's a title, like it should carry a whole catalog of attributes and legends. I don't know it. The rails are an alien land to me, one that I visit as rarely as I possibly can. He sees my lack of understanding in my eyes, because he shakes his head and says, "It doesn't matter. We have to get out of here. Can't you see that we're in danger?"

"I picked up on that, yeah. What the hell's a tithing train?"

Now the look he gives me is pure disgust, strong enough to slice through his fear. "Do they teach you *anything* on the road?"

"Yeah." I fold my arms. "They teach me that rail ghosts are dicks. What's a tithing train?"

"I'll explain while you help me pry this open." He turns back to the door, where his fingers still cling fast to the wood. I need to know where I am, and so I go to him and lend my phantom strength to his. It's hard, harder than I would have ever dreamed. I do it anyway, and to my relief, the boy starts talking again.

"When the rails were new, trains used to break through to the Underworld all the time."

I forget to pry for a moment while I stare at him. "You mean the ghostroads?"

"No. The ghost*rails* aren't in the Underworld." The boy glares at me. I get the feeling he's been dead longer than I have. "But lots of people died every time that happened and it helped to feed the rails. Kept the trains moving smoothly. The more the rails were used, the thicker the soft places got, until trains stopped breaking through. It was still all right for a little while, until rail transport started to become less popular. The trainspotters had to do something if they wanted to protect the railways. So they created the tithing trains, to keep feeding the rails."

"What?" I look behind me, at the oblivious passengers. "You mean the trainspotters are going to kill all these people?"

"Not the people. The people haven't gone far enough. They're not heavy enough for the rails. The trainspotters are going to kill *us*. Unless we get this door open. Now help me!"

I want to go back to the ghostroads. This ecology is too brutal for me. The roads support and keep the ghosts they make; they don't destroy us to feed themselves and the routewitches certainly wouldn't help them if they tried. But then, the roads are older than the rails, aren't they? Maybe this is how it worked for us too, millennia ago, when a road was still a miracle cutting through the hills.

We throw all our insubstantial weight against the door, trying to force it to open, trying to force our way through. The boy is almost crying in his frustration. That's the trouble with tithes. No one ever thinks it's going to happen to them.

I am not a railway ghost. I do not belong here. And it is *not* going to happen to me. Persephone's brand is burning on my back, *danger danger danger*, but I'm not tasting anything, no lilies or ashes or cherry cough syrup to tell me what's coming. I suppose that's beyond me too, here in this place where the rules were made for other circumstances. I back away from the door, moving halfway down the train. Maybe if I run and throw myself against it, I can get a little more momentum behind me. I'm not sure what good that will do. It can't hurt to try.

"Where are you going?" demands the boy. He twists to face me, his hands still flush with the door. "We have to get this open! We have to—"

Whatever he was intending to say is lost in a rising wail of panic and desperation as ink-black hands with fingers that taper into trails of coal smoke thrust through the wood and grab him by the shoulders. He struggles, this little lost boy who died on the rails, but they're stronger than he is, and a second pair soon joins the first, this one thrust through the bottom of the door, grabbing his ankles. He screams. It is the sound of an impossible death, of something that is already dead seeing the end of everything. It is the sound ghosts make when they are exorcised... or, I suppose, when they are used as fuel for an infernal engine.

The hands yank him through the door that was impassable only a moment before. His screams cut off as soon as his face passes through the wood. The sounds of the living around me are so muted that they might as well be silence. I sink to the aisle, trying to make sense of what I just saw.

I never learned his name. He was dead for decades; he lived once, long enough ago that he's probably forgotten to all who knew him in his life. I never learned his name and now he's gone.

I have to get off this train.

Any hope I might have harbored that the tithe has been paid dissolves when I cautiously approach the door, staying out of grabbing range, and see that the lines are still glowing. Whatever turned this train into a ghost trap hasn't been cancelled out yet. "Shit," I hiss, through clenched teeth. Then I turn and all but run back to the middle of the car, staying as far from the doors at either end as I possibly can. If those hands come reaching for me, they're not going to find me easy prey.

How long is this train supposed to run before it makes a stop? I don't know how long it takes to ride the rails between Albuquerque and Ann Arbor, but I have the horrible feeling that whatever the answer is, it's too long for me.

This isn't how it was supposed to end. I'm a road ghost. If I wasn't going to move on to whatever lies beyond the Last Dance Diner, I should at least have run afoul of the dangers of the road, not the dangers of the rails. This isn't right. This isn't *fair*. This isn't...

This isn't a good time to sit around feeling sorry for myself. According to the dead boy, this is a "tithing train," and that implies that someone made it this way. Someone who probably wasn't dead, since ghosts have real trouble constructing ghost traps without getting caught themselves. That meant that whoever it was would have been thinking like the living, and that's a problem when you're playing with dead things. I take a breath I don't need, close my eyes, and try to drop through the floor of the car, down into the twilight.

Nothing happens. I open my eyes and scowl at the faded carpet under my feet. They must have put wards under the train, to avoid just that sort of trick. Fine, then: if they weren't going to let me have the easy way, I'd take the hard one.

Where there's an under, there's an over. I walk to one of the open seats, step up onto the armrest, and grab the nearest overhead luggage rack, pulling myself up. No one really seems to notice. They're all lulled by the rails, these sleepy passengers, oblivious to what's really happening around them. That's probably for the best. There are a lot of things that can't touch you if you don't know they're out there, and these people are innocent. They deserve the protection.

I climb as high as I can before reaching for the roof of the car. My hand slides through the steel like it's no more consequential than a cobweb. I grin and start to pull myself up, grabbing the outside of the car for leverage. Don't ask me how that works, because I don't know; it's not like they taught this shit in school, and I probably wouldn't have paid attention if they had. All I know is that I am getting *out* of here.

The wind outside the train can't touch me as I pull myself through the roof. Persephone's mark starts burning as I get my chest through. I start moving faster, but it's not fast enough to get to safety before something grabs my ankle — something that burns and chills at the same time — and yanks me back down. I scream.

There's no one here to hear me.

I fall through the train roof and back to the floor, landing hard. The creature that's holding my ankle doesn't let go, and the impact wrenches my leg painfully in its socket. I *hate* feeling pain when I'm insubstantial. It's just not *fair*.

Neither is the thing that's holding me. It was terrifying when it was just a pair of hands. Now, seen up close and personal, it's a nightmare given roughly human form. It stands nearly six feet tall, and is made entirely of smoky dark, like a moving hole in the world. I scream again, kicking against it. It doesn't seem to notice, or to care— and another is moving up behind it, ready to help it contain me.

More than anything, I don't want to see where these creatures will take me, or what happens to the railway tithes. The hobo nickel is a heavy weight in my pocket, all out of proportion with what it should be. Sudden rage washes over me. This is all the fault of railroads.

"Get the hell away from me!" I shout loudly enough that several of the passengers look around, suddenly aware that something is going on, even if none of them can see it. I pull the nickel from my pocket and fling it at the thing that holds my ankles. "I'm not paying your debts for you!"

The hobo nickel flies through the head of the first creature, only to be caught by the second. Much to my surprise, the first one drops me to lunge for the second, smoky fingers scrabbling for ownership of the nickel.

I'm not the kind to wait around and see if an opportunity changes its mind. The two shadow-things are locked together, fighting for the coin. I scramble to my feet, ready to try climbing through the roof one more time

I don't have to. The door at the end of the car is no longer glowing, maybe because both shadow-things are here with me. I run for it, flinging myself through the wood and into a perfectly normal-looking dining car. A few people look up, startled by my sudden appearance. The trainspotters I came here to see, no doubt.

"Fuck you," I shout at them, as I run past, heading for the far door. This one doesn't stop me either, and neither does the next, or the next, until I leap through the final door of the train and find myself falling to the tracks below. I land in a painless heap, rolling onto my back to watch the train recede into the distance.

There is a man standing atop the last car, dressed in an old-fashioned conductor's uniform. He's too far away for me to see clearly, but it feels like he's watching me. Judging me. The little road ghost who dared to set foot on his train. I know a train-spotter when I see one. He's tossing something up and down in his hand, and I think I know what it is. Fishermen reclaim their hooks after the prey breaks loose, after all.

Just to be sure, I stick my hand into my pocket. No nickel.

I watch the train until it's gone, taking the trainspotter — and the hobo nickel — with it. "Oh, thank fuck," I finally moan, and let myself collapse, lying exhausted where I fell. When I feel like I can walk again, I get back to my feet and start toward the distant lights of the highway. Maybe I can't get back to the train yard barbecue, but after the night I've had, I deserve a burger, and a ride on the clean tar highway where no trains will ever run, and where all the ghosts will be familiar.

WHEN I DISCOVERED HOW *far this particular coin of chaos had traveled, even I was surprised. Shocked to tell the truth. It was the first time I discovered that one of my nickels could grow beyond this mortal plane. Even as that one man sacrificed himself to rid the world of my coin's influence, he opened up vast new worlds for it to explore. Now my coin travels the roads that once were and may never be again. I don't understand this mystery and that, in and of itself, is worth more than I can express.*

—The Carver

SKULL OF SNAKES

GLENN ROLFE

IT WAS THE SUMMER of 1989. School vacation was in full effect and we loved every second of it. A quick stop at Boynton's Market for our penny candy and pop rations was always among the first orders of business. Once fully stocked with our daily supply of sugar, we'd bike back to our little fort in the woods out back of Kirk's house.

'Fort Eat My Shorts' was painted on the poorly constructed sign above the club house door. Its runny red letters were supposed to look like blood. We thought its resemblance to the camp blood signs in the *Friday the 13th* movie series helped to keep the younger kids away.

On this particularly hot and sticky June morning, we were all fired up for the Hanson Union River Run. It was part of our small town's celebration of itself. Hanson Union Weekend featured a parade, a battle of the bands at the Hanson Union Common, a bunch of sidewalk arts and craft things that we paid absolutely no attention to, two nights of fireworks, and of course, the Hanson Union River Run.

The river run consisted of anywhere from twenty-five to fifty homemade floats cruising down the Jessup River. It started up in Dutton and wound to its usually dramatic finish at the boat landing here in Hanson Union. It was mostly grown-ups who took part in the race, but this year, Kirk's brother Gary would be participating. He and his football buddies had spent the last two weeks building a pirate-themed float. That meant that this year, we'd finally have someone we actually knew, and liked, to root for.

"So, can we see it?"

Paul was referring to Kirk's brother's float.

"It's not here, dummy. They took it up to Dutton," Kirk replied.

"What time does the race start again?" Mike asked, to no one in particular.

"It starts at noon, but they won't get down our way until around 12:30-12:45." Kirk answered Mike with a little more patience.

"Shit, you mean we gotta find stuff to do between now and then," Paul said as he popped a fireball in his mouth.

I had the morning planned out already and decided it was time to let the boys in on it. "We can go back to my house and watch MTV until lunch. My mom's out running errands. I'm sure she'll make us some lunch when she gets back too. Then we can head over to the tracks."

No one argued. We were back at my house by 9:30.

The few hours flew by faster than we feared they would. We watched cool music videos from Guns N' Roses, Skid Row, Poison and Madonna while playing air guitars and wrestling around until my mom got home. We helped her bring in the groceries and other odds and ends she had picked up while she was out and, just as I knew she would, she made us burgers and fries for lunch.

We all thanked my mom before heading out the door and riding our bikes down to the tracks.

The tracks were the train tracks out behind Jenner's Grocery. We had watched the river run from this very spot the last two years. The location was perfect. The tracks ran across a bank that rose about twenty feet above the river and followed straight down to the boat landing. The trees that dressed our side of the river gave way and opened up to a perfect view of the river and its annual parade of canoes and motor boats dressed as floats. The other side of the river, which was tree-free, was where most of the town gathered to watch the race's conclusion, leaving us and a few other kids from our side the perfect perch to witness the grand finale.

Paul, who was staring out at the rushing waters, spoke up, "Should be coming down any time now, huh guys... guys?"

Kirk and Mike were both standing around me. I'd been walking on the rails, imagining myself as one of the tightrope walkers from the circus, when a shine from the ground caught my eye. I reached down and plucked the shimmering nickel from the rocks between the tracks. It was old, real old. I brushed the dirt off revealing a buffalo. The most intriguing part of the coin was on its reverse side. I had to scrape the hardened dirt on this side with my fingernail, but what I found was both amazing and a little creepy. Rather than an old president, this coin featured a skull covered with snakes. There were snakes coming from its gaping mouth, a snake protruding from its left eye, and snakes as hair along the entirety of its wide crown. The detail in the carving was brilliant. The guys saw me staring at the coin and wrapped around me to see what I was so lost in.

"Whoa, that's creepy," Mike said. "What the hell kind of coin is that?"

Even Mike's dog breath couldn't distract me from the beauty of the coin. "I don't know, man, but it's old. Look at that— 1913. This could be worth some real money."

"Hey, guys. What are you lookin' at?" Paul asked from his post. He was probably catching a hint of the excitement reverberating from our huddle. The lure of our find still wasn't enough to make him abandon his perch.

"It's a buffalo nickel," I said, trying to sound confident. "Mrs. Oxford talked about them in social studies last year." At least I thought I'd remembered her talking about them.

Kirk backed me up, "Yeah, yeah... I remember that. Aren't they supposed to have an Indian on them?"

"Yeah, I think that's what she said... I'm not sure *what* this is?" I swiped my thumb over the skull and could feel the smooth edge of every detail.

"Guys—"

"Jesus, Paul," Kirk barked. "Shut up and get your fat ass over here if you want to see—"

"—the floats are coming."

There they were. Gary and his football buddies dressed to the gills in pirate regalia— eye patches, ruffled blouses (from Kirk's mother's closet), bandanas, and big dangling earrings.

The float was cool, too. The main sail was a bunch of sewn together tan and white sheets attached to a mast that was just a large PVC pipe. Jutting from both the bow and the stern were two giant black and white flags featuring the Jolly Roger skull and crossbones design. Kirk, who possessed a hidden talent as an artist, had confessed to me three days earlier that he had hand painted the flags himself at his brother's request.

More PVC piping and a bunch of stretched and connected bungee cords served as the ship's handrails (although to me they looked more like the ring ropes around a World Wrestling Federation ring). To further enhance the overall ambience of the ship were a couple of papier-mâché cannons and a hope chest that served as their booty.

The boys were running in second place behind a lame red, white, and blue American-themed boat and had their treasure chest, which turned out to be filled with water balloons, wide open for a last chance attack.

"Whoa," Paul's excitement peaked. "They're gonna bombard those old guys with water balloons." He was hopping up and down like a kid in a candy store as he pointed out the obvious. The rest of us fell in behind him and began hooting and hollering for *our* ship, the creepy, old coin momentarily forgotten.

As if on cue, Gary and his pals began grabbing and launching the multi-colored balloons at the lone team they were trailing. The white-haired group of geezer's decked out in pink and lavender windbreakers, who had been ignoring the encroaching motley crew of misfits, were caught by surprise. The shouts and warrior cries from the high school footballers scared and pissed off the elderly group, who no doubt, had been ready to begin celebrating their forthcoming victory. The old guys were shouting back only to have Gary's crew up the ante by hauling out a couple of large Super Soakers. The old men had no choice but to duck and cover while their captain veered their Lee Greenwood-inspired ship away from the encroaching football pirates.

We roared from the sidelines, running along the tracks, following our ship down the river as it passed the last of its competitors, and headed towards the finish line.

That's when Gary fell into the river.

One minute he was there laughing, screaming, and throwing balloons. The next— he was gone.

I didn't see it happen, but Kirk told us later that he had.

The race, along with our collective hearts, ceased as all of the closest competitors closed in and began searching the rivers surface for the fallen student.

We had to hold Kirk back from running off to the river to help. He was shouting for his brother, shouting he could swim, and that he had to save Gary. We knew the river was way too dangerous, even for a good swimmer like Kirk.

Gary's body was never found.

That night, much to our surprise, the town still held the night one fireworks display. Though, in light of our best friend's tragedy, we weren't sure whether we should be there or not. My mom made us go. She had said that Kirk would need a while with his family and that the rest of us should try to do something to get our minds off of "it." Gary's drowning would be known as "it" by my mother for the remainder of the summer.

We decided to go to the fireworks, but we all agreed that it wouldn't be any fun.

"I just wanna switch into some jeans," I told the guys as I hurried back into my house.

I passed my mother talking in hushed tones into the phone receiver and rushed upstairs to my bedroom. The day had been hot and humid, but the night, as if somehow sensing the mood of the day, had cooled. I grabbed the jeans my mother hated with all the homemade incisions and pulled my shorts off, throwing them towards the foot of my TV. I heard something ping against my Nintendo.

I walked over in my underwear and picked up the coin I'd found earlier by the tracks. I had forgotten about it.

Gazing into the freaky skull of snakes, I felt both in awe and sick. A strange feeling crept over my emotionally wracked nerves pricking the hairs upon the nape of neck to life.

"Lenny!" I jumped as my mom bellowed from the bottom of the stairs. "Your friends are waiting for you."

Freed from the weird trance, I put the coin on top of my TV and started pulling my jeans on. I stopped, noticing a burn mark on my upper right thigh. A red circle, similar to…

I picked the coin up from the TV and held it to the mark. It was a perfect match. *What the hell?*

"Lenny," My mom yelled for me again. "What the heck are you doing up there? Your friends don't want to watch the fireworks from our driveway. Hurry up."

I threw the coin, along with the six dollars I had left in my Superman piggy bank, into the front pocket of my jeans, grabbed my blue hooded sweatshirt, and headed out the door.

Nobody said a word as we cruised down Beaumont Hill towards downtown with the cool night air blowing against our faces and through our hair. Gary and Kirk were on our minds, but my mom was probably right. It wouldn't do any of us any good just sitting around thinking about "it." So downtown we rode; the four horsemen minus one.

Down on Main Street there was a mix of blissful ignorance from the younger kids of Hanson Union, running and laughing with sparklers in hand, their carefree thoughts wrapped tightly around the fun of the evening, while a good number of the older kids and most of the adults that were present, wore somber faces; their hearts heavy laden with the day's earlier tragedy. We met up with Bryce Cooper and his sister Lana.

Bryce helped us break our silence.

"What's up guys? How's Kirk?"

Bryce Cooper, and his twin sister Lana, weren't part of our little tribe per say, but they were the next closest thing.

Paul and I both looked to Mike to answer; Mike stared at the ground.

He was taking it harder than either of us. I spoke up, "He's at home, obviously, with his folks."

Lana put her arm around me and rubbed my back. "I just can't believe it," she said soothingly. "I feel awful for Kirk. I mean, I didn't really know Gary, but I heard Kirk talk about him so much I almost feel like I did. Ya know?"

"Yeah," I replied. I hated myself for a moment. My best friend's brother was dead, and here I stood, slightly red in the face, quietly enjoying the fact that Lana Cooper was rubbing my back. I couldn't help but feel like a piece of shit. "Have you guys seen Kerry or Tony?" I asked.

"Nope, I guess some of the parents didn't want their kids coming out tonight and are pretty pissed at the Mayor for having the fireworks still. I mean Christ, they set 'em off over the river, ya know?"

Out of the blue, Mike snapped.

He threw his bike to the ground, stomped his way over to the side of the street and picked up a pile of bricks from in front of Kent's Hardware and Garden. Before any of us could stop him he just started screaming and throwing the bricks against the front window of the store.

On the third brick, the giant pane of glass smashed sending shards every which way.

Mike had tears streaming down his face and his cries were so deep, they made it sound as if his soul was tearing its way up through his insides and coming out his mouth. My heart hurt listening to him, watching the sad scene play out seemingly in slow motion.

Bryce, who was bigger than either Paul or I, and only slightly bigger than Mike, tackled him to the ground as Mister Kent came running out through the storefront door.

There was a sudden pain on my leg, but before I could check it out, Lana screamed.

Mister Kent pulled Bryce off of Mike; Mike didn't move. As Bryce tried to break free of Mister Kent's grasp, a circle of people stepped into the scene. I noticed the blood on Bryce's white Winger t-shirt, and wondered where it had come from. Out of the corner of my eye, I saw Lana drop to her knees. Also, one of the people suddenly kneeling by Mike was Doctor Howard. And then, Officer Gilbert and Mister Newman were standing next to him. I couldn't see Mike. Even worse, I couldn't hear him.

Paul appeared next to me, "What's wrong with Mike? Duffy, what's wrong with Mike?"

Lana was crying and rocking back and forth on the street. Bryce was in tears, too. Mister Kent's eyes were welling up, his face scrunched up in an ugly mask of sorrow.

"What's wrong with Mike?" Paul's voice sounded on the verge of breaking.

I had to see. I had to know.

I ran forward, ducking from Mister Kent's outstretched arm and shoving past the couple of people who had come running.

Officer Gilbert noticed me appear over his shoulder and turned to shield my view of Mike. He ushered me away from the scene, but not before I saw what had happened.

Mike's eyes were open, but there was nothing behind them. A large sliver of glass from the window he had smashed only moments before was protruding from the front of his throat. There was a massive pool of blood spreading out from beneath him.

As Officer Gilbert ushered me to his patrol car, I could hear Paul, poor lost Paul, yelling to me. "Duffy, what's wrong with Mike? What's wrong with Mike?"

As I sat in the back of Officer Gilbert's cruiser, I felt cold and numb. My life had just been slammed not once, but twice with tragedy in the same day. I had never known anyone who had died. Within twelve hours I was provided with the first two worst experiences of my life.

My dad was waiting at the end of the driveway for me as we pulled up.

"Thanks, Danny," He said to Officer Gilbert.

"No problem, Craig. For whatever it's worth, I'm sorry. You'll have to excuse me— I've got to get back downtown."

My dad just nodded as Officer Gilbert climbed back behind the wheel and pulled away. My father looked more broken than I'd ever seen him look before. Mike's dad had been dad's best friend in high school. Mom no doubt was over at the Leach's right now with Jenna, Mike's mom. I could see another cruiser at the end of the block sitting in their driveway.

I went into the house and ran up to my room. My dad didn't even bother to try and come after me. We both had some tears to shed and he knew us Duffy's were better at crying alone.

I burst through my door and threw myself on my bed. The tears flowed without hesitation, instantly soaking my Superman pillowcase.

I'm not sure how long I cried, only that I fell asleep somewhere between the tears and the strange dream I was awoken from by the tapping on my window.

Unbelievably, it was Kirk.

As I opened the window, I stretched towards the corners of my half-awake mind grasping for fragments of the dream I could see evaporating more and more by the second. In the dream, there had been a house and a young Native American boy who had been mouthing something to me from the porch of the house... then the sky turned black. Despite my best efforts to retrieve the visions, the dream memory slipped away.

Kirk slipped in through the half-opened window; the cool chill of the night followed, "I hope you don't mind me waking you, man."

"Nah, don't worry about it," I said. "I'm just surprised to see you."

He looked tired, old even. His steel blue eyes were red-rimmed and bloodshot. His shoulders were hunched forward like a fighter sitting in his corner between rounds that's got nothing left to give. He was still dressed in his Simpson's t-shirt and black jeans from earlier in the day and his hair was pulled back in a ponytail, the loose strands wafted, like wheat in a lazy summer wind, around his face as he stood before the box fan I constantly kept running at the foot of my bed.

I tried to think of something to say. I tried to find the right words that would take away my friend's pain, the pain that had aged him so much in the course of this one horrible day, this day that had started off as every summer day should, so innocently, so carefree. I searched, but all of my best lines weren't even close.

I watched his worn-out eyes staring out the window he'd just climbed through as he sat broken at the end of my bed. I took the spot next to him and threw my arms around him. Our embrace was more than something shared by best friends; it was one of brothers. In that moment we transcended the bonds of our physical beings, our souls clinging to the remnants of the innocence that had been stolen from us.

"I can't believe he's not at home right now waiting for me to sneak in and kick my ass and threaten me with mom and dad..." More tears flowed from Kirk's seemingly endless well.

Suddenly it occurred to me that he may or may not know about Mike. Before I could broach the subject, he wiped the wetness from his cheeks and produced a folded piece of paper from his pocket.

"What's that?" I asked him.

"I needed to do something, ya know? I've been crying all friggin' day." He wiped a fresh tear from his eye. "I remembered that coin you found, the one with the skull and snakes?"

I nodded.

He continued, "And I remembered last summer when my dad took me to that Cryptozoology museum in Danvers."

He held the folded paper in his hands, and drifted off, lost in a memory.

I waited for him to work through whatever was running around behind his burnt out eyes.

"I remembered that coin you found, and then I remembered the story that grizzly old fart at the museum told me." Kirk unfolded the piece of paper and handed it to me.

In big black bold print was a headline that read:

THE LEGEND OF THE "SKULL OF SNAKES" COIN

"Read it." Kirk's voice was like background music as I was already devouring the words before me.

> In 1914, Jeffrey Tuttle and William Hubert robbed men, woman, and children up and down the Jessup River. That summer, they also raped and strangled two Native American sisters, taking a satchel of coins from each. In the elder sister's satchel they found thirteen buffalo coins; one stood out over all the others. This one particular nickel had been chiseled, changed from its original form and transformed into something darker, more menacing. Where the Indian head once had been, now sat a darkly crafted skull. Protruding from the skull were seven serpents. The detail was incredible, and for William, its lure proved irresistible. He tucked the sinister looking coin in his coat pocket before Jeffery had a chance to see it.
>
> That night, William snuck away from Jeffery to find a buyer for the impressive coin on the way, he suffered a severe heart attack, and dropped dead in the street. His body was found early the next morning. Jeffery took the rest of the score and jumped a train heading south. His body was discovered two days later in Chettenwood, Tennessee, his tongue swollen within in his mouth, his eyes bloodshot and bulging from their sockets.
>
> Meanwhile, the "Skull of Snakes" coin was discovered by Edgar Tomlin, the mortician who took care of William Hubert's body. That afternoon, while peeling potatoes for supper, Tomlin's wife slipped with her sharpest knife in hand, cutting her wrist wide open. She bled to death while trying to make the relatively short trek from their home to the town doctor's office. Edgar Tomlin, compelled either by the

great loss, or the dark force attached to the coin, slit his own wrists two nights later. The "Skull of Snakes" coin was later found by Tomlin's young apprentice, Travis Hicks. Hicks sensed the curse imprinted upon the coin, and felt it his obligation to dispose of the coin and whatever evil it possessed. Hick's body was found floating down the Jessup River the next day. The "Skull of Snakes" coin was lost to time.

I couldn't believe it. I brought my eyes up to meet Kirk's and was completely speechless. My guts sank like a ton of bricks. I felt responsible for Gary's death, for Mike's.

"Where is it?" Kirk asked as he rose to his feet.

"It's…" I remembered that Kirk still didn't know about Mike. "I have to tell you something—"

"Whatever it is, it can wait. Where's that damn coin?" He began scanning my room from where he stood.

I decided not telling him about Mike wouldn't be the worst thing right now. He'd been through enough today, and if I could spare him any additional hurt for a few hours, then so be it.

I reached in my pocket, and came up empty.

Impossible!

Kirk noticed the franticness in my reaction. "What? What is it?"

"The coin… it was in my pocket—" I stopped as I touched the bottom of the pocket lining. "There's a hole in my pocket. It must have slipped out."

"What did you do when you got home today?" He put on a hand on my shoulder. "Did you go anywhere?"

Without thinking, I answered him. "Yeah, I had it when we went downtown. It might be anywhere between here and Main Street." A thought struck me. I raised my eyes to meet his, "Or it could be in Officer Gilbert's cruiser."

"What?" He shook his head trying to wrap his head around that one. "Wait, why would it be in Officer Gilbert's cruiser? What did you guys do tonight?"

Crap

I knew I should tell him what happened to Mike, but there were more pressing matters to tend to. Chances were that the coin was in the back of the cop car. I would have heard it ping off the street had it fallen out of my pocket while we were downtown.

Suddenly, I recalled the burning sensation I'd felt on my leg right before Mike lost his shit. I pulled my shorts down.

"What the heck are you doing, man?" Kirk brought his hand up to shield his eyes from the unannounced view of my near nakedness.

I got the shorts off, pulled the liner up to examine it, and found the hole. The exit aperture was charred; the coin had burned its way through my pants.

"It's in Officer Gilbert's car," I stated without a second thought. "We need to find him. That's where we'll find the coin."

"How again, did you end up in the back of a cop car?" Kirk looked a lot like a guy that didn't get a joke.

"I'll explain later. We need to get the coin before something else happens." I was struck by the thought of what re-possessing the coin might mean for us. Would we be better off to just let it go? I thought of Mike. I thought of Gary. I thought of Officer Gilbert.

"What is it?" Kirk asked as I paused before my bedroom window.

"Nothing," I replied. "Let's go find that coin and get rid of it."

Obviously we couldn't just walk out my front door. There was my dad and my mom to contend with, and there was Mike's house. Out the window and through the backyard was the only option.

As we hit the ground, grabbed our bikes, and got ready to depart, Kirk made the inevitable suggestion: "Let's go get Mike and Paul."

I had to turn my face away from him to hide the tears. I bit my lip, shook my head, and peddled forward, away from my street. "No time, man. It's just me and you this time. Just me and you."

I was half way to Cross Street before Kirk could argue.

As we reached the far end of Main Street, I said a silent prayer that the area in front of Kent's Hardware and Garden where Mike's accident had occurred had been cleaned up and would be devoid of any trace of the night's earlier event.

My heart nearly stopped as I saw a chubby kid on a neon green BMX, one just like Paul's, head off west on Emerson Street past Izzy's Flowers. I was hoping I was the only one to have spotted him.

Kirk's voice came from behind me, "What? What is it?"

"Na-nothing," I managed to spit out. "Let's hurry up. I don't wanna miss Officer Gilbert."

He bought the line, never even bothering to look down Emerson. I wondered what the hell Paul was doing out here. He had run away from his mom and step-dad's a couple of times last summer. Maybe with all of the crapola of the day, he was at it again.

There were three bright yellow wooden saw horses and a mess of police line around the storefront, but there were no stragglers, no police and *no body*.

Kirk's voice broke the replay going on in my head. "What the heck happened to Kent's? Did you have anything to do with that?"

"I'll tell you later," I said.

We zoomed past the closed shops lining both sides of the sleeping street. The police station sat quietly at the other end.

We reached the station only to find one of the four squad cars parked out front. Officer Gilbert's was among the missing.

"He could be anywhere. How are we supposed to track him down?" Kirk's voice sounded tired, ready to quit.

"Follow me," I said as I marched towards the front door of the station.

"Where are you going?" He sounded worried. "We can't go in there; they'll... wait up, man."

I walked through the station's front door and saw Officer Mattingly parked behind the Plexiglas window.

"Hi Officer Mattingly," I tried to sound as calm as possible. "Is Officer Gilbert around?"

Kirk filed in behind me. The look on Officer Mattingly's pudgy face told me that something else awful had happened. There was sadness in his old brown eyes giving him a look that reminded me of Betty, my grandpa's Lab, whenever the rain prevented us from playing out in the yard during these summer days. He tried to mask his obvious distress with mock irritation.

"What the hell are you boys doing here?" He tilted his head to look past me and saw Kirk. "This isn't the night for... whatever it is you kids are up to. Go home."

"We need to find Officer Gilbert," I spoke up. "It's an emergency."

He was about to respond when a voice came over the two-way. "Station. Officer Pratt to station. Over."

"Go ahead, Pratt." Mattingly instantly forgot about us.

Pratt's voice came back, "This is a mess. We're gonna need the Jaws of Life over here on Herman. It doesn't look good."

I began to back up; Kirk didn't want to stick around either.

"Will do, Pratt." He stopped as he caught us backing away. "Hey Duffy, you kids get back here. Hey!"

We ran through the doors and jumped on our bikes.

"Where we going, Duffy?" Kirk asked.

I could tell his adrenalin was kicking in. There was a hint of excitement in his voice. "Herman Street," I yelled back over my shoulder. "I think something bad happened to Officer Gilbert."

I didn't want to be right. I wanted this to all be part of some messed-up crazy dream. I wanted everything to go back to the way it had all been this morning. As we crested Beaumont, we saw two other police cruisers, two fire trucks, and an ambulance.

At the foot of Beaumont where it t-boned with Herman, was a smoldering, upside down cop car. Just off to the right of the cop cars was what looked like a mangled neon green bike frame.

"Holy shit, Duffy. Look, is that—" Kirk's voice stopped.

In the middle of the road was a lump under an off-white canvas covering. There was no doubt a body was under that covering. It was either Officer Gilbert or the owner of the mangled bike frame. Without knowing; I knew. I knew it was Paul.

"Let's go home," I said flatly.

"That thing in the road, that bike frame? Don't you think it kind of looks like Paul's? I mean, I can't be sure, I mean, it can't be his, right? That's somebody else's." He sat there thunderstruck, waiting for me to respond. When I didn't he asked, "Duffy, what about the coin?"

"Trust me, Kirk; we're safer if we forget about it." I began peddling for home.

I looked over my shoulder and saw Kirk staring at the accident. Tears were sliding down his cheeks as he zoned into the destructive scene below.

I was getting ready to turn back around when he wiped his eyes and nose on his sleeve and started in my direction. It was a long, silent bike ride back home. I still had to tell him about Mike… and now, well, it wouldn't be confirmed until daylight, but my guts told me we were going to be mourning Paul, as well.

That night I decided I'd let Kirk's parents tell him about our friends. I didn't think I could handle another crying session, not tonight. When I got home, my dad was sitting, head down at the kitchen table, with an empty bottle of whiskey next to his hand.

I couldn't imagine he'd gotten the news about Officer Gilbert or Paul yet. He probably turned to the bottle in light of all that had already happened. If I were a little older myself, I'd have been sitting right there next to him.

As I started up the stairs towards my room, I caught a glimpse of my mom curled up on the living room sofa. This day had sucked the innocence and fun out of a habitually good time around this neighborhood. I just wanted to sleep. And I didn't care if I didn't wake up for months, I didn't want to feel like this tomorrow, but I knew I would. June 24th would stay with me, my family, and my small (even smaller) group of friends for the rest of our lives.

IT IS OFTEN THE INNOCENT *who lose the most when chaos is involved. I think it's because of the potential lost. The younger the victim, the longer and more potential my life has. Oh, and it might interest you to know that Hicks did not have the "Skull of Snakes" on him when he cast himself in the river. His death was nothing more than despair at the loss of his friends and his job. Really, until then, life had been simple and uncomplicated. Sometimes, bad things just happen.*

— The Carver

Searching for a Hero

DYLAN BIRTOLO

BRENT STOOD IN FRONT of the freezer section of the conven-ience store, debating which of the previously-cooked entrees would service for dinner after another late night at the office. Realizing they all tasted about the same, he opened the door and picked up the dinner seated at eye level. He wandered to another aisle looking for a beverage. As he turned the corner at the end of the row, he had to twist his shoulders to keep from running into a woman standing there. She gave Brent a nod and he apologized for almost running her over. His words sounded loud in the empty store. Besides the clerk behind the counter, they were the only two there.

The door chime went off, signaling a new arrival. Brent looked over at the noise and saw a young man, probably in his mid twenties, walk briskly up to the counter. The clerk looked up from his magazine just in time to see the newcomer pull a gun out of his pocket. His hand visibly shook as he pointed it at the clerk.

"Gimme the money!" he snapped.

Brent glanced at the woman he almost ran over. She stood there watching, but her eyes were on Brent, not the conflict. Brent walked forward slowly, creeping behind the guy with the gun.

"Hurry up! Shove it in a bag!"

The clerk had opened the cash register and was stuffing the money from it into the garbage can kept under the counter. Brent was almost directly behind the robber now.

"Faster!" The guy waved the gun back and forth. From here, Brent could see it was a revolver and the hammer wasn't pulled back.

Brent rushed forward, keeping his head low and moving as fast as his legs would carry him. The criminal heard him coming and turned, but Brent was too close. Brent grabbed the man's wrist in both of his hands as the two of them crashed to the ground. The impact knocked the gun loose and it clattered on the floor as it slid out of reach.

The criminal tried to get up to his feet and scrambled in the general direction of the door, but Brent grabbed his ankle and tugged. He got kicked in the face as the other man dropped. Brent held on with one hand, using his other to try and protect his head as a heel came at him multiple times. It was not the planned strikes of a fighter, but the desperate struggles of a beast trying to get free.

The clerk came out from behind the counter and picked up the gun on the floor. He pulled the hammer back with his thumb and pointed it at his former assailant.

"Freeze! The cops are on their way, asshole."

The would-be thief stopped his struggles and lay on the floor with his hands raised as high as he could make them from his compromised position. The clerk eased the hammer down and then walked over to help Brent up to a sitting position.

"Thanks, guy. You saved my ass."

Brent started to smile but winced from the pain around his eye. "Just doing what anyone else would do," he said as he backed across the floor to rest against a shelving unit.

"That ain't true. You're a hero, man." He looked up at the woman standing off to the side. "Hey! Can you get this guy some ice or somethin'?"

The clerk went back to standing guard and waiting for the police to arrive. Off in the distance, Brent could hear the sirens. The woman walked over to him and knelt down to hand him a pack of frozen vegetables. He noticed she was wearing thick black gloves as he took the package from her. He pressed it against his face but quickly pulled it away when it got too cold. There were traces of blood on the bag.

"You were very brave," the woman said, speaking in a soft voice that Brent could barely hear even though she still squatted next to him.

"Thanks."

"It's rare to see that kind of courage these days," she continued.

Brent didn't know what to say. He was sure he was blushing and hoped that the makeshift ice pack and bruising hid it.

"And humble, too."

He glanced up at her and was surprised to see that she wasn't smiling. Even though her words were complimentary, her body language and tone were flat. She reached inside her jacket and pulled something out. With her other hand, she took Brent's free hand and pulled it close. He felt her put something small and metal in the palm of his hand.

"I think you should have this. I've been holding onto it. It's a luck charm. I think it would be better off with you."

She curled his fingers around what felt like a coin and then stood up. He looked down and opened up his palm. There was a nickel resting in the center, but it was unlike any nickel he had seen before. The face had been radically changed. The nose was lengthened and pointed down towards the character's neck, a neck which looked about half the size that it should be. The man's lips we curled upwards in an unnatural smile, revealing too many perfectly shaped teeth. The side of his face was covered in what looked like swirling tattoos. Brent barely could recognize it as a nickel at all, and wouldn't have believed it if it weren't for the backside which was completely unaltered. The date on the coin said 1913.

The door chime made him snap his head up just in time to see the woman walk out of the store. He saw flashing lights reflecting off the buildings across the street and knew the cops would be there soon. Sinking back against the shelving unit as much as he could, Brent tucked the nickel into his pants pocket.

As Brent walked into the office the next day, several of his coworkers began to clap. A grin spread across his face as he made his way to his desk. Shortly after the police arrived at the store, a news crew appeared on the scene and wanted to interview him. He didn't get to see the segment, but it was clear that at least a few of his coworkers had. After recounting the story three times to different groups of people, Brent was finally able to sit at his desk and begin his work for the day. That only lasted a few minutes before his boss requested his presence.

Brent knocked on the open door as he stepped into his boss's office.

"You wanted to see me, Victor?"

"Yes. Please, come in and have a seat. Would you mind closing the door?"

Brent closed the door and sat down across from his boss. "What did you want to see me about?"

"Brent, as I am sure you know, you are a very influential employee with a very good track record at Mutual Investments. It's been, what, three years now?"

"Three and a half."

"Ah yes. As you're aware, we pride ourselves on an image of stability and steadiness. Our clients feel comfortable investing and working with us because of how they view us. They know that even in these turbulent times, we are the rock that they can cling to. We are the voice of reason that tells them what to do and reassures them that everything will be okay in the morning."

Brent squirmed in his seat.

"We pride ourselves on being the best risk-analyzers in the business. It's what sets us apart and why we have the largest corporate accounts of any investment firm in the entire Northeast. You know all of this though. After all, you wouldn't be here if you weren't good at cost-benefit analysis."

Brent reached into his pocket and pulled out the nickel from the previous evening. He played with it, rolling it around one finger and feeling the grooves etched into the face with his thumb. It helped him relax.

"So, let me ask you something, Brent. What was the cost-analysis of your actions last night that have made you something of a local celebrity?"

Silence hung in the air for a few seconds. Brent's skin crawled—this was not the conversation he expected. He stopped playing with the coin and held it in the center of his hand. It felt oddly warm and the sensation made him sit a little straighter in his chair. "There was no 'analysis.' I was just helping out the clerk behind the counter."

"Interesting. Was the criminal about to shoot the clerk?"

"No, but..."

"And isn't it possible the gun might have gone off with your actions?"

"Not likely."

"But it is possible. You also could have been shot."

Brent pressed his lips together and nodded once.

"The store is also insured, something you could have assumed since it is a nationwide chain. This means that even if the criminal did get the money, it would have been returned. So clearly, the best thing to do according to cost-analysis would be?"

"There was no time for that. I just did what was right." Brent's hand clenched on the nickel, pressing it into his hand.

"Please, Brent. Stay calm and answer my question."

Brent took a deep breath and relaxed his grip. He tucked the coin back into his pocket. "The best thing to do would have been to not get involved."

"Exactly. And that is the image that we wish to convey to our customers."

"Understood, Sir."

"Unfortunately, you have tarnished that image with your actions by allowing yourself to be plastered all over the news. While some people may consider you a hero, our customers will see you as a hot-headed liability. That is something we cannot abide."

"What are you saying?"

"I'm saying that while I personally applaud your actions, questionable as they might be, professionally I can't have you scaring away our large clients."

"You mean you're putting me back on entry-level contracts? Individual accounts?"

Victor shook his head. "I'm afraid that our HR department believes we need to make a stronger statement than that. Because of your actions last night, you are being terminated, effective immediately. You have until the end of the day to clean out your desk. I'm sorry, Brent."

"Thanks for coming out," Brent said to Travis as he walked up to the front of one of the many bars on Main Street.

"No problem. The work will still be there in the morning. That just sucks that you got canned. And for such a bullshit reason too."

"I know." Brent shook his head as he pushed through the bar. "As far as I'm concerned…"

He was cut off when someone in the bar recognized him and let out a cheer. "It's the mini-mart hero! Get him a drink!"

Despite it being only four in the afternoon, the bar was reasonably crowded. As soon as they recognized Brent, half the people in the bar crowded around him, and he found more than one beer offered to him. He accepted the offer and sat down at a table. Travis had to push his way through to sit next to his friend. Before he finished the first drink, the bartender walked over.

"Any man who sticks up for the little guy gets a free pitcher in my place. What do you want?"

Brent drank for several hours, well into the evening. Every time he offered to pay, another patron picked up the bill. By the time last call rolled around, he had retold the story more times than he cared to count and drank enough that the entire room rocked back and forth constantly.

"Let's get you home." Travis said as he slid under Brent's arm and helped his friend stand. "Considering how little you drink, you're gonna have a hell of a hangover tomorrow. At least that's one upside to not needing to go into work."

The bartender waved as the two men stumbled through the door.

Brent sat at the table at what had become his favorite bar, rolling the nickel across his fingers. He almost was able to make one continuous path around every finger, but he kept dropping it when he tried to go around the pinky. A half-empty glass sat next to him. He didn't look up from his latest coin-rolling attempt when Travis dropped into the chair next to him.

"How's it going?" Travis asked.

Brent grunted in response.

"No news on a new job?"

"Nope."

"Well, give it time— it's only been a couple of weeks." Travis offered. He took a sip from his drink. "You might want to get cleaned up though before you try any face-to-face interviews."

"Shut it."

Travis froze. "What did you say?"

Brent stopped playing with the coin and tucked it away into his pants pocket. He took a breath, and then looked up at Travis, one corner of his mouth curled up in a smile.

"What, you don't like the bearded look? I was going to go the whole Viking route. I figure if I can't get a job in insurance or investments, I might as well go the other way and take up conquering and pillaging. The beard is step one."

"Uh huh. You keep telling yourself that."

Travis looked at Brent long enough to make the latter feel uncomfortable. He looked away, grabbing his glass and becoming very interested in watching the liquid swirl around the edges as he spun it.

"How many have you had?"

"Just a couple tonight. I don't exactly get free drinks anymore."

"How long did you think you were going to be able to milk that horse?"

"As long as they let me."

The two of them chatted for several hours, having a few drinks. When the bill came, Travis paid and the two of them got up and left the bar. They started the long walk to Travis's car. Rather than drive in the city, he kept his car at his office several blocks away and walked to the bar. He offered to give Brent a ride home since it was clear Brent was in no shape to drive.

As they made their way down the city streets, several other people were also making their way home as all the bars closed at the same time. They had traveled three city blocks when they heard shouting across the street. Three men were shouting at each other just past the entrance to an alley. It looked as if two of the men were doing most of the shouting to a third man who visibly cowered in front of them. Other people on the streets deliberately looked away and walked faster or watched in silence.

Brent stopped and turned to watch the scene. "Can you believe this?"

Travis looked around as if expecting someone to jump them for stopping. "Come on, Brent, let's go. It's not our business."

"What do you mean?"

"I mean it isn't our problem. We can call the cops, but I bet one of the other people watching already did."

"How can people just stand there and do nothing?" His hand slid into his pocket as he thought back to the night at the convenience store. His thumb traced over the now-familiar etchings of the nickel.

Travis tugged on Brent's arm to get him to start walking again, but Brent whirled on his friend and stepped into his face forcing Travis to back up until he hit a wall.

"What do you mean it isn't our business? He's a person, just like us! They shouldn't be pushing him around like that. You can't just pretend it isn't there and it will magically go away!"

Before Travis could say anything in response, Brent turned on his heel and strode across the street without checking for traffic. As he neared the other side, a car swerved to miss him and laid on its horn, but it didn't faze Brent. He continued to walk toward the three men. The two bullies were now shoving the victim between them.

"Hey!" Brent called out as he broke into a run and charged.

All three of the guys looked over to Brent. The first one took a step forward and held one hand out. He started to say something, but at that moment, Brent lunged forward leading with his fist. His knuckles landed solidly across the other guy's jaw and the bully dropped to the ground like a rag doll. Brent landed on his side and quickly scrambled to his feet before the other man could attack him.

Brent managed to stand and get his arms in front of his face just in time to block a punch. It connected just above the elbow and his entire arm went numb. Another shot struck him in the shoulder as he tried to turn and protect his head. The impact sent him stumbling and he put one hand against the wall to steady himself. As the bully came in, Brent pushed off the wall and tried to hit his opponent in the face. The blow missed and Brent slid to his face on the concrete in front of a pile of trash. He felt a kick land solidly in his ribs forcing him to roll over. He kept rolling, getting just out of the way as a foot slammed down into the ground.

The thug came close and looked down at Brent.

"Should've kept your nose outta my business."

Brent reached into the pile of trash above his head and searched wildly for something hard. His hands curled around what felt like the handle for a baseball bat. As the bully brought his foot back to deliver a kick, Brent swung what he found as hard as he could and closed his eyes. He felt the impact up his arm and heard a distinct crunch as the thug fell to the ground when the piece of pipe collided with his knee. He screamed, and the other thug, just getting back to his feet, ran off and never looked back.

Using the wall for support, Brent got up to a standing position, still holding the pipe in his hand. He looked down at the man rolling back and forth with both hands grabbing his knee. Brent walked around until he was standing next to the man's rib cage.

"You shouldn't bully people," Brent said, his voice calm. "It isn't right."

He brought his foot back and kicked the man in the ribs as hard as he could. The man's screaming renewed its intensity and he brought a hand up to press against his side.

"It doesn't feel good does it?" Brent shouted, delivering another kick.

He raised his hand with the pipe in it and was about to bring it crashing down when he felt someone holding onto his wrist. He whirled but stopped when he recognized Travis.

"Geez, let it go, man! He's done!"

Brent looked around and saw that the three of them were alone in the alley. Both the other assailant and the victim had run off. Even the onlookers had retreated and were deliberately not looking in their direction. Brent uncurled his fist and the pipe dropped to the ground.

"What the hell were you thinking, Brent?"

"I don't know." Brent said under his breath.

Brent rubbed his fingers up and down his cheek stroking his beard as he looked through the windows. He had a full beard now and saw no reason to shave. It had been a couple of months of searching, but no one would even give him a phone interview, let alone a face-to-face. And his limited funds had already dried up. A few months ago, immediate unemployment was not in his life plan. If he could just survive a few more months, something would come through. It would have to.

He waited until the last of the people left the convenience store, and then walked in. The clerk behind the counter didn't even look up from his iPad. Brent spent some time wandering the shelves of the store, looking at things that he couldn't afford. He resisted the urge to help himself to a few free samples. He couldn't do anything that would draw attention to himself. As he stood in the aisle, he slid his right hand into his pants pocket and pulled out the nickel that he always carried with him. The woman said it brought her luck. He was hoping she was right. He tucked the coin back into his pants and slid both hands into his jacket pockets. The cold metal of a handgun rested against his knuckles and made him hesitate.

It only lasted a few seconds until he walked up to the counter. He reminded himself that the gun wasn't loaded, so no one was really in any danger. And, once he was back on his feet, he would make up for it. The clerk looked up from her iPad when he approached the counter.

"How can I help you?" she asked, the boredom clear in her tone.

"Well," Brent said and then paused. The woman looked up at him and blinked a few times, raising an eyebrow when he didn't say anything.

He chewed on his bottom lip hard and then whipped the gun out from his pocket and pointed it at the girl. She jumped back hard enough to make her chair clatter to the floor.

"I want all the money in the register and in the safe!"

The girl nodded vigorously and opened up the drawer. Brent slid a garbage bag across the counter and she began filling it. He looked around, but didn't see anyone or even the telltale sign of headlights moving down the road. When he turned back to the girl, she had just finished emptying one cash register.

"Can you open the safe?"

The girl shook her head back and forth. Some instinct in the back of his mind told him she was lying. Brent leaned across the counter and pushed the gun forward until it was almost touching her face.

"I don't believe you. Open the safe!"

"I can't!"

"Do it!"

The girl started sobbing and Brent eased back to his side of the counter. She curled up in the fetal position and begged for him not to hurt her. Brent's whole body felt numb as he grabbed the bag and shuffled backwards toward the entrance to the store. He couldn't take his eyes off the counter and could still hear the girl's sobs. It almost drowned out the sound of sirens as a few police cars rushed into the parking lot. As if from far away, he heard something over a speaker, something about a gun.

Brent turned around holding the gun out in front of him. There was the crack of a gunshot, and it seemed as if the world moved in slow motion. He felt the bullet rip into his body and leave the other side, but the expected pain didn't arrive immediately. A second bullet pierced his body and then a third as he started to fall. There were no more bullets, and just as the pain was arriving, it passed into the calm oblivion of death.

A tall woman walked through the crime scene and came directly to Brent's body. A press badge was attached to one of the pockets of her jacket, plainly visible. She crouched down next to the body on his right side. She looked around and waited until no one was looking in her direction. With a very smooth practiced motion, she reached into his pocket with her gloved fingers and retrieved the nickel. As she held it in her hand she looked down at Brent's body.

"It's a shame really. I was hoping that you would be able to overcome it." She let out a sigh. "I'll have to keep searching."

As she stood up, she pulled a small coin purse out of her pocket and unlocked it. She dropped the nickel inside where it clinked against several others.

THERE ARE ALWAYS THOSE IN life willing to sacrifice others in the name of good. Hypocrites. Every last one. No person ever does a deed with an altruistic heart. There is always something in it for them. To seek out would-be heroes and damn them to failure is wondrous irony. She never gave him a chance to fight, never let him know what he was up against. Instead, she cursed him. Perhaps, that is how my nickels have stolen her life.

— The Carver

SOMETHING IN THE BLOOD

KELLY LAGOR

"DO YOU HAVE ANY VELVET?" I ask the thrift store clerk as I arrange the pile of clothes on the counter. "Curtains or dresses or anything?" I'm not sure if she hears me over the Smashing Pumpkins or Soundgarden or something similarly loud and distorted that's playing on the radio next to the register.

The clerk, a slender woman whose tattoos creep from the edges of her black t-shirt, turns down the volume and peeks over the pile at me. She looks like what I imagine my best friend, Jessica, will look like when we're in college, with her short, dark hair and thin nose. The clerk's eyes, rimmed with thick, black eyeliner, fix on mine. I look away and pretend to rummage in my backpack for my wallet.

"I think we've got some velvet paintings of tigers or clowns or something," she says.

"That won't work," I say. "I'm making Halloween costumes for my family."

I catch a glimpse of three thin scars on the inside of her forearm as she starts to ring up the clothes. My envy unhinges me.

"What are you guys going as?" she asks without looking up.

I struggle to keep my voice steady, using the practiced nonchalance I learned from my father. "My parents are going to be Nicolas and Elizabeth Medina, and my twin brother and I are going to be Roderick and Madeline Usher."

The corner of her mouth twists up into a smirk. It's the same look Jessica gives me when I say something she thinks is amusing.

"*The Pit and the Pendulum* and *House of Usher*," she says. "Big Poe fan, eh?"

I let my hair fall in front of my face to hide my burning cheeks. "I'm more of a Vincent Price fan," I say.

She pulls up the sleeve of her t-shirt to show me a tattoo of a raven perched on a knobby, twisted branch. "I love Poe," she says. "He makes going mad feel like falling in love. Like they're both inevitable and inescapable."

I want to run away, but I set my wallet down on the counter as she rings up the last item. "How much?" I ask.

"Twelve-fifty."

I pour what money I have on the counter and sort through the coins and bills until I find I'm short. I set aside a few items and pay with exact change.

As she folds the clothing and loads it into a trash bag, my eyes keep drifting to the marks on her arm. I try to imagine what drove her to do that to herself, how she earned the scars, the eyeliner, the black clothes; but I can't get beyond what it would be like to have marks like that on my own arm. Marks like that are like tattoos. They invite others to see pain written plainly on the skin.

I notice she's watching me. She smiles again and puts the last of the clothing into the bag. I move to gather it into my arms, but she leans in, her face inches from mine.

"How old are you?" she asks.

"Thirteen," I say.

"Thirteen," she says. She reaches into her pocket and wraps her hand around something. I notice the way the fabric stretches, how it pulls down the waist of her pants so I can see the line of her hip. I've seen Jessica's hip jut out of her hem when we're changing for gym. Jessica didn't use to have that line, or at least I didn't notice it when we were younger. More ink peeks above the fabric. I look away, down at my fingers clutching the garbage bag, my nails painted red-black with Sharpie. My faded black jeans. My stretched-out black t-shirt. I want this moment to end.

"You remind me of me when I was your age," she says.

I change the subject. "What are you gonna be?"

"Not sure. My girlfriend landed me a gig, but I don't have any details yet."

Girlfriend. My face burns even brighter. I scoop the bag of clothes into my arms and turn to go when the clerk calls after me.

I consider running for the Belmont train stop, away from her, but she reaches over the counter, touches my arm, and presses something small and warm into my hand. She leans in close to my ear. I can smell her skin over the thrift store's ever-present smell of mothballs and corn chips. She even smells like Jessica, flowers with a tang of dried sweat beneath it.

"This helped me fix things," she says. "It can help you, too."

I shove whatever it is in my pocket and I'm out the door, but I still hear her wish me a Happy Halloween.

It isn't until I'm on the train that I look at what she gave me. It's a nickel, but instead of Jefferson's head, there's a Native American man's face in profile. I run a finger along the coin's surface. It feels different than it looks, like there are holes where the man's eyes should be. I nearly drop the coin when the train's fluorescent lights flicker as we go underground. I swear I catch a glimpse of a skull.

Mom's home tonight, so we're having a real dinner with roast chicken and mashed potatoes instead of the frozen dinners Dad makes for us when she's out of town. I look out our apartment's dining room window, beyond the alley and the parking structure that make up our view, to the persistently grey October sky, stained a sickly red by the dying sunset.

"How are the costumes coming along, Amy?" Mom asks.

I shrug and turn my attention back to my plate. "I couldn't get some of the things I needed for your dress."

"I'm sure it'll be wonderful. You're so creative. You'll think of something."

I shrink down in my seat at the compliment. I wish I could believe she doesn't really mean it, like she said it out of guilt. There's something rotten in me that doesn't deserve to be complimented. But there's nothing rotten about her. She means every word. I stab at the mound of mashed potatoes on my plate until the gravy bleeds over the side onto the pile of untouched chicken.

"I still don't want to go as some Victorian asshole." Aaron crosses his arms in front of him.

"It's a masquerade *ball*," Dad says. "You can't go to a ball dressed like a hobo. It's a formal event."

"Yeah, a formal event thrown by the *Davenports*," Aaron says. "We're gonna look like hobos next to them no matter what."

"It'll be fun," Mom says. "Ted told me he and Jessica have something special planned for midnight."

I see the covert smile on Aaron's lips in response to Jessica's name. I don't like that he likes her that way. Aaron and I are two halves of the same whole, split at birth. Outside, we are similar, with the same dark hair, light eyes and slim build. But he's an outgoing, well-liked skater kid with girls fawning over him. I'm the inward-facing movie nerd. There's nothing wrong with him. He's happy. I'm not. I don't understand why we became so different. I should be happy like Aaron. That's how I was when I first met Jessica. But now, with how she looks back at him, I'm afraid she's...

"When did you talk to Ted?" Dad asks.

The familiar nonchalance in his voice snaps me out of my reverie. There's suspicion lurking beneath it.

Mom avoids Dad's gaze and I lose what little interest I had in my dinner. Something might actually be happening.

"On Michigan Avenue. He was with Jessica. They were getting things for the party."

I see Dad relax, but now I can't. I ask to be excused.

Later that night, I sneak out of the apartment and take the emergency exit stairs down to the mezzanine where the storage lockers are. I turn on the dim fluorescent lights and climb into our family's storage unit. A few of the lights flicker. No one else comes down here much, so the lights never get fixed. I sit with my legs dangling off the sides of the metal cage and pull the box of family photos beside me.

I know these pictures well. I'd gone through them again and again looking for some outward sign of decay. I flip through the sepia pictures of Mom and Dad when they were my age, my mom elegant and self-confident, my dad all awkward angles and forced smiles. Pictures of his parent's grocery store. Her grandfather's law firm. Pictures of new old cars. Everything mundane. Normal. Nothing to indicate there's any kind of madness in our family.

I get to the last picture in the set. It's not a photo of my family, but one I stole from Jessica's house of her and her mom in the hospital just before her mom died. I try to make myself feel what she must have felt, but I can't.

I pull my legs up to my chest and feel something in my pocket press into my leg. It's the nickel. I run my finger along the face and I still feel indentations where none should be. I want to fling it across the room when the lights flicker again and I catch another glimpse of the skull.

"You're hiding something," I say to the coin.

I sigh and close my hand around it, feeling my stolen body heat in it.

"I wish I were hiding something. I wish there were a reason why I feel the way I do," I think about Jessica and the pain she must have felt when her mom died. Sometimes I wish someone I loved would die.

A small itch grows on my forearm. I scratch at it, but the sensation is rooted deep beneath my skin. I hold my arm up to the light and I see what looks like a thin red line.

The next morning, Aaron is lying on his bed beneath the pilfered street signs and CTA subway map that decorate the wall on his side of the room. He's playing *The Legend of Zelda: A Link to the Past* for the hundredth time. My side of our bedroom is decorated with cut outs from the fashion magazines Mom brings home for me, sketches of outfits I'll make when I can save up enough money, and sketches of Vincent Price from his various movies. I try to ignore the monotonous video game music and focus on putting the mock-up outfits for our Halloween costumes onto my dolls. The itching on my arm stopped sometime in the night. Despite me not scratching, it left behind a long, thin cut. I try to ignore it.

The outfits are passable, but I did a poor job making Roderick's tailcoat. It bunches at the armpits and sits crooked across the doll's plastic shoulders so one of the tails keeps creeping over his thigh. I straighten the coat once more and move the doll's arms into his lap.

"Madeline and I are like figures of glass," I say in my best Vincent Price and move one of the doll's hands over his heart. "The slightest touch and we may shatter." A knock on the door interrupts me. Dad sticks his head in.

"Amy, you should come here." He leaves the door ajar behind him.

In the living room, Mom sits on the couch, hands in her lap, eyes fixed on me. Entertainment Tonight is playing a clip of Vincent Price from Return of the Fly. There's a momentary thrill as I wonder what he's doing on the news, but then John Tesh comes on.

"Hollywood today is remembering the leading man of horror movies, Vincent Price. He died last night in Los Angeles of lung cancer at eighty-two."

The grey morning light fades and a red-black darkness irises in around my vision. The sound of the television becomes smaller, further away. A ringing grows in my ears. I can't conceive of anything beyond the sound and the dark. But then there is a word. A single word.

Overwrought.

I am overwrought.

I can't stop crying the next day at school. The tears are a consolation, at least, like I am part of a larger ritual. The comfort and pain feel complementary, like love and hate, two sides of the same coin. I avoided Jessica after I saw her talking to Aaron. My jealousy makes the pain worse, so I clutch the coin in my hand. The metal digging into my flesh overwhelms any other sensations for a while, but when the physical pain fades, the emotional pain returns.

I am copying lines from *The Raven* out of my English textbook into a notebook when I recall the tattoo on the thrift store clerk's arm, the smell of her as she leaned in to give me the coin. I remember the three cuts on her forearm and I look down at my own cut, still fresh and angry. The clerk was right. The coin is helping me. My misery finally has a cause.

After school, Dad and I watch Vincent Price movies while Mom brings me tea. Dad tells me about seeing these movies when he was about my age, and how he immediately liked Vincent Price because his characters were always broken and alone. Dad says you can't condemn the crazy things those characters do because they did them out of love. It makes me feel my loss more potently, so I retreat to my room to work on our costumes. Every cut and stitch makes me feel like I'm bringing something of Vincent Price back from the dead. I work until my fingers and my mind go numb.

The next day as I throw my books in my locker for lunch, my melancholy is so overwhelming I don't notice Jessica until she wraps her arm around me. The contact sends an arc of excitement through me, but I ignore it and shrug off her hand.

"You doing okay?" she asks.

"Yeah."

"You want to go to Goudy Park for lunch?" she asks. "We can see how far we can jump off the swings."

"Sure."

I don't talk on the way over. The historic mansions of Astor Street squat resolutely on one side, dwarfed by the luxury skyscrapers of Streeterville that surround it. This is where we first met. Now, just as then, we swing back-and-forth, side-by-side.

"My dad thinks you're going to get a kick out of the party on Saturday," she finally says.

I don't respond. Instead I listen to the familiar squeak of the chains. The rubber seat digs into my hips in a way it hasn't before.

"I'm sorry about Vincent Price. I know he meant a lot to you."

I look over at her. Jessica's eyes are sad. I want to think she's giving me that look out of empathy, but there's something else there. Is it pity? I allow Jessica's sympathy to sooth my hurt because it's a connection. "I know you understand with your mom dying a few months ago."

"I don't think it's the same thing."

I realize Jessica doesn't get it and I let my swing go out of sync with hers. I'm angry. It was pity. Grief is grief. Always inevitable. Always inescapable. I slam my feet into the ground and stop. Jessica drags her feet and stops too.

"Just because it was your mom who died doesn't mean your pain is more legitimate than mine." I don't realize I've snapped at her until the words are out of my mouth. They feel good.

Jessica's face goes red. "Losing your mother and an actor dying are not the same thing."

She has no right to be angry. I want to hurt her more. I say the first thing that pops into my head. "Your dad's been sleeping with my mom, you know."

I can see the hurt in her eyes before her anger returns. "You shouldn't joke about that."

I persist. It feels good to hurt her. Like something is finally balancing out between us. "I'm not joking. My dad's been suspicious of them for a while."

Jessica gets up and slings her backpack over her shoulder. Her voice is cold. "What's wrong with you?"

I start swinging again and remember the things my dad told me about being motivated by love and how Vincent Price used it to justify doing crazy things. "My dad has a dark side, you know. I'd hate to see what would happen if he gets any proof.

You might tell your dad to lay off. And you should stay away from my brother, too. I don't care if he's in love with you. The same madness runs in his veins."

As the lie comes out of my mouth, my anger deflates. I'm afraid of what I've done to our friendship. The pain that's left is sharper and more immediate than the grief I feel for Vincent Price. Maybe Jessica was right about there being different kinds of loss. I hang my head and stop swinging.

When I look up, she's gone. I could run after her and apologize, but I'm not sure she would forgive me. The implications of what I said are enough to make her uncertain of anything I say. But if there were no uncertainty… If our parents were actually having an affair…

I pull the coin out of my pocket. She'll have to forgive me when she finds out what I said was true.

I run my finger over its face when I finish making my wish. My arm starts itching again.

"What were you thinking skipping school this afternoon?" Dad says.

The itch in my arm is unbearable, but I cross my arms and try to ignore it. I consider telling him about my fight with Jessica, but the thought of it makes me angry. I wouldn't have said those things to her if he hadn't thought Mom was cheating on him. "Why shouldn't I? It's not like Mom goes to work. You know she's sleeping with Mister Davenport."

Dad slaps me. He's never slapped me before. The shock of it overwhelms me and I need to be anyplace but here. I grab my backpack and run out the front door. Halfway down the stairs to the lobby, I realize I don't know where I'm going. I've never run away before and I can't go to Jessica's, so I go to the storage room.

I sit in our locker and dig out the photos again. I feel bad for what I did to Dad, but I already know he's been suspicious of her. Maybe it will be better for all of us when it's out in the open. They can work through it that way. But maybe not. Maybe Dad's jealousy will scare her so she leaves us. But if she understands the only reason he's jealous is because he loves her… I can't risk her leaving, not if I have the means to remove any uncertainty.

I pull the coin from my pocket when I hear the storage room door open. It's Aaron.

"Thought I'd find you here." He leans against a locker across the aisle.

I shove the coin back in my pocket.

"You stirred up a helluva fight between them. What did you say?"

I don't answer.

"He's throwing things."

I shrug and swing my feet against the storage cage beneath ours. Aaron sits down on the floor. "Why are you doing this?"

I try to think of an answer, why I keep making the wishes I do, and I come up blank. "Why do any of us do the things we do? There's never any reason for it. All of us eventually become monsters for no good reason."

"You're not a monster."

We sit in silence for a while and listen to the pipes burping. We used to play hide and seek in this room, but we got too big for it to be a challenge anymore. Even if we turn the lights out, we would always find each other in the dark.

"You know she doesn't like girls," Aaron says.

Something small and indistinct in my chest breaks at his words. "Who?"

"Jessica. I don't know if that makes anything easier for you."

I become acutely aware of the feel of the metal grate beneath my hands as I press my fingers through the holes and squeeze until I can't feel my fingers. The gurgling pipes and the hum of the florescent lights become a cacophony of sound that overwhelms the sound of blood rushing through my ears.

"I'm gonna go back upstairs," Aaron says.

He leaves and I slowly unwind my hands from the grate. My fingers ache. Spots of blood well up from where sharp imperfections pierced my skin. I pull the nickel out of my pocket. Aaron doesn't understand anything. He never will. He'll pass through life completely unaffected. If my father and I are meant to suffer, he should be made to as well. After all, he and I are two halves of the same whole. I close my hand around the nickel and wish for the madness to be something in the blood, passed down from father to daughter and son.

When I open my hand, my blood has settled into the indentations in the coin and I can see each and every tooth on the damned coin's face. The itch is maddening.

None of us talk on the way to the party. They fought about going until I tried to burn our costumes in the bathtub. My dress was damaged beyond repair, so I'm wearing the first failed attempt at the coat I made for Aaron. Aaron lags behind us, trying not to look embarrassed in his waistcoat and slacks. He should be grateful the shoulders are right on his.

We turn past Goudy Park onto Astor Street and come up to the Davenport's 19th century neo-gothic townhouse, a pillar of pale grey stone set back from the street. In my neighborhood, the building would have been split up into apartments. But here, a family can live in perfect isolation in a house with as many square feet as an entire floor of my apartment building.

Garish colors bleed through the French windows. There's muffled music playing within. Something old and dusty, like the house itself. We knock.

Mister Davenport opens the door. He's wearing a blood-red robe and cowl. Standing beside him is Jessica, done up as a peasant girl. I recognize them as characters from *The Masque of the Red Death*. Pale blue light extends down into the foyer from the second floor, while a purple and a deeper violet light bleeds in from the living room and study. I see now why Jessica thought I would be excited. They recreated Prospero's ill-fated party from the movie.

Dad pushes between them and disappears into the living room as Mom plants a light kiss on Mister Davenport's cheek. The two of them go to the study.

I watch Jessica to see if she sees the truth in what I said, but when her eyes lock on mine, all I can see is anger. She turns her back and follows after her dad. I want to talk to her, tell her that I'm doing all of this out of love, but she'll understand. In time.

Each room on the first floor is lit with flickering torches encased in stained glass lanterns. Adults mill around the bar and the buffet table as the kids and teenagers find the corners of the rooms to gather in. The effect of the lighting is eerie, as though the real strength is in the shadows. There is the blue foyer, the purple living room, the green dining room, where the booze and adults are, the orange kitchen, where chafing dishes perch atop flickering sternos, the white breakfast nook and the violet study.

I wonder where the black room with the red lighting is, the one from whence the Red Death came to take them all in the movie. I move to open the door in the foyer that leads down to the wine cellar when I hear the clanking of metal on crystal. I follow the sound into the green room to find Mister Davenport holding a wine glass aloft above the gathered crowd. I let the crowd press past me as I move toward the periphery. The music dies and fog begins to roll down the front stairs.

"Dearest friends," he says, "I would like to thank you for coming to our annual Halloween Masquerade. I only ask you forget yourselves tonight. The way is not easy, I know, but when the clock strikes midnight, I will take you by the hand and lead you through the cruel light into velvet darkness."

The door to the wine cellar bursts open and figures dressed in black bodysuits and featureless white masks emerge. Some dance. Some perform small feats of acrobatics. Others, magic tricks. They settle in open spaces in each room and set to entertaining the guests. Amid the chaos, I see Mister Davenport and my mom slip upstairs. A moment later I see my Dad follow after them.

I think to investigate when I spot Jessica and Aaron through the crowd. They're in the breakfast nook. I squeeze between the other guests for a better view. Aaron moves in to kiss her, to demonstrate his love for her with his hands as they wander over her skirt. My heart twists in my chest. I see her slap him across the face. She slips from view and I hear her footsteps on the rear stairs. A moment later, Aaron follows.

I move toward the rear stairs when a black figure steps in front of me. From the swell of the hips, I can tell it's a woman. She reaches behind my ear and, with a flourish, produces a quarter. She presents me the coin, but I ignore her and push past her to the stairs. She blocks my way.

"Guests should stay on the first floor," she says.

"I'm family." I push her hard. She catches herself on the wall, but the momentary imbalance is enough to get around her. I take the stairs two at a time.

At the top, there's no sign of Aaron, but Dad squats in front of Mister Davenport's bedroom door, staring through the keyhole. I can hear squeaking beyond the closed door. I want to touch his shoulder, to tell him I'm doing this out of love, but I can feel the tension casting off him like heat.

I turn down the hall toward Jessica's room. The door is locked. I bend down to peek through the keyhole but there is something blocking it. I press my ear to the door, trying to hear what Aaron might be saying to her.

159

"She won't let you in." Aaron emerges from the bathroom behind me. He holds one of his hands behind him.

"She could never love you." I cross my arms and jut out my hip. "You don't understand what pain is. Not like she and I do."

He crosses his arms and shifts his weight to mirror me. "But she doesn't love you either."

"At least I didn't try to grope her." I move to get around him, to leave him to his pathetic vigil, but he grabs the sleeve of my jacket.

"You think I don't understand pain?" He lets me go and pulls up the sleeve of his coat. I see three long cuts, still weeping on his arm. I move to get away from him but he grabs the sleeve of my coat again. I try to pull away, but he's stronger.

"You've never lost anyone." I'm shaking. "You couldn't possibly understand."

I jerk myself backwards. The seam rips and my sleeve comes free. I run down the back steps and out into the backyard. I slam the door behind me, expecting Aaron to be coming after me, but after a few heartbeats, I know he isn't. There's only the cool autumn night. Thick clouds obscure the stars and the backyard is bathed in orange light from the party.

I sit on the back steps. My frustration is making the back of my head itch. Everything I wished to happen is happening, but I get no relief from it. If anything, I'm angrier than ever. I pull out the nickel and look at it. There is still dried blood on its face from my last wish.

"What are you doing out here?"

Jessica jumps down off the trellis that extends from the flower-bed up to the base of her bedroom window. The wind is pushing her hair all around her head like a halo.

"Nothing," I say.

She approaches me. I can see the tension in her step and I realize I'm afraid. I don't want her to yell at me. I just want things to be okay between us, like they were before. That's all I ever wanted. Her stare is sharp enough to cut me.

"I'm sorry," I say, but the words slip past her.

"Sorry? Sorry for what? Wait, did you put Aaron up to this?"

I wonder what answer would make her less angry. If I say it's a prank, if he does anything else tonight, she'll know I was lying. But if I tell her the truth? "I didn't want him to hurt you."

"Why have you been so mean to me lately?"

I open my mouth, but nothing comes out. I look down at the grass. It looks gray under the orange light. Like ash.

"Answer me."

"No." My voice is small and far away.

"Tell me!" Her voice tears through me like tissue paper.

"Because I'm in love with you!" I scream back. A knot in my chest loosens and I feel a little lighter. But it's replaced with anxiety. She still hasn't said anything. She's just looking at me. I wish I could take the words back and shove them back down my throat. She looks angry.

Jessica steps around me to go back in the house. I grab her dress.

"Please don't leave!"

She kicks me away and dislodges the nickel from my hand. I don't pay attention to where it lands. Instead, I watch the door slam behind her.

I'm not sure how long I sit on the porch. The party becomes more raucous, but I focus on the sound of the wind blowing through the desiccated trees. The sounds of the party have died down considerably when the cellar door opens and a black-suited figure emerges. I recognize her as the one who did the coin trick. She pulls off her mask and I immediately recognize her as the clerk from the thrift store. Her face is painted like a corpse.

Rage overcomes me and I am in front of her before I can recall crossing the lawn. I push her backwards. Her lighter falls to the grass but she catches herself on the doorframe.

"Hey! What's your prob—" She looks at my face. Recognizes me. "I knew that was you I saw tonight. What's with the pushing?"

"It's all your fault!" I yell at her. "She'll never speak to me again!"

She bends over to pick up her lighter and grabs something else in the grass. It's the nickel. She looks down at my arm, sees the cuts.

"What did you do?" She reaches out for my arm, horror growing in her eyes.

"Don't touch me!" Tears are running hot down my face.

Her voice is weak, her eyes far away. "It was supposed to help you become who you wanted to be. It helped me."

It's her fault. All her fault. A wind gusts behind her, sending her hair flying around her head like a halo. She looks so much like Jessica, even with the makeup on.

Jessica will never speak to me again. There is no life without her in it. This woman took everything from me.

A calm descends over me and I know what I need to do. I push her. She stumbles backwards again, but this time she grabs empty air before she falls. There's a crack, like a branch snapping when she hits the bottom. I look down after her. Her head is stuck out at an odd angle. She isn't moving.

There is a long moment between my breaths as I dimly register someone screaming. Dead faces stare up at me from the basement. I snap out of my trance and run back through the back door.

Inside the air is hot and thick. A siren sounds off in the distance at nearly the same time the smoke alarm begins its wail. The house is on fire. I have to get out. Away.

I pull the hem of my shirt over my nose and run toward the front of the house. The smoke is thicker in the living room. I shut my watering eyes against it and trip over someone on the floor. I see them when I open my eyes briefly to regain my balance. Mom and Mister Davenport and Jessica, eyes open, staring but not watering. All three wear deep cuts along their throats. Mister Davenport's costume is missing. I drag my eyes away and stagger toward the front door.

The handle turns, but the door sticks. I look down. There are nails driven into the floor. As the grandfather clock begins to toll midnight, I run back to the kitchen. I don't even try the backdoor. I can see it's been nailed shut since I came back inside. There's only one more option.

I open the door to the wine cellar and half-stumble down the stairs. The wine racks are draped in thick black velvet. Red light spills from two more decorative lanterns. There's movement— figures in black, their faces painted to look like the dead, pushing each other to flee up the back stairs.

I know now what Mister Davenport's surprise at midnight was going to be. He was going to stage a recreation of the final scene of the movie, with the actors made up to look like victims of the Red Death.

The actors don't notice me as they push their way out, just like they've stopped noticing the clerk still lying at the foot of the stairs. But I notice her. In fact, I can't look away. I am vaguely aware of a rapping on the stairs behind me as it plays a counter-point to the final tolls of the clock.

After the last of the actors disappear into the night, I will my legs to move. To take me to her side. I didn't even know her name. I look away, up and out toward the clean night air through the still-open cellar door. I see my father in Mister Davenport's pilfered costume, his face dripping with red. He steps onto the cellar steps and shuts out the sky behind him. He comes down the stairs to me, laughing, and sweeps me up in his arms. I let him. I see Aaron climb the cellar steps with a hammer. Long nails held between bloody lips. He seals off the final exit and returns to us. Dad wraps us both in his red cloak.

Interred in this way, we wait for the house to come down around us.

SOME PEOPLE BELIEVE THEY *win over the coins. They never do. Eventually, they pass the coins on and, in that passing, doom themselves. The poor little Goth girl clerk. She had all of her desires come true. And each one led them to Mister Davenport's party. Just as giving Amy the nickel caused the path to be laid out the way it did. In the clerk's case, she was screaming in the trap from the beginning and had no idea.*

—*The Carver*

THE VALUE OF A YEAR OF TEARS AND SORROW

JASON ANDREW

WALTER WAITED, MOTIONLESS amongst the pigeons, at the top of the escalator. *Time is the enemy of the lost,* he thought as he carefully tracked distracted commuters as they stepped off the Seattle Metro. It was a game he played to burn through the morning hours of the weekday. He liked to watch the yuppies, businessmen, and wage slaves as they staggered through downtown at a frenetic pace, trying to down their tall cups of low-fat ambition. If he concentrated, Walter could read their lives from their weary faces.

Enduring the slow, consuming progress of the seemingly infinite hours of the day proved to be a Sisyphean task endlessly repeated in a strange blur. His contract specified a year's worth of sorrow and tears for the coin that would finally allow his son's dead soul to rest. It had been agonizingly vague on the details of his allotted suffering.

Walter watched and waited until he found a target that stirred the proper amount of loathing from his finicky heart and then started to stalk him. He learned to slip between the cracks in his target's perception to become practically invisible as part of the background. His presence was no more notable than a street light or a filthy garbage can. The homeless were rarely noticed unless they inserted themselves into the crowd.

Living within the system was a constant struggle to squeeze out every second to make it count. There was always something to do at any hour of the day or night as work, play, family, and strangers all blurred together like a favorite program on television that played only late at night on a static-filled nostalgia channel. It drained your ability to see the world or care for things outside of your finite dominion.

Walter made it his business to poke those blind to the world's ills. The bespeckled fat man wearing a polo shirt uneasily glanced over his shoulder, as though sensing the presence of a predator, only to meet his unflinching gaze. The slow dawning awareness of being hunted sprinkled across his expression like a sour smell that only became more pronounced as soon as it was noticed.

His response was a quiet, determined grin. The man clutched tightly to the leather satchel that he wore over his shoulder and quickened his pace. He had learned long ago that the first real instinct of prey was to escape and that if he wanted to continue the chase he would have to anticipate his opponent's actions.

Walter hated weakness. He thought of the visceral pleasure of wrapping his fingers around his target's throat and slowly squeezing. Letting the hate bubble in his blood like a shot of caffeine, Walter adapted his pace ensuring that his target never exceeded his reach.

Crimson faced and huffing as though the very air thinned, the frantic man crossed Pike heading south onto Third Street. Worming his way through the mass of distracted flesh, he tried to keep track of Walter's position. Sweating and wheezing, he paused at the queue to enter the revolving door to the towering building in which he worked and desperately scanned the crowd for the face of his aggressor.

Walter stepped out of the crowd and faux-accidently bumped into his prey. He must have looked like a wild man that stumbled off a mountain somewhere. "Apologies."

The fat man with thick glasses fumbled backwards in a panic. With a tip of his cap, Walter continued along the sidewalk knowing that he would infest this man's nightmares for years. He checked his watch and noted with despair that he had only burned through fifteen minutes.

Walter took to life on the streets with an organized fervor that marked his entire life. He had calculated that he needed to collect a minimum of fifteen dollars a day to live. The generous nature of Seattle's culture made this goal easily attainable on most days. In fact, he worried about collecting too much on any single day least he break the contract.

Remington Borri demanded a year's worth of tears and sorrow and, much like the fabled Shylock, he would be exact when he collected. His pound of flesh could only be taken from his heart. If he had a good day and lived comfortably, would that invalidate the geis? Walter didn't understand enough about magic to take the risk. The death of his son had to be avenged or what sort of father was he?

Each day provided a new challenge in struggling to keep the motivation to live long enough to put his son to rest. Walter begged in the morning from mouth-breathing morons that he could have bought and sold a little more than a year previous. He learned from experience that worker bees were more likely to be generous in the morning before the day ground their spirits. Once the daily living allotment had been reached, Walter tried to find new ways to burn through the days.

The first several months of the contract, he took a walking tour through the winding streets, hidden allies, and strange catacombs of the city. Walter learned in elementary school that Seattle had suffered a horrible fire in 1889 that burned most of the city to the ground. Rather than move the city, the early Seattleites stubbornly built over the ruins leaving hundreds of strange underground tunnels and places to hide.

Walter learned that there was a secret city that lived just below the surface if you knew where to look. He learned a great deal about the creatures that lived in the shadows and outside of the system. On the corner, there was a prophet that cried forth warnings of doom in coded rants about the Seattle Police Department and Communism. He witnessed the strange ecstasy of the Esoteric Order of Heavenly Delight and their attempt to use pleasure and altered states of consciousness to peer through to the unknowable City of Leng. Walter communed with the hopeless cult of Mister Bang crying forth relief from the desolate life in the city.

Every day seemed to bring a new depravity as he surrendered to the world of the lost. He tried to keep his dignity intact the first few weeks of the contract by allotting a portion of his daily budget to purchase sanitation wipes for regular dry baths in an attempt to remain hygienic. As the days upon days of listless wandering burrowed into his brain, he lost himself more and more in the simple pleasures of a warm meal and occasional strong drink.

Boredom became Walter's worst enemy. He found ways to stretch moments of time to last the entire day. Sometimes, if he collected an extra seven dollars, Walter would visit the Chinese Room at the Smith Tower. Years ago, he had brought Wendy into the brass and copper caged elevators for a ride to the 35th floor. They gazed at the entirety of the Emerald City during a perfectly romantic summer sunset. He proposed to her that night.

The Chinese Room was a small room decorated with onyx and marble panels adored with hand-carved occidental art. The main attraction of the Chinese Room was the infamous Wishing Chair. A dragon and a phoenix were carved together out of a majestic dark wood that brought forth luck and fertility. Legend had it that this special chair could help you conceive if you wished hard enough. It might have been magic or the thrill of the romantic gesture but nine months later baby Michael was born.

He circled the Wishing Chair ritually while peering out to the city landscape. He always brought the same question to the chair. *How could he have ruined his life so completely?*

He had fallen in love with Wendy in college. Her parents named her after the girl from Peter Pan and it shone through in her eyes. Walter saw endless summers and happy children in her eyes. She walked through life gaily as though she had the power to fly. The thought of the woman that left him forever was usually good for an extra tear or two.

The memories faded some days, but the lingering boredom remained. He discovered the best times to visit the library and when there were free concerts in parks. A taste of music or a fleeing reminder of the world of glass and steel towers of industry only served to remind him of what he had surrendered for the memory of his son.

His father had been a drunk that marked time by putting out cigarettes on his arm. He thought of that nightly as he captured his tears of the day in an azure glass bottle he hid under the freeway bridge near the vast cement columns adorned with guerilla-style paintings of saints clad in togas. Borri told him that the tears collected would never dry and the bottle worked as promised.

Walter ritually ran through his checklist of sins and then began to cry. At the top of that list was this question: Why hadn't he spent more time with Michael? He remembered all of the excuses, but none of them meant anything in the haze of regret. Walter had seen the life he wanted on the faded color screens of his youth; wise fathers gently raising sons and daughters with good natured humor and love. There was an Old Norse proverb that he remembered from a story. *Wake early if you want another man's life.* He thought of that saying upon seeing Michael for the first time in the hospital.

Wendy had been in labor for five hours and it felt like he would never arrive. Holding that fragile life in his hands had been a sacred promise to do better for the family, to give them a better life that he had. Walter redoubled his efforts towards his work in an effort to get noticed by the partners. He never noticed that the lines on Wendy's face had grown thicker. Her feet became heavy on the ground from the countless lonely nights until she left. He tried to place blame on her if only to mitigate his own guilt, but couldn't. He still loved her.

How much of his son's life did he miss? The logical part of his brain had once calculated that out of the ten years on this earth his son lived that he had spent less than a year in total acting as a father. It sickened him. If he had paid attention, she never would have divorced him and married that damned drunk Frank Thompson.

Walter lived so much in that world of laws, numbers, and towers of steel and glass that he hadn't known his son had died until three days later. What had been so important that he failed to notice the death of his child? He remembered that there was a merger, but he couldn't even remember who was involved. Practicing law felt so distant that the memories might as well have been someone else speaking in tongues to strange foreign gods.

Once he stoppered the bottle, he realized that it was full. Was it possible that his contract had been completed? Had he manage to survive a year? He remembered the months of hiding in the sewers to keep warm from the snow. Spring had come symbolized by a naked parade of painted bike riders celebrating the arrival of the warm weather. Walter checked the column where he had been marking the days with scratches like a prisoner awaiting freedom. A year had passed and gone. His contract had been complete days ago.

Walter took the free ride bus to the Farmer's Market and descended down the cement stairs into the lower levels, passing by a street kid playing guitar with an open case and a hungry-looking kitten. He subtly dropped the rest of his money into the mix. He wouldn't need the funds after returning the bottle to Borri and it wouldn't hurt to do a last kind deed before blacking his soul.

The sweet tingle of magic and power tickled the back of his neck. He pulled out a cigarette and prepared to light it, but stopped short of the warning sign on the entrance. The sign carried the same message in half a dozen languages, some of them inhuman. *Smoking is banned in this establishment. Violators will be hung by their entrails.* "I suppose I should quit anyway."

Near the bottom of the stairs, he heard the soft murmur of a crowd of muffled voices and random pieces of conversations. At the base of the stairs, there was a set of double steel doors that he pushed open. A befuddlement spell had been cast down this corridor to keep out the mundanes. A few years ago, he wouldn't have been able to enter this place.

The Underground was narrow and cramped; every inch was occupied or used. The air was a bit musty, but everything else was surprisingly clean. There were apothecaries, demonic looking vendors peddling magical charms, fish restaurants, and book-binding shops. There were dozens of strange humanoids in a variety of different colors and bizarre clothing.

Borri's Curiosity Shoppe reminded him of a subway tunnel that had been transformed into a used bookstore with countless stacks and shelves arranged haphazardly. It was like a magician's workshop from the stories that Wendy read Michael. He tried to absorb it all, but could not. Every spare inch of room was crammed with artifacts of interest and various knickknacks from all over the world. There was everything from enchanted glasses, talking skulls, and dancing stone gargoyles. He held up a bizarre curved crystal decanter that seemed to hum at his touch and almost dropped it when a voice surprised him from behind. "That is boiled essence of knotweed and burdock. It can be used to cure certain unnatural poisons that certain creatures of the night are known to polish their fangs with."

Walter flinched with surprise at the verbal intrusion into his thoughts. The thin, frail-looking man with a messy mop of dark chestnut hair seemed to be able to appear anyplace within the dominion of his store at any time. He refused to be intimidated by the rumored mystical abilities of this alchemist. "My contract is complete, Mister Borri." Walter presented the azure bottle filled with his tears. "I've completed by end of the bargain."

Remington Borri accepted the bottle nodded politely. He pulled the cork free, held the opening closely to his nose, and then slowly sniffed. "I can see that you upheld your end of the contract, Mister Meloni. Congratulations."

Walter didn't want to know how Borri could judge the quality of the tears by smelling them and was afraid to ask. "If you are satisfied with the tears, I'd like the coin as promised."

His soft brown eyes were piercing as though he could see right through to your soul. There was no mercy or pity in them only a weary longing for rest. "Mister Meloni, I must admit that I am slightly disappointed. I had hoped against reason that when you failed to return on time that you had given up this wasteful vendetta. I should think that one in your quite comfortable financial situation would seek to avoid the pains of the streets as quickly as possible. Did you have problems?"

Walter shook his head. It was difficult to put his feelings into words. "I got lost in my head. I didn't know that the year had passed."

A brief flicker of recognition flashed across Remington Borri's face. It was a predatory, hawkish expression. "I thought perhaps that you had given up this dark business and returned to your former wife." He sighed and then added. "She has been looking for you for months."

Wendy hadn't talked to him since Michael's funeral. She could barely stand to look at him. "How do you know?" Walter asked.

"She visited here twice." Borri wagged a single finger towards Walter. "You left a trail, Mister Meloni. Quite sloppy."

"I'm sorry. Really sorry." The thought that Wendy had come for him was quite the surprise. "I told my company that I was traveling for a year. I didn't think that anyone would try to follow me. Or would care."

"It is a small matter, but it does change my perspective on this matter." There was a sparkle in Borri's eyes as though holding back a swell of emotion. Walter feared the potential landmines that might be waiting in his path. "There is still a chance for love and redemption in your lifetime, Mister Meloni. You can leave here now. Take what you have learned this year and find her. Kiss her as though your life depends on it and find a reason to be happy."

He couldn't remember Wendy's face. He had thought of her so often that that she became a dream of feelings burned away in the sorrow of the year. He thought of his son and his head pulsed. His heart was dead. "I haven't changed my mind."

Borri removed his glasses slowly and cleaned them with a white handkerchief. He opened his mouth as though to say something and then shook his head. Instead, he gestured to a large glass door near the back of the shop. "Please follow me."

Walter followed him into an elaborately decorated office. Borri sat at his oversized oak desk and began searching through a drawer. "I shall be with you in just a moment. I was just looking at the file this morning just in case you arrived."

Curious, Walter glanced around the office looking at the various photographs. Some of them were very old. One of them was labeled Great Seattle Fire, 1889. The photograph depicted several men searching through a burned out landscape. One of the men looked suspiciously like Borri.

"Yes, I am in that photograph, Mister Meloni," Borri said, without looking up from his drawer. Startled, Walter looked away. "No, it is okay for you to look at my photographs. I have displayed them, after all."

"How can you be in that photograph? Wait, are you an actual immortal?" Walter asked.

"There are many different paths to immortality, young man. Each with their own price."

"How old are you?"

"That is a very long story, Mister Meloni. I am the third eldest resident of this city. Perhaps I shall share my own sordid history with you in time." Borri rummaged through his files a moment until he produced a large legal folder and flipped it open. He scanned the page with his finger until he found the exact spot he was looking for and then laid it out on the table for Walter to read. "Now that I have verified the contents of the bottle, I shall sign the paperwork that frees the money in your accounts and then surrender onto you the infamous Dyson's Nickel. However, I feel that I must again strongly urge you against this action."

Walter waved away any additional warnings and cut directly to the heart of the matter. "Will the nickel do the job? Will it hurt Thompson?" Walter asked.

The look of dread fixated on the stoic features of Borri said everything Walter needed to know. "Mister Meloni, I promise you that the Dyson Nickel can indeed do everything that you've asked and more. The so-called Hobo Nickels are not mere appropriations of currency as urban art. It was a practice started during a difficult time in the world when work and food were scarce and faith was shaken to the core. Hobo nickels began as a method to alleviate boredom. There is nothing worse than idle hours when you are suffering."

He grunted intolerantly. "I think I understand the concept."

"Some realized that it might actually be considered artwork and thus increased the value of the coin. Speculators instantly realized that they could prey upon the survivor's guilt of the wealthy. This spiraled to create a strange market where an obsession grew. Men that would happily ignore a starving child on a street corner spent fortunes on a simple nickel to adorn their homes as a status of wealth."

"I know all of this, Borri," Walter complained. "Get on with it."

Borri held up a single finger to silence him. "Magic is governed by rules. One of these rules is that 'like is always attracted to like.' Some of the new artisans learned that the faith we place upon money is quite potent."

Walter shook his head with disbelief. He had been rich and poor. He knew which he preferred and where his beliefs lie. "Why wouldn't they have faith in money?"

"Money is separate from wealth. A lawyer such as yourself should know the difference. Money is but a promise of payment of gold. The value of said promise is determined by an opinion, informed or otherwise, of the institution making the promise." Borri gingerly placed a velvet box upon the desk and opened it revealing a small, tarnished coin. "In the days of the Great Depression, as in modern nights, some doubted the power of the once mighty institution. There was still faith in the America idea that any man can achieve wealth. Like is attracted to like. That faith in the dream transfers to the physical avatars in this world."

"And that faith powers the coins?" Walter asked. "You said this coin would bring suffering to anyone that owned it. Thompson is an avid coin collector. He won't be able to contain himself."

"The coins are empowered by the symbols carved with sorrow and pain," Borri replied. "The Dyson Nickel is more than up to the task, I assure you."

Walter glanced over the desk to examine the coin closely. At a glance it appeared to be little more than a tarnished buffalo nickel minted 1913. The face of the traditional Indian head had been molded and sculpted to that of a hollow skull-faced reaper grinning in judgment. "And this coin has never been released?"

"James Dyson was a veteran of a number of foreign wars, but never quite made it back to civilization. He learned strange things in foreign lands, but not how to keep a job. He roamed the streets as you did and made a living carving. He kept a very small knife to do this work. I contracted him to create this coin five years ago. He died shortly after completing it.

"Some whisper that Dyson didn't actually carve this nickel. He was just another poor soul trying to harvest the nickel's power for his own purposes and instead was ensnared into its trap. Some believe that a single man carved all of the coins and imbibed them with magic for an unknown purpose. Of course, rumors are just that— rumors. Perhaps true. Perhaps not.

"In any case, several policemen found him suspicious and asked him to drop everything. The coin had burned a hole in his mind. He couldn't drop it or the knife and thus the police dropped him. It was in the papers for a week, perhaps two, and then forgotten."

Walter snapped his fingers. "I heard about that on the streets. The Seattle Cops don't mess around."

Borri nodded sympathetically. "It is dangerous to walk the shadows and sometimes the lines between predators and prey are blurred. *'When beggars die there are no comets seen; the heavens themselves blaze forth the death of princes.'*"

The words were familiar, but the meaning long lost. "I know that from somewhere. It is hard to remember."

"I am unsurprised," Borri stated, his tone flat. "The Bard wrote it. Julius Caesar. In the scene just before he is murdered by the Senate. All men die. Some are mourned more than others."

Walter placed his hand over the box and clasped it shut with a determined finality. "Are you trying to scare me, Borri? I paid for this."

"I am merely reminding you of the warning already freely given," Borri shot him a look that could cut glass. His next words came out in a cold clip. "Like attracts like. If you put forth this sort of magic into the world, it will taint you."

Walter shook his head thinking of the year he spent on the streets. "If you thought this was such a bad idea, why help me?"

"The Dyson Nickel is tainted enough for my purposes. His murdered blood is part of it now. Until you came to me, I had completely forgotten it." The alchemist snorted derisively. "I could have turned you away, but you had will and power. You would have found another source in time. This way the damage done to the world can be mitigated and I required your tears for my own purposes."

"You are such a cold bastard." Walter's lip quivered at the thought of giving up after having suffered for an entire year. "How could you possibly know what I am feeling?"

Borri stood, quite angry. He adjusted his glasses. "I have buried three sons. One of them died less than three blocks from this very spot. Nine wives have faded to time. Three of them before their time. Time is the enemy of life, not death. We waste it in hollow pursuits and then wail with the emotional maturity of a child when it gone."

"He killed my son!" Walter slammed his fist upon the ancient desk. "My poor boy deserved better."

"Indeed. It is a sin Thompson will have to live with the rest of his life; however long you design to allot to him because of an accident that marked his soul as much as yours. Dyson's Nickel will absorb your hate. It will consume Thompson and then move along to the next target and then the next. It will not be sated. You understand?"

Walter's face turned crimson with barely contained rage. "What kind of father would I be if I didn't punish the man that killed my son?"

"A merciful one."

The doorman puffed his chest and blocked Walter's path as sternly as Cerberus. His nose twitched with disgust. "I'm afraid that only residents and their guests are allowed into this building."

Walter shook his head, hardly able to blame the man. His hair was long and unkempt. His beard with pocked with white hair. His nose had a row of thick black heads. His teeth had yellowed. One of them was likely rotten in the back which caused his breath to smell like fetid garbage. He flashed his ID. "I'm Walter Meloni. I have a condo in here. I've been traveling."

The doorman blinked, checked the credentials twice, and wondered how a man that smelled of urine could afford such lavish luxury. Walter ignored him. He was ready to return to the land of the living. The journey through the elevator to his floor felt strange as though it was the first time. He unlocked the doors with the keys Borri returned to him and stepped inside.

It was mostly empty, like his life. He never bothered to fill this place with new memories; not after Wendy left him, not after Michael died. He dug through the cardboard boxes until he found the photo album. He had forgotten what Michael looked like remembering only the pain.

Walter poured himself a glass of bourbon, filled the bathtub, and stripped naked. He cradled the album in his arms while he soaked in the warm water. His skin felt as though slugs had been duct taped to him for months. He drained his glass and then decided to skip the formality of refilling it and simply drink from the bottle.

He allowed the soothing warmth of the bath to ease his muscles and then set aside both the bottle and the album to focus on the business of scrubbing himself clean. His razors were dull, but after washing them and tapping them clean on the counter, he managed to trim down most of his scruffy beard. His hair was a frightening mop with white streaks like the Bride of Frankenstein. Tomorrow, he swore that the first thing he would do was visit the barber for a proper grooming.

Walter searched through his dresser trying to find a pair of pajamas that fit. He had lost over forty pounds on the street. Idly wondering if he could sell the rights to this story as a celebrity weight loss option, he grabbed the bottle once more and almost drank from it before deciding that he needed to return to drinking from the glass. He poured himself one last glass of bourbon, promised himself that it would be his last, and then sauntered over to the bay windows. He stood naked before the nighttime glittering landscape of Seattle and felt like a king.

He looked at Dyson's Nickel in the velvet box and felt a giddy sort of poisoned joy. Tomorrow would be a big day for him.

Walter Meloni felt the knife in his jacket for reassurance. He wasn't certain what sort of protection that Remington Borri had against personal attacks, but he was prepared to spend his miserable life to settle the score. He held his breath and then stepped over the threshold into Borri's Curiosity Shoppe.

It was quiet as a whisper.

The night customers seemed to sense the oncoming storm and left one by one with a sense of disturbing foreboding. The stone gargoyles covered their eyes as he passed. Chattering skulls bit down and turned towards each other. He stalked around the cluttered rows until he found his new prey taking inventory near the back office.

He pulled out the knife and moved to strike. He had never directly killed a man before, but he was quite eager to learn. Walter stepped closer to Remington Borri trying to remain outside of his perception. The delicate looking man knelt down over a collection of quills and parchments intent upon counting.

Walter raised his knife, eager to slip it around Borri's neck, and finally be done with it. A bolt of blazing white light struck down the blade. The metal exploded in a kaleidoscope of fire and shrapnel. The molten metal dripped onto his hand searing the flesh.

He screamed and dropped to the floor.

"You didn't think that trick would work on an immortal. We have nothing but time. You can't fade from our sight." Borri turned and then shook his head with a twinge of disgust. "A knife? Really? There are better ways to express dissatisfaction, Mister Meloni."

Words were too hollow to express the pain. "Wendy is dead." Borri said nothing. "Didn't you hear me? The coin didn't work. It was supposed to cause Thompson pain! To make him hate life!"

The alchemist stood and reached across the aisle for a bit of burdock root, snapped it in half, and then handed it to Walter. "This will help with the pain."

Walter accepted the root and applied it to the bubbling wound upon his hand. The root did ease the pain. He cradled his hand close to his chest and wrapped it with Borri's handkerchief. "It wasn't supposed to kill Wendy!" Walter protested. "This was for her and Michael!"

"Didn't you suppose that Thompson cared for his wife? That he loved Wendy as much as you?" Borri asked in a tone of voice one used for moronic children who asked stupid questions. "What better way to strike at his heart? Perhaps it was a kindness. She suffered the loss of a son alone without the comfort of his father or the man she loved."

"You have to bring her back!" Walter begged. "You have the power!"

"I have a number of powers, but that is not one of them. Death comes for us all in time. Some of us are merely better at delaying it than others." Borri gestured to the pictures on the wall. "It is a shame that any parent should outlive a son."

"What of Thompson?" Walter asked in desperation.

"He will suffer. You will find little joy in it," Borri warned. "Poisoned delight weakens the heart."

"What am I supposed to do now?"

"Live with it and what you've done, if you can."

 I AM ALWAYS INTRIGUED BY men like Borri and his little "Curiosity Shoppe." I don't think I could learn so much about magic only to sell it. Call me selfish — I am — but why bring so much power together only to barter it away? There must be something I'm missing. Though, I must admit, making his victim pay a year's worth of tears to get a cursed coin was genius. He also knew enough to handle my child with care. Perhaps I'll pay him a visit one day. And, as always, it thrills me when someone claims my work as their own. There's protection in the camouflage.

— The Carver

DEFINITELY DVOŘÁK

MAE EMPSON

*"The finale closes with a gradual diminuendo, like a breath…
the solo dying down to pianissimo. Then… the last bars are
taken over by the orchestra, which provides a tempestuous
ending. That was my idea, and from it I cannot recede."*

—Antonín Dvořák, on the ending of his cello concerto,
B minor, Op. 104, B. 191 (in a letter to his Czech publisher)

KATIE LUGGED HER CELLO down the front ramp of the music
building. The night air in Chapel Hill clung warm and thick.
She could feel herself sweating with each step, though the sun
had long set. She stopped to catch her breath and glanced at her
watch. *Shit.* She'd missed her usual 9:45 pm bus for sure. Was
there another one she could still catch? The schedule would be
posted at the stop up on Franklin Street, one block beyond the
music building, Hill Hall.

She'd just lost track of time. She needed to nail her solo in the
Dvořák at tomorrow's rehearsal, particularly the troublesome
octaves and double stops in the coda in the *Allegro*. Professor
Kenyon had selected the cello concerto for their spring program
specifically to feature "the freshman prodigy" as he'd called her
right in front of the older cellists he'd bypassed when he made
her principal. She wished he hadn't said it quite like that. They
resented her enough already.

If only someone else was still practicing, she could have asked
them for a ride. But the poorly muffled, competing sounds of

178

trumpet, violin, and clarinet from the other practice rooms had faded hours ago. Amateurs. The professors didn't give the majors much trouble so long as they practiced at least one or two hours a day, but she knew that wasn't long enough to stay on top.

Her roommate in the dorm, Alicia, insisted that she couldn't study with any background noise every time Katie brought up practicing at night back at the dorm. That left the practice rooms on campus. Of course, Katie couldn't help but notice that Alicia had no trouble concentrating over background noise of her own making, like endless tracks of R.E.M and They Might Be Giants, and the latest episodes of *In Living Color*, *Northern Exposure*, or *Twin Peaks*. It was the 1990's for goodness sake. Couldn't she listen to that noise with her CD Walkman? In fairness, practicing the cello in her dorm room would have likely aggravated all seven of the other girls in the suite, too. Four hours of Dvořák would make anyone crazy.

Katie reached the bus stop on Franklin Street. By the light of the streetlamp, she could see that the 9:45 was the last bus. Did any other buses on campus have routes after ten that she could catch at a different stop? What choice did she have?

She knew that it was *possible* to walk to her dorm on the far south end of campus from here, but it would take about forty-five minutes under the best circumstances. She didn't think she could manage it with the cello. She could have left it in a locker at Hill Hall overnight, but her mother had made her swear that she wouldn't let her mother's instrument out of her sight. Walking probably wasn't safe, either. She'd seen fliers all over the place discouraging students from walking alone after dark after some recent incidents. Had the police caught the attacker yet? She couldn't recall.

She fished through her purse. Did she have any bus schedules? No. Did she have enough change to try to call someone to pick her up? She had her checkbook, a twenty, a wad of ones, and two dimes— more than enough cash to cover the bus fare, or even a cab if she called one, but not enough change for a pay phone. *Shitissimo.*

Now what? There had to be a place still open at ten o'clock on a weeknight on Franklin Street where she could get change, and find a phone. She hefted the cello and started walking. She watched the cars whizzing past to see if any stopped up ahead, suggesting a business that was still open. None did.

She found a pay phone outside a drug store that had just closed at ten o'clock. Too late again. If only she had a credit card. Her roommate Alicia did and used it to order pizza all the time. "You'll thank us when you graduate without thousands of dollars of credit card debt," her dad had said when she'd complained. "And without twenty extra pounds of pizza," her mom had added, and Katie had no trouble picturing her Mom's expression across the phone line. If Katie was going to follow in her mom's footsteps and play her cello and live her discarded dreams, she'd better damn well look like her mother's memories of her own glamorous college self while doing it.

Would a cab company take a collect call? That seemed unlikely. At least the pay phone had a phonebook. She tore out a page of taxi service phone numbers, in case the next phone she found, once she had change, didn't have a phone book.

She flipped to the white pages. Would any students actually take a collect call from her? Alicia was right out. She'd bitch about the interruption and inconvenience for months, if she even took the call. Katie tried to remember the last names of the other cello players in the orchestra. They might resent her, but surely one of them would come if they knew she was stranded. She'd heard their last names before and seen them on the posted chair and desk assignments, but she hadn't read down past her own name on top. And even if she could remember, did she really want them to see her stuck like this? Better to call a cab company.

She turned back to her cello, and wondered how far she would have to walk to find a shop that was still open. She really needed a case with wheels, but she could imagine what her mom would say. *My case isn't good enough for you? Afraid of a little exercise, which, I might add, you sorely need?* If her mother could see her now out in public with her hair slicked tight to her skull from sweat, and the sides of her shirt stained damp and reeking, she might actually relent on the wheels.

Katie looked back at the phone, wishing she could make it work for free just by staring at it long enough. She really did not want to pick up the cello again.

Her glance fell on the coin return. Could someone have forgotten to pick up their own change?

Jackpot! She could feel at least three coins in there, and pulled them out into the light of the street lamp above her to confirm. A dime, a quarter, and... was that even a real coin? A nickel, by its size, but with a buffalo on it. She'd heard of buffalo nickels, now that she thought about it, but she'd never seen one. It was kind of cool. She flipped it over, trying to remember if it would still have Jefferson on the back. No, an Indian, right?

Instead, she found a man with a beard. The Indian's profile had been completely altered. The man's raised eye protruded slightly, under a bushy eyebrow, and an even more prominent cheek appled beneath. His thick mustache and beard had been carved bushy and wild with thin strokes, extending to the edge of the coin.

The carving looked exactly like the picture of Dvořák on the back of her sheet music for the cello concerto, if he had hid his balding forehead with a thin-brimmed bowler hat. She wondered if some street musician had carved it as a good luck token, or if all bushy-bearded pop-eyed men from the turn of the century looked alike.

No, she wanted it to be a picture of Dvořák. It was definitely Dvořák. The dime and quarter would suffice to call a cab company. She could keep the Dvořák nickel. She slipped the nickel into the right pocket of her jeans. She'd keep it for good luck. It was at least as likely to bring luck as not washing her hands for eight hours before a performance — her mother's tip — or putting a picture of Jesus in her case like that model-cute blonde sophomore in the viola section. Emily something.

That girl couldn't play for shit but the guys watched Emily as she wandered around the music building at least as carefully as they ever watched Professor Kenyon's baton.

Katie didn't need that much attention, but it would have been nice if Eric, at least, ever noticed her enough to remember her name. Eric played principal viola, and had the talent and looks, most closely resembling Luke Perry from *Beverly Hills: 90210*, to figure in her most closely guarded fantasies of what going on a date with him might be like.

Katie held the found coins. Which cab company should she call? On a whim, she flipped the Dvořák nickel. Heads, she'd call the first one listed: AAA Cab. Tails, she'd call the second one listed: Checker Cab. She really hoped she could get a ride. She did not want to carry that cello one block further.

Heads. She smiled at Dvořák. AAA it was. Naturally, he'd prefer a name that could be understood as a series of musical notes.

About ten minutes later, she saw the orange AAA cab approaching from the right, and waved. The cab did not slow, but suddenly veered directly towards her. Its horn blared. Tires squealed. She flinched and threw herself out of the way. A crashing-crushing noise. The cab slammed into the space beside her, barely missing the phone and the front wall of the drug store.

Katie stopped screaming long enough to confirm that she had not been hurt.

"Jesus, what did I hit?" she heard from the driver's seat through the opened window.

That voice. "Eric?" She'd heard him say he had a night job to help with bills, but she hadn't realized he drove a cab. Her hair! Her armpits! Oh God.

He stepped gingerly out of the cab. He stared at her blankly. "Hey, you, I didn't hurt you did I? Did you see what I hit?"

She looked at the wheels of the cab, and the debris around the front wheel. What? Oh. Oh no. No no no no. "My... my cello."

"Oh hey, I know you. The little cello girl. Ummm... Kayley? No. Katie, right?"

Katie moaned, and started picking up fragments of case and wood. No no no. That was her mother's cello. A David Caron. Her parents had insured it, right? Her mother was going to kill her. Her father was going to kill her. *Shitississimo.*

She sunk to her knees, and looked under the vehicle for more pieces. The bulk of the cello was still in the remains of the case, lodged under the cab completely crushed.

"That cello was a David Caron. My mother's cello." She could hear herself saying the words, but it almost seemed like someone else was speaking. Was she already dead? Was this hell?

Eric flinched. "A Caron? Christ. I don't know what happened. I was just driving through here to pick up a caller and I just... I completely lost control of the cab. There must have been something slick on the road."

"Are you drunk?"

"What? No. Of course not." He looked angry that she would even suggest it. He didn't smell like he'd been drinking. "Don't say that. Look, when we talk to the cops, you can't say something crazy like that."

The cops? What could the police do? She was going to be dead when her parents found out. Dead. Should she call the police? She was out of change again, but weren't you supposed to be able to call 911 without paying? Eric probably had enough change for the call if not. He'd remember her after that for sure. The sweaty little cello girl who called the cops on him. This was not how she'd pictured spending time with him. And the police might want to talk to her parents tonight. She wasn't ready.

"Look, you admit that you destroyed the cello, right? I think it's insured." And the cab company had to have some kind of car insurance that covered damage to property like this, though they probably would balk at the price tag of a Caron cello. His cab did not appear damaged. If they sold the cab, would that be enough money to replace the cello? Almost certainly.

Even with insurance, though, she probably wouldn't get a new cello in time for the concert. Maybe the school could provide a loaner instrument and bow in the meantime. She knew it would never sound as rich and full as the Caron.

"I'm so sorry. I'm just glad you aren't hurt. I'll find a way to make it up to you. I'm sure the cab company will be able to do something. I'll call them when I get home. I promise."

Right. Should she ask him to sign some sort of paper admitting that he'd driven over her cello, at least? Would he try to lie about it later? She wanted to get back to her dorm room in Hinton James, to the shower in the four-room suite which was the one place where she let herself cry on campus, hoping the sound of the water masked her sobbing. Decision time. What would Eric think watching her flip a coin at a moment like this? Well, it had to look cooler than crying about it. Heads, she'd just go home. Tails, she'd call the police. Dvořák came up smiling again.

"Look, could you at least help me gather up the pieces, and give me a ride home?" Her dorm was only about ten minutes away by car, on the south side of campus.

He nodded, and helped her load the broken cello into the trunk of the cab.

They rode in silence, as he drove around the outer edge of campus towards the high-rises down on the far end by the athletic fields, including Hinton James, where she and other lucky freshman who weren't cool enough to pledge sororities up on the north end of campus got stuck for their first year. She wanted to bring up the idea of having him sign some kind of confession, but she wasn't quite sure how to say that, or what it would actually require. What a horrible night.

She heard a sound like a bullet, and the car lurched suddenly, throwing her towards Eric. Her neck and chest jerked against the seat belt. The cab skidded to a halt, wheels and brakes screaming.

"My tire! I should have checked it more carefully. It must have been damaged by the uh… by driving over your… Oh Jeez." Eric got out of the cab to check the driver's side tire.

Katie stared out the window, at her dorm up ahead. So close.

She let herself out of the cab, and walked around to the driver's side to see what Eric was doing. "Can you fix it?"

She couldn't see his expression clearly enough to tell if it would be good news or bad news in the dark. He had a flashlight out. "I can't see very well but the tire's blown. We drove on the rims, pulling to the side of the road, and I think that's screwed up the tire well too. I probably need to call a tow truck."

She nodded. They were farther from the potentially open bars and restaurants and pay phones now. "The closest phone is probably at my dorm at Hinton James. I can see the building from here. It's maybe a ten minute walk. Do you want to come with me and call from there?"

Katie knew she'd feel safer walking to the dorm with Eric than alone, particularly since he had a flashlight. This area of campus wasn't well lit at all. It was just a series of huge parking lots, and they were awfully dark.

"Sure, I guess."

Katie waited while he turned on some kind of flashing hazard lights on the cab, composing a mental list of topics that she could ask him about as they made their way across the road and parking lots towards the dorm. His music classes. His other classes. Where was he from? Did he have any plans for spring break? Did he have any pets back home? Would he sign a confession that he'd destroyed her cello?

Eric had little to say, as they began to cross the parking lots between the road and the high-rise dorm. His music classes were "fine." His other classes were "tough, but okay, and kind of boring."

She was trying to think of a way to ask "where are you from" that would take more than one word to answer, when a man stepped out from behind a van and grabbed her, wrapping a thick arm around her neck and yanking her back against his chest. His arm and clothes stunk of cigarette smoke.

She heard a click to the right side of her head.

"Don't be a hero, kid. I've got a gun. Put your money on the ground, and get out of here."

She realized he was talking to Eric, and tried to catch his eye. *Don't leave me here.*

Eric didn't make eye contact with Katie. He tossed something on the ground that was probably a wallet and ran back in the direction of the cab.

"Put your wrists together. Behind you."

Katie didn't want to put her hands any closer to the crazy man than she had to but she didn't want to get shot either. She reluctantly crossed her hands behind her at the wrist. Her purse slipped off her shoulder and onto the pavement.

She felt a hand circling her crossed wrists, tight as a manacle. Where was the gun? Had he set it down? Slipped it in a belt or pocket? He let go of her neck, and she felt a second hand wrapping some kind of duct tape around her wrists, tying them together.

She could feel both hands working on binding her wrists. If she was going to run, she needed to do it now, while he didn't have the gun at the ready.

She bolted for the dorm.

She heard a shot, felt a sharp pain in her leg, and fell forward, crashing face first onto the pavement, unable to brace or protect herself with her hands bound behind her. Had Eric heard the shot? Would he come back? Was he fetching help? He couldn't even get into the dorm if he did circle back that way alone but he could maybe talk to the security guard at the front desk.

Katie felt a hand tangle in the back of her hair and yank her up by it.

"You have pretty hair. I'm going to take most of it."

No. No, this was not happening. She could feel him sawing at her sweaty hair with something. A knife? Did that mean he'd set the gun down on the ground somewhere or holstered it back into a belt? She needed her hands free.

When he finished chopping at her hair and rolled her over to face up to the sky, it was too dark to see much more than the outline of her attacker. She could make out most of her hair clutched in his left hand, and a knife in his right hand. Where was the gun? He shoved her hair into a pocket of his coat and zipped it shut.

She could feel the cold pavement against her palms, flat against the ground under the weight of her body, pushing her belly up into the air. At least her body now shielded her hands from him. If he didn't hurt her hands, she could still play. She wondered if her leg was bleeding. Probably. At least she didn't play bass. She could still play cello even if she never walked again.

He cut the front of her shirt open with the knife. She stiffened. She needed a plan. She needed to get away right now. What could she do? Think.

He sliced her bra in half, through the narrow point, and pushed the padded cups out of the way.

Katie screamed and tried to twist and squirm out of his reach. She kicked at him with her uninjured leg. Maybe she could propel herself to one side and try to roll out of the way. Could she hide under a car? Was there a big enough car that she could hide under where he couldn't quite reach her?

He re-positioned himself over her, so he had her hips trapped between his knees. Not good. She tried to kick him in the crotch with her uninjured leg, but he was positioned too high up her body. She couldn't get the leverage with her hips trapped, and, at best, she could try to kick him in the back.

She screamed as loud as she could.

He shoved a hand over her mouth. That at least had to slow him down.

She continued to twist and squirm but with a new objective. Could she rub the duct tape on her wrists against the pavement until it abraded? He hadn't quite finished securing her wrists, because she'd tried to run. She just needed to get her wrists free.

He held the cold metal of the knife against her throat. "You are going to stop screaming and lie very still."

Like hell she would. Better to die. She reared her neck up, letting the knife bite into her throat.

He flinched and pulled the knife back.

She expected she was bleeding from her leg, neck, and the skin of her wrists now. How long could she just lie there and bleed without losing consciousness? She kept wriggling against the asphalt, letting it tear her skin. That much she could feel. But was it tearing the tape yet? She felt like she could stretch her wrists a bit farther. Almost there.

"You're one crazy bitch."

He set the knife down and reached into his right pocket. Was he trying to find his tape to silence her? This was as distracted as he would be. He didn't have the knife or the gun in hand as far as she could tell.

She tore her right wrist free and punched him as hard as she could in the crotch, like in the self-defense video that the dorm had made all the freshmen girls watch.

The tension of his knees trapping her thighs lessened. She wriggled up out of his grip, and crawled for the protection of the closest car. If she hid under a car, he could still shoot her, but at least he couldn't *touch* her.

She huddled under a van, reminded of how her cello had been in a similar position under Eric's cab when she finally caught sight of it. She couldn't think about the cello.

She listened for footsteps or the sound of a car door or a car starting.

Silence.

Then, she heard the wail of a siren. Had Eric found a security guard and called the police? Would that scare her attacker off? Oh thank God.

A hand grasped her ankle and started pulling her backwards, out from under the van.

Katie screamed and tried to hook her arms around the front left tire to brace herself, digging her fingers into its tread.

The thought struck her that everything had twisted horribly since she picked up the Dvořák nickel. If she took it out of her pocket, would things get better? Could she spare a hand off the tire to reach for it, or would that give him the edge to yank her out from under the van? She hesitated.

The siren screamed louder and louder. The police car had to be close, searching the dark parking lot for her. She tried to scream over the siren: "I'm here! Here!"

Over the crescendo of the siren, she heard the sudden sound of metal crashing into metal, and the tire she clutched turned and lurched forward, crushing her arms and the bones of her hands.

Katie heard herself screaming through the excruciating pain and loss, but her screams got softer and softer, strangely muffled and muted, until she couldn't hear anything at all.

Katie's parents spent a lot of time arguing with the various witnesses of their daughter's bone-crushing ordeal, to try to assign fault, and set the bearings for the lawsuits to follow. Was it the school's fault for having such poorly lit parking lots? The overzealous rookie cop who managed to clip the back of the van with his police car, while searching for their screaming daughter, unaware that she lay under its wheels? The tearful boy who left their daughter to face a man with a gun, alone, in order to run for help? The lunatic who cut their daughter's clothes and hair and chased her under the van, and was currently the subject of a multi-county manhunt? The last seemed most deserving, but least likely to have the personal resources to make a lawsuit worthwhile.

One thing was clear. Katie would not be able to play again for a long time. If ever. Her mother did not look forward to telling her that, should her daughter's mind heal enough that she could comprehend the damage to her hands and arms.

For now, they could afford a nurse to watch over her at home, and wipe her tears and clean her up in those hideous adult diapers. The doctors thought the shock would eventually wear off but were careful to make no promises. The lawsuits would ensure their little girl had access to care as long as she needed it.

Katie's nurse observed that she was most responsive when listening to music and became particularly animated at the sounds of the Dvořák concerto that, according to her mother, she'd been practicing on the night of the attack.

At the sound of the Dvořák, Katie would scream and gesture incoherently, and then grab a crayon in the stiff swollen fingers of her right hand that protruded like blackened sausages out of the heavy white cast on her hand and wrist.

She drew awkward looking circles on page after page of blank white printer paper, or even the walls, if the nurse was slow. In the circles, the troubled young woman drew the rough profile of the face of a man with a wild beard.

The nurse quietly replaced the stacks of blank paper and kept a file of the crayon drawings in case Katie's parents wanted to see how much their daughter was still haunted by what the nurse could only conclude was a rough sketch of the face of Katie's attacker.

◇◈◇

THE PASSION OF THE CREATIVE *soul is one of my favorite in this world. Mostly because the creative is as obsessive about their craft as I am about mine. There is a kinship I feel as I eat their lives. A power that adds to mine. Sometimes, for a short while — one or two decades — I can do what they did: play an instrument, paint, sculpt, write. I've learned from these souls to appreciate the talent I've consumed. In a way, I give it back to the world.*

—The Carver

JUSTICE IN FIVE CENTS

RICHARD DANSKY

THE VOICE ON THE PHONE was exactly what Harold had anticipated, gravelly and a little rough, and tinged with some sort of accent he couldn't quite identify.

"Rouskopf Coins," the man said. "Steven Rouskopf speaking. How can I help you?"

Harold cleared his throat. He'd rehearsed this a few times, but it always sounded silly to him, having to ask a professional a question whose answer might be "nothing at all."

"Hi. Mister Rouskopf. My name is Harold Green and I have a question."

There was a pause. "And that question is?" said Rouskopf, with just a twinge of impatience.

Suddenly feeling self-conscious, Harold coughed, then cleared his throat again. "Ah, yes. I mean, you come very highly recommended, according to a few websites I checked, and, I have a question. About coins."

"I see."

Was that a dry chuckle? "I have one. A very strange one. And I was wondering..."

"If it was worth something. Aha. So you want to bring it in and have me tell you if it's valuable."

"If it is, it's for sale." All of a sudden, Harold was back in elementary school, up in front of the class, the teacher demanding recitation of a book report on something he hadn't read. "I mean, I don't collect coins. I don't know how I got this one. It just looks old, and it looks weird, and, I don't know. The internet

190

isn't helping," he ended miserably, and mentally cursed himself for sounding like an idiot.

There was a faint rumble on the line. After a minute, Harold realized it was Rouskopf, laughing.

"Look, Mister Green. Normally, I don't deal with single coins. I buy collections. And looking "weird" generally doesn't mean much. But, if you really want, I can take a look at it for you. Say, Friday? Four o'clock?"

"Could we make it six? I've got a meeting, and—"

"I close at five."

Harold swallowed again. "Right. Four it is."

He heard Rouskopf hang up.

The shadow falling over his cube was the only warning Harold had that Bobby Helmer was inbound. Helmer was the boss, of course; a legend on the claims floor who'd climbed the corporate ladder with a metaphorical knife between his teeth. Now he was The Man, tasked with overseeing Harold's department and two others, and he made a habit of swooping down from above without warning or pity.

"Harold," he started, "I see you're leaving a little early on Friday."

Harold swiveled his chair around. Helmer was standing behind him, arms folded across his chest, grinning. "Yes, sir. A little over an hour. Put in for it with HR and they said it would be no problem." He paused, coughing into his hand. "I've already made up the time."

"Oh, very nice. What's got you running out early?" Helmer's voice was still jovial, but there was the faintest hint of an edge to it, a warning to the wary.

Harold was many things, but wary was not one of them. "Yeah. I've got to get a piece of… an inheritance checked out. It was the only time the appraiser was open." Which was true enough, as far as things went. "Like I've said, I've made up the time."

Helmer nodded. "Inheritance?"

"A coin. Here, take a look." Harold reached into his pocket and pulled out what looked to be a small circle of silver. "Weird, huh?"

Stepping back, Helmer waved him off. "Maybe next time, after you find out what it's worth. But I need you to remember something, Harold. We're not running a flextime operation here. I need you at your desk during working hours."

"I understand, sir." Belatedly, Harold realized he was still holding the coin out and tucked his arm in against his body.

"Good. Because your work is good but nobody gets special treatment around here. Not even the guy who broke my record for best month. Mark Friday as a day off."

Harold blinked. "You... want me to take the whole day?"

Helmer shook his head. "No, it's getting marked against your vacation. I expect you in at eight, I expect you to make up the time that day, and then you can go check out your inheritance. But since you're leaving early with insufficient notice, policy says that the whole day is forfeit."

Suddenly, he was all smiles again, clapping Harold on the arm. "But hey, these things happen. Enjoy that time off. Hope you get good news on that coin thing."

With mechanical ease, Helmer spun on his heel and stalked off toward the elevators. Harold stared after him, open-mouthed, then dropped his gaze to the coin in his hand. "But I made up the time," he said to no one in particular, before slowly turning his chair around and getting back to work.

Thursday night, Harold had bad dreams. The one he remembered was about a small child slowing eating its way out of his belly. He woke up in the morning, drenched in sweat, and dead certain that the ones he didn't remember were worse.

Rouskopf's shop was in a dingy strip mall in New Haven, far from gentrified districts around Yale. Squeezed in between a martial arts academy that promised an unlikely sixteen varieties of instruction and a second-hand furniture store, it wore its name proudly on the faded awning above and in gold lettering on the heavy door. Bells jangled when Harold pushed it open, and he stopped, blinking as his eyes adjusted to the shop's gloom.

"Come in, come in, you're letting the air out. Or in. Or something," said a lumpy shadow in the back of the shop, one that resolved into the slump-shouldered shape of a man stepping forward into the light.

Harold stepped in, the door thumping shut behind him. "Mister Rouskopf?"

"That I am. Come. To the counter. Let me see what you've got for me." Rouskopf was visible now, an older man carrying too many pounds around his waist and too many sad stories in his face. His over-full beard was shot through with the same gray that streaked his hair, and while he wore a suit, it looked as if he didn't own many others. He tromped over to the counter that ran along one wall of the shop; coins of various vintages and conditions sat under glass on faded velvet. The opposite wall was marked by shelves holding accoutrements of the numismatic hobby, none of which looked as if they'd been touched in years.

"Nice shop." Harold looked around and tried to assign a color to the carpet's spectacularly dull shade of yellow.

"It's a dump," Rouskopf replied. "I stay here because the rent is cheap and I like my neighbors. Ninety percent of my business is online these days. Now, you have a coin to show me?"

"I have a coin." Harold brought out the coin and laid it on the counter. "You see why I thought it was weird?"

"Ah." Rouskopf leaned in, his massive, shaggy head blocking Harold's view of the coin for a moment. "OK. First things first, I'm gonna give you something for this." His hands disappeared below the counter, then came up holding a cardboard square with a circle cut out of the middle. "Put the coin in the sleeve and I'll tell you about it."

Harold did as he was told. The hole in the cardboard was actually clear plastic, and the coin nestled into it nicely. "Now what?"

"Now I tell you what you've got. Take a look at it. What do you see?"

Harold held it up between his fingers, trying to find a little light in the dingy shop. He'd seen it before, of course. That's why he'd called Rouskopf in the first place. But Harold felt oddly compelled to impress the old man, to show that he'd really looked at it like he was serious. "Huh. Well, it's got a buffalo on one side. I think it's a nickel, or I would, if that's all I saw." He flipped the coin in its holder over in his hands. "But this side, I don't know. I don't know what that is."

"It's a skull," Rouskopf supplied helpfully. "Now stop trying to be smart and tell me what you see."

Harold coughed, reflexively. "OK. I see, umm, a skull. It looks like a skull."

"Very good," said Rouskopf, his voice dry. "What else?"

193

"Besides the skull? What else is there?"

The old man sighed. "The date, anything else that would look out of place on a coin, you name it."

Harold sniffed. "Why don't you take a look at it?"

"I've seen it. Now I want to know what you see."

Harold looked at it again. "It says 'BERT'" he blurted out. "Is it supposed to say that?"

Roukopf gave a sigh. "Enough. Let me just walk you through this. Then you can decide what you want to do with it. What you're holding is what's called a hobo nickel."

"A whatbo nickel?"

"Hobo nickel. It's folk art. People used to take coins and make their own little sculptures out of them, turn them into self-portraits or pirates or whatever. The one you've got is a decent example, but it's scuffed up to hell and gone. No serious collector's gonna touch it."

"But it's got a skull on it," Harold said. What was supposed to be a bold counterargument came out as a plaintive whine, and he winced at hearing it. "It's a coin with a skull. And, and maybe that skull's named Bert?"

Rouskopf shook his head. "The skull's not named Bert. It's just what someone carved on it. The coin isn't worth anything and we're done here. Sorry I couldn't give you better news." He made shooing motions with his hands toward the door. "Now go. I'm closing."

"But—"

"You got what you came for and you got it for free. It was lovely meeting you, now go."

Harold stood there a moment, then put the coin down on the counter. "If it's not worth anything, you keep it." He slid it across the counter. "All yours."

"Get that thing out of here," Rouskopf's voice was ice. "Leave my shop and don't bring it back. I deal with real coins, valuable ones. You take that thing and you go. Now!" He brought his fist down on the counter for emphasis, hard enough that Harold thought the glass might crack. It didn't, but Harold scooped the coin up anyway and scurried out the door, bells jingling behind him.

The last he saw of Rouskopf, he was standing in the doorway, scowling out into the parking lot until Harold drove away.

Harold didn't dream of a child eating him from the inside that night. Instead, it was the coin, the exquisitely detailed skull-face that was doing the chewing. It took tiny bites. Each one burned, and it chewed with elegant patience.

The coin really was beautiful, Harold decided. Early morning light sneaking in through the blinds of his bedroom window illuminated it, showing off the magnificent detail on the face of the skull. There was no hint here of the tools used to alter the original creation, no grooves or pits to show that this hadn't come stamped from the mint with death's grinning face upon it. Hollow eyes, too-long teeth, cheekbones sharp enough to cut a man like a knife; that was the face that death showed here. To look at it too long made Harold nervous. Still, the carving was so elegant, the lines so clean, that he found it hard to look away. Whoever made it had known their craft and had mastered it.

A quick search online showed him what the coin was supposed to have looked like. Buffalo on one side, Native American on the other. He thought about looking up a couple of price guides to see what it might be worth, but Rouskopf's words discouraged him. It had clearly spent a lot of rough time in a lot of rough men's pockets. There were rough spots and nicks along the nickel's edge that the sculptor had never added.

With a sigh, he put the coin down on his nightstand and headed for the bathroom. Monday morning, and the office called. Helmer's numbers weren't going to make themselves. And the coin, it wasn't going anywhere.

"You, Harold, look like crap. You'd better not tell me that you're upset over that vacation thing, because that sort of grudge-holding is not what we're looking for here."

Helmer hadn't even waited for Harold to turn around before starting in. Harold turned around anyway.

"No, Mister Helmer. Just having trouble sleeping." And that was as true as anything else Harold told Helmer. "Bad dreams, that's all."

"Ah. Get someone downstairs to write you a prescription for lorazepam. It'll knock your ass out so that the only thing you dream about is the inside of your eyelids. I need you sharp, and if you can't sleep without a nightlight, that doesn't help me."

He grinned below the eyes, and then stampeded off in the rough direction of the break room.

Harold watched him go.

That night, Harold took twice the recommended dosage of lorazepam, for which he had been duly prescribed by one of the on-site doctors at Helmer's insistence, and collapsed onto his bed within seconds.

He did dream, though. He was in a box that he somehow realized was a coffin, and he was alive and couldn't move. As he fought and struggled, something flensed the still-living flesh from his face in thin, bloody strips, until the face that he wore and the one on the nickel were the same.

By Thursday, he couldn't take it anymore. He called in sick, fully aware of what that was going to cost him in terms of Helmer's attention when he returned, and sat on the edge of his bed with the coin. He'd taken it back out of the wrapper because he wanted to feel it between his fingers, marveling at how it always seemed to stay cool, no matter how long or how tightly he held it.

The nightmares were getting worse, to the point where he wasn't getting any sleep. The drugs, he'd thrown away after a couple of nights of abject failure and mornings of bleary-eyed hangovers. He couldn't eat, he couldn't concentrate, and every time he closed his eyes, he could see the grinning skull, waiting for him in another of its manifestations.

He'd tried getting rid of the coin. Vending machines wouldn't take it. When he left it behind, people ran up to him to give him his missing change. When he tried to spend it, cash registers broke and legal tender was no longer an option. He'd even tried dropping it down a sewer. It had hit something and bounced right back up, landing heads-up on his shoe.

Which was, of course, impossible. But there was a lot of impossible going around these days, and there was no way that this was just another hobo nickel. Not when it wouldn't be parted from him. Not when the nightmares wore its face, the nightmares that only started when he'd found it. Not when it stayed cool as the grave.

That meant that Rouskopf had lied to him. Which meant that Rouskopf knew something. And that meant that he had to go see Rouskopf. No warnings, no phone calls, no appointments. He'd just walk in and demand the truth. Because Rouskopf knew something and it was time Harold knew it, too.

The dramatic entrance Harold was hoping to make at Rouskopf's shop was hindered somewhat by door sticking as he tried to open it. On the second shove, it swung inward in a jangle of bells, and Harold stepped inside.

"You lied to me, Mister Rouskopf. I want the truth."

Rouskopf stood behind the counter, facing the door with his hands behind him. "You are an exceedingly rude young man. I never lie to a paying customer."

"I didn't pay you anything." Harold stalked toward him. "Now I want the truth about that nickel."

"Really?"

"Really."

"OK. Just as long as you're sure." He shrugged, then reached underneath the counter. When his hands came up, they were holding a pistol.

"You," he said. "You really want to know what's going on? Fine. Lock the door, turn the sign around, and pull the shade. You and me, we're gonna talk."

Harold stared at the coin dealer for a moment, then at the gun, then at the coin dealer again. "You're nuts."

"I'm nuts? You're the killer in here," Rouskopf said, and waggled the gun suggestively toward the door. "If you run, I won't shoot you. But you never get to come back."

Slowly, Harold put his hands in the air. "I have no idea what you're talking about. But I'll play along. Just give me a minute."

"It doesn't take that long." Rouskopf moved along the counter toward the back of the shop, where a small table was set up with two chairs and a tottering pile of ancient coin guides. "Come back here when you're done."

The coin dealer had seated himself and propped the gun on the stack of books by the time Harold reached the back of the store. "Take a seat. Put the coin on the table. Then put your hands where I can see them."

"I'm not going to do anything stupid. You've got the gun."

"Hah!" was all Rouskopf said, even as Harold carefully pulled the nickel out of his pocket. It caught the dim light for a second, a gleam of something bright in the shrouded gloom of the shop, and the dealer hissed out a muttered "Jesus."

Harold looked at him, coin still between his fingers. "What is it? You told me it was just a coin." Taken by a sudden thought, he stretched forward ever so slightly, holding the nickel out toward his host. "You want to take it."

"Put it the fuck on the table!" Rouskopf shouted. "There isn't a cop in this city who won't believe me if I tell them I shot your ass in self-defense. Now you stop fucking around and put it down, or I pull the trigger. We're too far gone for you to back down now."

"All right, all right. Putting it down." The click of the nickel on the table seemed to calm Roskopf somewhat.

"Good. Now, hands in the air." Wordlessly, Harold did as he was told. "Okay. Now we can talk. First things first, who'd you kill?"

Harold exploded. "What the hell is wrong with you? I haven't killed anyone. You're the one with the gun in someone's face."

Rouskopf adjusted his aim slightly, making it very clear to Harold that the safety was in fact off. "I haven't used it. Yet. You, on the other hand… only one way to get your hands on that nickel, kiddo. One way. You off somebody."

"That's ridiculous. You said it was just some, what, hobo thing? Carving the coins?"

The dealer leaned forward. "I said that to get you out of my shop. That coin? It's death."

Harold shook his head. "You're crazy. And I'm leaving." He slid his chair back, and it scraped along the floorboards evilly. "Keep the nickel."

"No!" Rouskopf was around the table in an instant, the cold metal of the gun barrel pressed up against Harold's temple. "You're not putting that on me. Now who did you kill?"

"I didn't kill anyone, I swear! I've got a desk job! I've never even been in a car accident. I got beat up all the time in school. I swear, I haven't killed anyone!" Sweat dripped down around the gun where it met Harold's skin. "Please," he whimpered. "Please."

"The coin's never wrong. The coin is death. The coin, hell, it's a legend. 1913 buffalo nickel, carved by Bertram Wiegand. You look at it, you see he put his name on it."

Harold nodded, and Rouskopf prodded him with the gun. "Look!"

Harold looked. "He chopped three letters off "Liberty. It says "Bert" now. I saw that last time."

The dealer nodded. "Saw. Didn't notice, which was sad. Greatest carver of hobo nickels ever. You can always tell a Bert. And this one, it was one of his first, and he made it special. If you believe the story, he carved it at a camp in Florida. Some railroad bulls beat one of his friends to death, and Bert, he took it on himself to do something about it."

"Couldn't he call the cops?" Harold asked, acutely aware of the pressure still lodged against his temple.

Rouskopf laughed. "It didn't work like that. Tramps and hobos? Not human, no rights. You beat one to death and you were a railroad cop, you made sure you got rid of the body and nobody would do a damn thing to you. Cops did the murder, kid. Cops did lots of murders, and Bert, they say he finally had enough."

"Can you put the gun down?"

"No. You want the rest of this, you shut up and you listen. Bert made the nickel, made *this* nickel, and the story goes he got a little help on it from a hoodoo man he'd met down Louisiana way. Hexed it. Made it so that to have the coin was death, and that it would get passed from killer to killer to killer. A little piece of justice, five cents wide. You understand now?"

Harold held very still. "No. Please. Put the gun down. I won't do anything."

Rouskopf jabbed the gun cruelly against the side of Harold's head. "Oh, you're going to do something. You're going to put that coin back in your pocket and you're going to keep it away from me."

"I can do that." Gingerly, he reached out for the nickel, inert and dull against the wood of the tabletop. "But I have a question. If the coin was supposed to go from killer to killer, how'd it get from this Burt guy to… whoever?"

"Bert," Rouskopf corrected him. "Bert made it, so Bert was immune. He made it, and he took that coin, and he hitched a ride on the Florida East Coast Railway, back and forth for three weeks until he finally found the bulls that killed his friend. Then he let them beat the crap out of him."

Harold shuddered. "Why'd he do that?"

"Part of a beating was getting rolled. Jesus, you don't know anything. The bulls, they took everything he had, including the coin. And that was the whole plan."

"Oh."

"Six weeks later, one of them murdered the other one. Dumped his body along the track, but went through is pockets first. Took everything."

"What happened to him," Harold asked, dreading the answer.

"He had it for six months. Had bad dreams, started drinking, tried to hijack a mob liquor shipment down from Canada. You want to guess how that ended?"

"I think I know." The coin went into his pocket. "Look. See? It's away. You can put the gun down."

After a moment, Rouskopf did, and he stepped away. "All right. You're probably thinking this is crazy. You're telling me you didn't kill anyone. But the coin, if the stories are right, the coin's never wrong. You may not think you killed anyone, but you sure as shit did, and they had the coin when you did it. That's why it found its way to you, and you got no way out. You having bad dreams?"

"Uh-huh." The whole conversation felt surreal; a trip into a funhouse world where crazy men with guns could tell magic stories in strip mall storefronts, and the reality of paperwork and claims discussions and life at an insurance agency was an impossible distance away.

"That's how it starts. That's why you're here. You get bad dreams, then you get bad luck, then you get dead. That's how it ends, and the guy that offs you, he gets the nickel, and it starts all over again."

Harold sat very still, his hand still wrapped around the coin in his pocket. It was cool, cooler than it had any right to be. "I didn't kill anyone," he said, and his voice sounded very small in his ears. "I don't even know how I got it. It was just... there one day. On my desk. In the change cup."

"Uh-huh." Rouskopf moved back behind the counter, but the gun stayed out. "You sure about that?"

Harold nodded, once. "I mean, there was a meeting that day, but that was about it. Angry customers on site with a lawyer. They kept me out of that one. Had me work up on the fifth floor until they left. Keeping me away from the lawyer, I guess. They tell me it got intense."

The coin dealer frowned. "Over car insurance?"

"No, no. Health insurance. I work for a health insurance company. The people in the building, there was a big argument over their coverage. Some kind of treatment for pancreatic cancer. Denied. I saw them as they came in. The guy, I guess he was the one with the cancer. He looked like a mummy. Pancreatic moves fast. But he'd violated his policy six ways from Sunday, so we had to drop the coverage. That's the way it works. Right?"

He turned to Rouskopf, a terrible flower of fear blossoming in his gut. "Wait. Is that how it works? Oh, God, don't let that be how it works."

With infinite care, Rouskopf put the gun down on the counter. He took a step back and then another. "I think I know who you killed."

"No. It's not like that. There are rules and this guy didn't follow them. If we let everyone just do what they want, they'd all be running up million dollar peach pit bills and—"

"You denied his treatment, didn't you? You made the call?"

"It's not like that!"

"Did you make the call?" Rouskopf's voice filled the room.

Harold blinked. "Yes. I found the reason we could drop him and I made the recommendation. Because that was— that is my job. Find those things. And we saved a couple of hundred thousand dollars. I got a pat on the back, and my boss told me I'd be seeing that in my bonus, and I went back to work the next day and did the same goddamn thing all over again."

"Ah," said Rouskopf. "You do know I was never going to shoot you, right?"

A nod. "Because of the nickel?"

"Because of what the nickel carries. Now get out of my shop and don't come back."

Mechanically, Harold stood, and stumbled toward the door.

"Change the sign back, would you," said Rouskopf. "And one more thing."

"Yes," said Harold, his hand on the door handle.

"Start thinking about who's gonna kill you."

Something punched Harold in the gut as he stepped out of the elevator, a hard sharp pain that came from the inside. It was serious, he was quite certain, and most probably fatal. He'd get it looked at, most likely, but then again, maybe not. Talking to Rouskopf had cleared his head, cleared his dreams. He was sleeping well now, knowing that the end was coming. The nightmares were no longer necessary.

A personal assistant looked up as he strode past her desk. "Mister Helmer is busy," she said. "You can't go in there."

Ahead of him was the heavy wooden door to Bobby Helmer's office. It was closed, but not locked; Helmer always said that his door was open.

And now was the time to test it.

"It's okay," Harold said. He waved a sheaf of papers, held tight between his fingers. "Bobby wanted to see these. I'll just drop them off with him and go."

"I'm not sure—" the receptionist started, and then Harold was past her and through the door and on his way inside.

Inside the office of the man who'd hired him.

Who'd encouraged him in his work.

Who'd told him to find the loophole that had brought the nickel to him.

Who, now that Harold thought about it, had killed him.

Helmer looked up as Harold slapped the pile of papers down on his desk. "This month's rescissions," Harold said, before his boss could get going. "I think you'll find the numbers interesting."

Helmer leaned forward, a predator stalking fresh meat. "Interesting? In a good way, I hope." He started thumbing through papers.

"I think so, yes." He turned to go. The nickel, he'd tucked securely into one of the files. He was sure Helmer would find it... eventually.

Harold was sure it wouldn't be coming back to him this time.

AH, YES. BERTRAM WIEGAND. *I do so love it when others take credit for my creations. There is safety in the falsehood. I love how the story of what happened between Bertram, the nickel, and the railroad cops continues to grow. That's not what happened at all, of course. But, telling you the truth might undo the lovely camouflage Bert has brought me. As has been noted before, those who ride the rails are not pleasant people. I am content for Bert to have his glory with my blessing— such as it is.*

— The Carver

TITHES

PETER M. BALL

1.

LAST STOP, GOULD'S ANTIQUES, up on Wickham Terrace. The three of them skulk in, trying to disappear amid the furniture and the ball gowns and rows of glass display cases. The same routine every visit: Angie slinking to the rear of the store, breathing in the scent of the ancient leather jackets; Byron down by the glass-fronted cabinet, crouched so low his coat brushes the concrete floor, peering at the flintlocks and gasmasks and colonial knives; Nate just kind of wandering around, not really looking at anything except his watch, fretting about the possibility of missing their last train home.

Nate's only there because they are a team, the three of them. Refugees from the land of misfit toys, as Byron's so fond of calling them, sharing a shitty fibro shack in a city that has no use for them. They spend their days, three against the world, the punk-girl, the Goth-boy, and whatever Byron calls himself, a witch or a warlock or just strange weird.

They come to Gould's because Byron wants to, telling stories about the occult paraphernalia auctioned to secret bidders. But Nate's never seen any magic here, never seen much of anything but antiques and junk. He's not even sure there's a difference between the two. He hates Gould's because Brisbane's supposed to be a break, one damn day in a city where their pale and black-clad existence doesn't stand-out amid the sea of tanned surfers and overweight tourists. And Gould's is the one place they go on these trips where the stern gaze of the owner makes Nathan Heaney feel like just a child playing Halloween dress-up.

The owner is an old man, squat and heavily jowled, with thinning white hair brushed back from his scalp. Despite sitting there, day after day, surrounded by the grandeur of ancient ball gowns and uniforms, he seems content with his drab cardigan and the gilded bifocals that enhance his already formidable scowl. Nate finds himself meeting the stare, caught and almost trembling, weight shifting from foot to foot.

"So," the owner says. "Just browsing?"

"No, I, uh—" Nate looks away, searching for back-up, but the others are gone. "I'd like to buy something. I mean, I've got..." He thinks about his wallet, empty except for a ten dollar note. Fingers dart into his pockets, searching for change. "I've got money."

"Right." The old man picks up a newspaper, folds it in half. The side facing upwards contains the crossword, the white boxes half-filled with messy scrawl. Nate stands there, hands plunged into pockets, face burning. He forces himself to step towards the counter, heavy boots clumping against the concrete floor. There's jewelry in the display cabinets; rings, earrings, and antique lighters. Old coins arranged on velvet displays, faces turned towards the heavens. He crouches, peering in, eyes drifting from face to face.

He stops when he spots the nickel. It's small; an interloper among the disused halfpennies, shillings, and sixpences. Nothing antique about it, just an American coin with a skull carved into the face. It's the details that catch Nate's eye, the silver metal buffed until each jut of bone and hollow socket is visible. The old man still sits on his stool, scribbling words onto his paper.

Nate can't say why he wants the coin, why he does what he does, but he leans forward, hands pressed to the glass, and feels the door slide sideways beneath his fingertips. He lets go, breath hissing as he inhales, fingers thrown back. Feels the world slide into freeze frame as he hovers there, waiting for someone to notice the cabinet left unlocked and open, the old man showing too little attention, the skinny little Goth-boy crouched down and waiting to see what happens next.

Nate exhales, fingers back against the glass, easing the door open millimeter by millimeter. Angie squeals, sharing some joke with Byron on the far side of the store, and the old man glances up, once, in irritation, before going back to his crosswords. Nate's fingers tremble as he slides the glass pane back, creating a space wide enough to fit three fingers.

For a moment he hesitates. In their trio, their little team, it's never been him that's done the stealing. Angie walks off with candy bars. Byron is more ambitious. Nate is always the nervous one, too distracted, too fretful of the consequences.

And yet Nate sees the nickel sitting there — the grinning skull sitting side-by-side with the faces of dead queens and kings — and calmly slips a hand inside the cabinet, claiming it. It's cold and small against his palm as he nudges the glass closed, eases his way back. He tries to remember Byron's lessons: stay calm; don't rush things; wait for a distraction.

Then Angie squeals again, and there's a crash as a rack of dresses give way, and Nate slips out of Gould's while the old man shuffles off to investigate. He waits outside, pulse hammering in his ears, until the exhilaration of the theft wears off.

Hours later, on the train home, the steady click-clack of the wheels lulling them into sleepiness, back to the Gold Coast where there's no place for things like flintlocks or ball gowns or antiques. Brisbane aspires to be a city, to house things that are laden with the burden of history, but the Gold Coast is beaches, tanning salons, and tourists by the hundreds. It measures its history by minutes instead of years. Nate gets out the coin and stares, puzzled by his desire to steal the damn thing. The skull seems less distinct in the murky light of the train carriage, the nickel oddly unpleasant to hold now that it's been warmed. He holds it and the shadows in the carriage grow longer, deeper, and a little darker than they were before.

The others don't seem to notice. Not right away. Byron is staring at the window, watching his own reflection. Angie's asleep, the shaved half of her head resting on Byron's skinny shoulder, the half left to grow long hanging like a purple veil over her face. Nate knows better than to trust Angie when her eyes are closed. Sometimes it means Angie's sleeping, sometimes it does not. He can't tell which until he begins to ease the coin back into his pocket and Angie's eyes flick open, wide and eager, grinning as if she's caught him doing something illicit.

"What's that?" she says.

"Something I picked up." Nate hesitates, coin in hand, then opens his fingers to show her. "I think it's an American nickel."

Byron shrugs Angie free of his shoulder and leans forward. "Where in hell do you pick up a nickel in the middle of Brisbane?"

Nate closes his fist around the coin. "Gould's."

Angie's eyebrows rise. Bryon snorts. "No way. No way did you rip that place off."

"Cabinet was open." Nate closes his other hand around his fist, working his thumb back and forth along the knuckles. "You and Angie caught his attention for a minute."

Angie clicks her fingers, opens her palm to accept the coin. Reluctantly, Nate gives it up.

Byron whistles. "Jesus," he says, voice muted in respect, "you did."

"I figured they wouldn't really miss it."

"Jesus." Byron glances at the coin, shakes his head. "Cabinet full of antique shit, and you steal a five cent piece?

"Maybe it's magic." Nate's grin is wolfish, eager to embarrass Byron with his own bullshit.

It doesn't work. "They don't keep that stuff on display." Byron crosses his arms, tattooed wrist peeking free of his sleeves. "You should have grabbed something cooler. Something we could sell."

"Sell where?" Nate says. "Who buys this shit back home?" He sits there, watching Angie examine the nickel, unable to take his eyes off it. Byron looks out the window again, face set into a scowl.

"I don't think I like it." Angie prods the coin on her palm, her face sour. "It's cool an all, with the skull, but...."

"But?" Nate tilts is head, watching her.

"But it's weird." Angie rubs the coin between her fingers, frowning at the way it feels.

"So I'll keep it in my room." Nate reaches out, plucks the coin from her fingers. Secures it in his pocket and glares, daring both of them to say a damn thing. "Neither of you need to see it again."

2.

I hate this place, Nate thinks and takes another hit of the joint Bryon rolled for them; a little something to get them through the afternoon heat and the oppressive humidity of summer. The three of them gathered on the back steps of the house, clustered there with the joint and bottled water, watching the breeze catch the hills-hoist clothesline and the unwashed grass. Nate is dressed up in his black shirt and jeans. Byron perched, stork-like, on the step above him. Angie pressed against his knees, taking a hit on the joint, the long hair on the left side of her scalp died pink in the three weeks since Brisbane.

Nothing ever happens here, not down on the Gold Coast. Nothing but summer and rain and the heat that turns their fibro rental slick and humid as a sauna. The neighbor's cat climbs over the fence, a flash of grey fur disappearing into the long grass, its presence only heard because of the jaunty, tinkling bell on the collar. Nate stares at the grass, at the shadows, looking for the creature, but all he sees is their overgrown yard and the weeds growing in the shadow fence line… a shadow the cat seems too cautious to go near. Not that Nate blames the feline, not since he started carrying the coin. There's something about dark places — hallways, ditches, the leeward side of buildings — something about their presence that leaves him uneasy.

"Jesus," Byron says, "I'll almost be glad when uni starts again. At least the classes have air-conditioning."

Angie nods, breathing against the joint, the same agreement they've made every time one of them makes that complaint. Nate grunts, bored with the exchange, digs through his pocket in search of the nickel, sorting through the shrapnel of unspent coins until his fingers find the one that feels as warm and dank as a mangrove floor. He doesn't pull it out, just runs his fingers across the surface, tracing the skull. A bad habit that's formed in the last few weeks, ever since he made off with coin to begin with.

"We should go to the movies," Angie says, reeling off another plan for the sake of filling the empty spaces in their conversation. "Go see something stupid and get out of the heat."

And again there's agreement, silent and universal. But they're all broke: too broke to go out, too broke for anything but smoking their last joint. *Jesus*, Nate thinks and he slips the coin out of his pocket without really meaning it. Just pulls it out and holds it in his left fist.

"Hey," Angie says, "what the hell's that?"

They follow her finger, eyes searching the fence-line for God knows what.

"What's what?" Byron says, standing to get a better look. His eyes are bloodshot and his shirt hangs open.

"Next to the second missing slat," Angie says, "down by the clump of dandelions."

Nate sees it: a twitch of movement in the overgrown weeds, a flicker of darkness. He tightens his grip on the nickel and the movement stops, the thing in the shadows halting. But now they can all sense its presence. Sense, but not see, like the shadows themselves are a living thing, hunkering in the overgrown grass. Something that watches, its presence tangible and everyone's struck by this feeling that's cold and terrible and empty as a lost soul. Angie, at least, starts shaking.

"Let's go inside," Nate says, and he knows Byron is nodding. Byron who's already standing but not willing to look away. Then the darkness, the emptiness they're looking at without really seeing, congeals and spreads through the overgrown weeds, creeping forward like a rising tide, until Nate finally panics and pockets the coin, letting it drop down amid the twenty and fifty cent pieces. The panic that gripped them melts, all of them breathing and slow to move.

"Jesus." Angie's still shaking, wild eyes going from the fence to Nate. She edges towards the house, clutching at the old stair rail. "Nate, that was you. What the hell did you do?"

"Nothing." Nate reaches for the dropped joint, rescuing it from the rotting step.

"Bull," Angie says. "Get out your nickel again."

"I don't got it on me," Nate lies.

"You've got it." Byron's voice still shaky. "You've always got it."

Nate turns to Byron, stares him down. "So what?"

"So it's doing something," Angie says. "It made that thing come, it made it go away."

"Like magic?" There's nothing friendly in the way he says it.

"Yeah." Angie's voice is very small. "Yeah, just like magic."

"Jesus, Angie, you're fucking stoned."

"She's not," Byron says. "No more than you and I are."

"It's just a damn coin."

Angie glares. "You saying you didn't see that?"

"No," Nate screws his eyes shut, holding back the irritation. He takes a deep breath before meeting Angie's gaze. "I'm saying—"

"Fuck you," Angie runs her hand across the stubbled half of her scalp, fingertips teasing the side left long. "Fuck you, Nate, for trying to make me feel crazy about this. Fuck you very much."

She stands and retreats, preferring the sweat-box heat of their house than sharing the steps with him. Nate watches her go with his mouth clamped shut, fighting the urge to shout that he's sorry, to give in just like he always does whenever Angie doesn't get her way. Byron waits, shakes his head, then disappears to comfort her, leaving Nate out there alone with his joint, the brewing storm, and the nickel he doesn't dare touch.

They spend four days avoiding one another, facing a silent detente. Nate finds himself touching the nickel without noticing, feeling the same cold terror. He tries to leave the coin alone and discovers that he can't, that he'll absently pick it up and fondle it until he feels something watching from the shadows and lets go. He smokes endless cigarettes to cover his nerves, prowling the house like a caged beast.

"This isn't fair," Nate argues, cornering Byron in the kitchen. "She can't expect me to take her seriously, right?"

Byron doesn't turn away from the counter, attention focused on spooning instant into a chipped and dirty coffee mug. "She's scared, Nate. Something weird happened. Has been since you got the nickel."

"That doesn't mean it's magic."

"We both saw something."

"We all saw something," Nate says. "I don't think the nickel's the cause. It's, I don't know, an illusion or something. A natural phenomena. A coincidence."

"That's three things." Byron's voice is steady and even. He picks up the kettle and pours, stirs gently. He drinks while staring out the kitchen window, watching the fence and the long grass. "So how do you really explain what happened?"

"I don't," Nate says. "Not in this house. Shit, the amount of—"

"Nate."

It cuts him off mid-rant. His name said softly with gentle calm. Byron slowly turning to look at him, dark eyes open and wary. "Nate," he says, "what's up? Why's it so important that this have nothing to do with the coin?"

"'Cause it doesn't," Nate says. "It's just some bloody metal."

"Maybe," Byron says, "but it's more than that to Ang. It's more than that to me. I think you know that as well. It's doing something weird, Nate, and it worries us both. What we saw, it wasn't normal."

"We didn't actually see anything," Nate says.

"I know people," Byron persists. "People who'll take it off our hands."

Nate clenches his fists and stares Byron down, forces the taller man to look away.

"All that shit you used to tell us about Gould's selling magic shit, that was just talk. None of us took you seriously. You know that, right?"

"I know people," Byron repeats, but Nate isn't listening. He charges out of the kitchen, disappearing into his room where he knows he can hide.

Later, hours later, Nate walks up to Angie's door. He says her name, not shouting it, but forcefully, says he just wants to talk, and eventually she opens up, standing there in the doorway of her cluttered, clothes-filled room, looking at him with wounded eyes.

"Well?" she says, hands on hips, her jaw set and ready in case he decides to be an arsehole.

"I'm sorry," Nate says. "I'm really sorry. I didn't meant to imply you were, you know…"

"You saw it, Nate. You felt whatever was out there."

"I saw something." Nate leans against the mould-covered wall and wishes it wasn't so damn hot in the house. "But I don't think it's the coin, Ang. I have it out all the time, Ang, and…"

"And what?" Angie reaches for the door, one hand on the brass knob.

"And nothing," Nate lies, trying not to think about the sensation of eyes upon him, the nightmares he has every night. "Nothing happens with the shadows. It's just a coin, yeah? A little freaky lookin', kinda cool, but just a coin."

For a moment he thinks she buys it, 'cause she doesn't slam the door. Lies have always been Nate's talent, the thing he brings to the house. Angie leads, Byron does, Nate creates the half-truths that allow them to stay friends.

"Show me," Angie says. "Get the coin out and show me nothing happens."

For a moment Nate hesitates, 'cause he can feel the coin in his pocket, warm and getting warmer like it anticipates coming out. His instincts tell him not to do it, that the lie is surely over once she sees that the shadows are omnipresent, that Nate has seen them time and again since he acquired the coin and given them too little notice.

But he reaches into his pocket and produces the nickel, opens his fingers to display it to the world. The shadows in Angie's room start to congeal, faster and thicker than they were in the daylight, far quicker than the dim fluorescent bulb can truly slow down.

"Fuck, Nate," Angie says, voice soft with fear. "Fuck just put it away, okay?"

Nate tries to close his fingers, tries to conceal the coin once more and return it to hiding. But his fingers won't cooperate and the shadows start reaching forward, stretching like the wings of some great bird trying to envelop Angie. She tries to run but Nate is in the way, blocking the easy path out. The shadows grab her, envelop her, bulging and swelling as she struggles. He can hear Angie screaming, but the scream is very distant, like she's in another house instead of an arms-length away.

Through it all Nate can't close his fingers, can't lock the coin away in a tight fist until the screaming is even fainter, so faint it's almost lost and gone within the swirling darkness.

Then Byron arrives, following Nate's own screams, and Byron's strong fingers work against Nate's hand, forcing him to drop the nickel against the hardwood floor.

"What happened?" Byron shouts. "Nate, where's Angie?"

Nate points to the centre of Angie's room, where the shadows are thinning and retreating to their usual place, where Angie lies amid the puddle of her dirty clothes, cold and pale and barely breathing— like something almost dead, waiting for its funeral shroud.

Angie lies in the hospital bed, all wires and tubes and pale skin. The room beeps, beeps, beeps, constantly beeping and hissing, reminding you that the machines are doing part of the work that keeps Angie breathing. Nate hates this place. Sand-colored walls, sand-colored curtains; another fucking permeation on the endless beige the Gold Coast embraces.

"Hey," Nate says. "Hey."

He's holding the nickel, has it coiled tight in his fist, thumb tracing the ridges cut into the side. He wants to give it to her, to tuck it into her hand for luck, to do whatever magic it can to help her out. But the coin is moist, unpleasant to hold, and he knows in his gut it'll just make things worse. He reaches out with his other hand, places it over Angie's still fingers. She's smaller here, in the hospital, but Nate is ready for that. Hospital's reduce people, shrink them away to nothing.

"Hey," he says, "just, don't die, okay? Hold on a bit. Hold on. Byron's got a plan."

He leans forward and kisses her forehead, just in case it helps. It doesn't. Angie keeps on sleeping, keeps on breathing and beeping and hissing away. He can feel something watching her sleep: the same empty feeling he had in the yard. Nate keeps the nickel clenched in his fist as he exits, finds Byron in the hall with a cigarette in hand, unlit but nervously fiddling with it, giving the nurses cautious looks.

Byron looks up, stares at Nate with glistening eyes, fighting back tears. "We're getting rid of your fucking coin," he says, high forehead covered in a sheen of sweat.

Nate bites his bottom lip and tightens his grip. "It's just a coin," he says. Damned if he knows why. It's just another untruth he can't help himself speaking.

"That's bullshit, and you know it," Byron says. "I'm making the fucking call."

And he disappears down the hallway, cigarette still in hand, making his way to the bank of payphones only pensioners and dero's ever end up using. Nate stands there, watching him go, unwilling to open his hand. He's afraid that letting go will free the thing that watches him, let it retreat back into the room, and savage the sleeping Angie. He's afraid that maybe what Byron's saying is true, and that everything that's happened is all his fault.

3.

Byron lines up a meeting for three in the morning, drags Nate down to the lot out front of the local shopping centre. Australia Fair is close to water, like everything on the Coast, nestled next to the highway that runs down the beach-front. Beyond that is the estuary where river meets ocean. It's the dodgy end of the Coast, home to junkies, students, and the mentally ill. The parks on the far side of the highway are a camping ground for the homeless.

Nate stands there, waiting, nickel in his pocket, wondering if someone is really going to show, if Byron is really serious when he says *he knows people*, and why they have to meet in the middle of the fucking night. "You sure about this?" he asks, not for the first time, and Byron's frown is all the answer Nate needs: angry and nervous at the same time.

"I've been thinking," Byron says, "about you and the coin. About how you ended up with it, up at Gould's. I think they let you steal it. I think they wanted it gone."

"Maybe," Nate says, because he doesn't want to agree, because he still wants to pretend that the there's nothing wrong. "You never said who we're meeting out here or why they'd want to take the coin."

"This guy's a friend of a friend." Byron searches his jacket for a cigarette, casting furtive glances down the street. It's dark there, in the shadow of the shopping centre, and the soft tick of the streetlights seem loud and alien in silence. "Not someone I know, but he's probably, you know…"

"Dangerous?"

"Maybe. Definitely not above board. Definitely not white magic."

"Definitely?" A voice asks and they realize too late that they aren't alone. The figure that walks down the car park ramp is one of the biggest men Nate's ever seen. Six-five, broad-shouldered, head shaved down to grey stubble. His dark suit blends seamlessly into the gloom of the night and there's a short, stubby weapon in his right hand. Not a gun, not quite, but its shape is close enough. "So," the big man says, "which one of you has the coin?"

"That depends," Byron says. "You Sabbath?"

The big man snorts. "Sabbath doesn't make house calls, mate. He sends me."

Byron hesitates, chewing over the information. Nate's eyes twitch back and forth between the stranger's weapon and the cheerful grin. He makes the circuit three times before Byron digs deep, finds the courage to say, "You got a name?"

"Randal." It doesn't suit him. There's a feral, misshapen beauty to the big man's face, a predator's grin and an unsettling fire in the eyes. Nate's putting some thought into running, but Byron isn't ready to leave. Nate watches his friend adopt a grin, stepping forward to meet their visitor.

"I'm Byron. He's—"

The big man, Randal, fires and two darts thump into Byron's chest. He falls to the ground, twitching, the steady click of electric current breaking the silence.

Nate backs away. "What the hell?"

213

"Taser," Randal says. "You've got the coin. You make the decisions. I didn't want this munter getting in your head."

"The coin—"

"The nickel." Randal makes a tiny O with his thumb and forefinger. "Little thing, skull, ugly as sin. You do have it, right? I'd hate to reload and go through this again."

"I've got it," Nate says, hand dropping to his pocket. As he does it Randal darts forward, strong fingers wrapping around Nate's wrist, pulling it up and away and around, locking it up behind Nate's back where it hurts.

"None of that, mate," Randal offers up the threat casually, confident it'll be obeyed. "No touching it, not out here. Trust me, it's better for all concerned. You got that?"

Nate nods.

"I want it said aloud, mate."

"I've got it," Nate says. "No touching the coin."

Randal lets him go. Nate stumbles forward and ends up on his knees on the concrete sidewalk. "I don't get it," Nate says. "It's just some weird-ass nickel."

"Lots of weird things in this world. This one's a long way from home." Randal produces a cigarette and lights it, flame blossoming without any lighter that Nate can see. "Can't say we're fond of it, me and Mister Sabbath. Too bloody disruptive, you know?"

Bryon stirs, coughing, whimpering like an injured animal. Randal takes a short step, builds momentum for a kick that catches Byron in the teeth. Nate flinches, looks away.

"That's—" Randal turns and the words die in Nate's throat, stick there until he coughs them free and forces himself to speak. "That's not exactly going to convince me to … you know … deal."

Randal smiles, transferring his cigarette to his left hand. "Look at the stones on you," he says. "Good for you, kid. Good for you." He buries a punch in Nate's stomach, folding Nate over in one smooth movement. "Now stop being a fucking idiot, yeah? I'm not here to deal with you. That coin, it's all kinds of bad news. One curse if it's stolen, another if it's given away. More effort than I'm willing to put in, mate, all things considered."

Nate coughs, splutters, forces himself to breathe. "Then… what…?"

"What do I want?" Randal lifts the cigarette to his lips, breathes with casual ease. "I want you to give it back to the original owners. You want rid of it, they want it back. Seems easy enough, yeah?"

No, Nate thinks, *not easy at all,* but what comes out of his mouth is a small, reluctant, "Yeah, I guess."

"Good call." Randal heads across the highway with long and easy strides that carry him away from Nate and the sucking, unpleasant sound of Byron trying to breathe through his wrecked lips and teeth. Nate hesitates, just a moment, hand hovering over his pocket, but Randal calls out and he finds himself moving, jogging across the empty highway in an effort to catch up. He follows the big man down to the riverside park, along the pebble paths no one but the homeless use regularly.

"Whatever you do," Randal's, voice floats back through the darkness, "don't throw a ciggy into the water. Damn shit'll go up in flames if you give it half a chance."

Nate's already wheezing with the effort of keeping pace, staying close enough to see the vague shape of Randal's silhouette in the shadowy night. He can barely think of smoking, think of anything but the coin, the big man leading him into the darkness, and the prickly points of fear digging their tines into his intestinal tract. He's so focused on it all that it catches him by surprise when Randal stops, settling down on his heels, and lights a small candle.

"We're here." Randal nods towards the path, the thickly-packed pebbles leaving the shoreline and winding towards the underpass that runs beneath the highway, a convenience no-one bothers to use.

There were stories about the tunnel, local tales about rape and murder and worse, stories that may be bullshit for all Nate really knows. But standing there, next to Randal, with the flickering candle lighting up the concrete mouth and the urine scent in the air, he can't help but acknowledge that there's something wrong, some aspect of the tunnel mouth and the darkness that seems too thick to be real, obscuring the far end just two hundred meters away where Nate knows, instinctively, he should be seeing the light of a streetlight.

Randal kneels down, sets the candle on a patch of grass, using his body to shield it from the wind. Nate stands by, arms slack at his side, legs hollowed out with a fear he can no longer explain. He takes two uncertain steps, stands at Randal's elbow. The big man smells of cigarette smoke and cologne and, very faintly, of a mixture of sugar and sulfur.

"This here," Randal says, "it's very do-not-try-this-at-home, yeah? One of those things that's going to happen. You're going wake up tomorrow, your sheila'll be on the mend, and you're going to pretend like none of this happened. You understand what I'm saying, mate?"

Nate offers him a mute nod.

"Out loud," Randal says.

"Yes."

"So here's what you're going to do." Randal points. "Get up there, close to the tunnel as you can, and leave the coin on the fuckin' ground. Once that's done, you're done. You get out of here before anything else can happen, right?"

Another mute nod, this one met with a stare, and it takes Nate a few seconds to realize he should be moving instead of saying yes. He takes a few uncertain steps up towards the tunnel mouth, leading the way with the fist holding the nickel tight. He blinks uncertainly, trying to get his vision to adjust, to penetrate the darkness of the tunnel. There are meant to be lights in the tunnel, a few inches of moonlight at least. But there is something impenetrable about the wall of black he's facing. No matter how his pupils adjust there's no peering through it.

"In and out, kid," Randal says, voice pitched low so only Nate can hear. "Don't fuck around."

Nate nods and takes a few more steps forward, but that's as far as he gets before he does see something: a kind of thickening in the darkness. Frost-touched air flows out of the tunnel like an exhalation and the sudden bite of it makes Nate open his hand, the nickel dropping and bouncing on the pebble path, rolling towards the tunnel mouth.

For a moment Nate watches it go, mutely trying to process what just happened, then he kneels and reaches forward, dimly aware of Randal shouting *something, something* he can't make out.

As he reaches, fingers stretching, the darkness in the tunnel congeals into a long and twisting tendril that slides across the ground and curves around the coin. Nate is still kneeling there, still leaning forward, frozen with a fear he can't quite explain. He can't make himself move when a second tendril congeals and slides across the path towards him, advancing with the same sinuous slither Nate associates with snakes.

"Hey." Randal is suddenly there, grabbing Nate by the shoulder, and hoisting him to his feet. "None of that, mate. Mister Sabbath made you a deal, got you back your coin. Leave the poor bastard alone, yeah? He's only the messenger."

For a moment Nate thinks he sees the tendril hesitate, poised in front of the big man, who shows no interest in giving ground, no interest in anything but staring down whatever it is that exists in the shadows of the tunnel.

And Nate, he sees the nickel going, sees it being dragged into the shadow. The part of him that doesn't want to let it go makes one last desperate dive and reaches for it, crossing the tunnel's threshold, plunging into the shadow beyond.

For a moment, the moment before he starts screaming, Nate marvels that what he feels creeping up his wrist isn't cold, not for all the ways it bites and numbs and chills him down to the marrow. No, not cold at all. But it's the only word he has for it; this feeling that's more like an absence. That's all he can really think before the pain becomes too much and he really starts to scream.

Later, when he comes to, Randal is standing over him, cigarette in hand. Nate blinks and stares at the shaved scalp, the little point of orange light that is the burning cherry. Randal leans down, forces one of Nate's eyelids open, waves the cigarette back and forth. "You'll do," he says. "Better get up."

Nate doesn't want to obey, but he does it anyway, levers himself into a seating position. They're back in the car-park, in the shadow of the shopping centre. Nate's hand is strapped to his chest with strips of white fabric. Bryon's leaning against the fence, shirt missing, hands pressed to his nose. There's blood splattered down his pale, skinny chest, and he doesn't look in Nate's direction.

"Just so you know," Randal says, "you truly are a stupid fucker."

He offers Nate a hand, hauls him to his feet with casual ease. "Really should have let the coin go, mate. It would have cost you a little less."

Nate stands there, nodding, taking it all in. He tries moving his fingers on the bandaged hand, fails completely. "I can't feel anything," he says. "My fingers. My hand. Nothing."

Randal exhales, drops his cigarette on the concrete. "Like I said, mate, stupid. Get your friend, go to a hospital, let the doctor's take a look at it. Get used to spending the rest of your life doing things with the other hand."

Nate opens his mouth to say something, then shuts it when he sees the look in Randal's eye. There is something burning there, something Nate can't quite place, but it scares him. Scares him almost as much as the darkness in the tunnel, the unseen thing that came for the coin.

"So, all this?" Randal gestures between them. "Never happened, yeah? Mister Sabbath isn't going to hear from you, or that dipshit, ever fucking again. Whatever happened down there, it was just a bad dream. Agreed?"

Nate says nothing. Randal steps forward. Steps and looms, a big man with the ability to inflict harm, and part of Nate wonders that he can still be afraid of that, still get that quickening of the pulse when he sees Randal's fingers bunch into a fist.

"Agreed," Nate says. "Just a bad dream."

Randal nods, once. "Good call. Now fuck off, mate. Call in on your girl. See if she's doing better now the bad voodoo's gone back home where it belongs."

Nate looks at him, stares at the eyes with the glimmer of red light in their pupils. "And she'll be okay, right? Angie, she'll be okay."

"Sure, kid, she'll be fine," Randal pulls out the pack of cigarettes, taps a new one free, and plants it in his mouth. He holds Nate's stare the entire way, as if daring him to call the bluff. "We're done?"

Nate nods, once. "We're done."

He turns and walks, leaving Randal and Bryon both, walking into the night that smells of saltwater and petrol fumes and the faint scent of brimstone. As he makes his way along the block, heading for the mall and the streets beyond, the path that'll lead him to the hospital, Nate's careful to move from streetlight to streetlight, spending as little time as possible walking through the dark.

He hears Randal laugh, a soft and gentle sound that's almost filled with respect, and soon, very soon, Bryon realizes he's left there, alone with the big man whose done nothing but hurt him. Nate hears his friend calling out his name out, again and again, as Bryon runs down the path.

Nate keeps walking, moving forward, sticking to the light.

NATE WAS ONE OF THE LUCKY ones. I mean that sincerely. This is another one of my coins that has surpassed my not-insignificant power. Even I don't know what ancient otherworldly thing has claimed it. I still reap the benefits of the shadows demanding their due but it leaves me cold, knowing that something so much older than I can link to me if it chooses. Fortunately, I am nothing in its eyes and I will keep it that way. Nate walked away with his life but without his hand. It is better than what happened to the girl. She lived but… let's just say she taught me why I want to remain hidden from the thing that has claimed my coin.

—*The Carver*

With One Coin for Fee: An Invocation of Sorts

GARY A. BRAUNBECK

"Crossing alone the nighted ferry
"With one coin for fee,
"Whom, on the wharf of Lethe waiting,
"Count you to find? Not me."
— A.E. Housman

ODD, HOW THE TOWERING figures of youth become peripheral shadows, growing less substantial in the memory, faces fading like an old photograph exposed too long to direct sunlight, while the idea of your own mortality emerges as less of an abstract concept composed of blurry characteristics and more of a sentient figure with definite form and recognizable features and an all-too-clear intent in the eyes. In one of its hands, this figure is rubbing something between thumb and forefinger, something small and round that glints when the sunlight catches its edge. The figure kneels down, extends its hand, and with a sharp flick of the thumb, does not so much toss as *fire* the small object outward, like a stone from a slingshot. It hits the street with a *ping!* and rolls forward, in a straight unwavering line, a zipper closing, a fault line cracking, its path underscored by a thin, almost musical rattling as it rolls nearer.

It is a coin, an old Indian-head nickel that someone has altered, carving or rubbing away at the engraved face until all that remains of its features are the death's-head skull underneath. Looking closer, we can see that there's a date, 191—. The last numeral has been worn away, perhaps by the figure's fingers as it rubbed against it, before stepping out of the realm of abstract concept and into the callous light of actuality and announcing that more of life is behind us than ahead.

Still, the coin rolls along, its almost-lighthearted musical rattling growing louder. We lean in for a closer look, eyes wide because it's moving rather quickly now — this street goes downhill, you know — and can see that there is something caked on the death's-head features, just below the jaw. Does it look like blood to you? Perhaps, or reddish clay, or a sun-baked fleck of mud. Still, we feel a soft whisper of — what? — dread? Dark anticipation? At the very least, anxiety.

But this is silly, isn't it? After all it's just an old coin, a hobo nickel it's called, isn't it? Just a coin, with no consciousness, no goal, devoid of intent good or ill. I know this, you know it, we know it. It's just a coin, rolling along, and maybe it does have a bit of caked blood on it, but that's not any sort of portent. It can't be a harbinger, a messenger of sorts, a form of fair warning, because in order to be any of those things, it would have to possess sentience, a sense of Self, and inanimate objects don't have these capabilities. For a moment, we feel slightly ridiculous for having ascribed such characteristics to the damned thing.

Still, there is that lingering, almost teasing, sense of unease. The sixteenth century German miners who first discovered the ore that looked like copper but yielded none when treated, they believed that the substance had been tainted when a sprite or demon entered the copper and, through some unholy alchemy, transformed it into this useless material. So they called it *kupfernickel*, "copper nickel," in which *nickel* was the Teutonic word for "demon." Superstitious fools. How could a simple ore be a demon, something with will, with purpose, its dark intent melted down and shaped into a piece of change one sees lying on the sidewalk? Impossible. Even after Axel F. Cronstedt figured out how to isolate the metal from it in 1751, are we to believe that the demon, the *nickel*, still existed within the chemical composition of the element. Of course not.

221

It's just a coin, rolling along, with no demonic purpose. Yes, there is that dried bit of blood — we're now certain that it was blood — on the thing, but there is undoubtedly an explanation for that; someone picked it up after pricking their finger; perhaps another person, whomever came into possession of it afterward, perhaps this person had a slightly bloody nose caused by allergies, and as they dug into their pocket to hand over some spare change to a beggar a few drops slipped from their nasal cavity and spattered against the surface. The beggar who took it wouldn't mind. What's a little blood when it brings you closer to having enough for a meal, or a bottle, a pill, some powder, or even a syringe?

Blood is neither blessing nor curse; it's just something dried to the surface of the coin, any coin, *this* coin that we watch as it rolls away, possessing no consciousness, no thoughts, no direction, soul, motivation, or focused intent. That would mean that there is some form of First Cause that directs its journey, some remnant of early Determinism that keeps it rolling along the straight and narrow, musically rattling toward something predestined, something planned, some inevitability that the coin, if it had consciousness, would already know but never reveal, its own little secret. Ridiculous, just like the German miners who believed that the *kupfernickel* was something demonic.

If that were true, does that mean the coin is destructive? Of course not. *Pshaw.* Don't be daft.

We step out into the street and chase after the coin. We manage to get to it before it reaches the downhill incline and we snatch it up before it gets away. We feel a mild tingling sensation between thumb and forefinger. And we know.

This coin has witnessed death, it has witnessed pain, murder, rape, disease, starvation, even genocide. Witnessed, but not *caused*.

But to witness, there must be some form of cognition, of lucidity, and an object such as this coin cannot hold such things in its mind and soul, for it has neither. That's right. Isn't it?

We turn around, stepping forward with deliberation, becoming less of an abstract concept composed of blurry characteristics and more of a sentient figure with definite form and recognizable features and an all-too-clear intent in our eyes. We rub the coin between thumb and forefinger, feeling the twinge of mild pain as we realize that, somehow, we've cut ourselves. We are smearing our blood over the face on the coin, but just as quickly as the blood spatters, it is gone, absorbed, disappeared. Except for a small speck that is caked just below the death's-head jaw. Looking up from the coin, we see another figure standing several yards down, standing by the curb, watching us as if we are some apparition, carrying auguries, whispering about the chaos of mortality, of intent, of demons in the ore.

Kneeling down, we extend our hand, and with a sharp flick of the thumb do not so much toss as *fire* the small object outward, like a stone from a slingshot. It hits the street with a *ping!* and rolls forward. The other figure leans in to stare at the coin as it rolls near. *It's just a coin*, we want to say but don't. *It has no purpose, no consciousness, no specificity of intent.*

After all, it's just an object, rolling along, with no purpose or meaning except that which we attribute to it.

Still, we hope that this other figure is careful when it chases after the coin. Its edges are sharp, like a demon's tooth. A person could cut a finger on something like that.

 OH, THIS ONE WAS SO CLOSE but so far. He knew enough not to get caught. His blood was sweet, hot, and full of knowledge. It is the ones that get away that we clamor for most, is it not?

—*The Carver*

THESE COINS OF CHAOS, SUCH *things of beauty, have surpassed my wildest expectations. I've come to learn that despite my arcane knowledge, what I have set loose on the world has grown in ways I cannot understand. At least one coin has traveled outside this mortal plane of existence and another has been claimed as a relic for a creature that even I cannot identify.*

My children surpass me. They outgrow me. They gather, collect, hoard power I cannot fathom. While each one has made me more powerful, each one has gained a life of its own and become more than a piece of the ritual I cast.

I cannot help but be proud, even awed, by my creation.

Still, I wonder what more these coins can do, where they will go, and how they will change. Already I have lived past my natural lifespan and seen wonders I could not imagine in my mortal days. I enjoy every moment of my stolen life. I will continue to do so.

And yet... and yet, I cannot help but think that, one day, this thing I have wrought will turn on even me. Perhaps it is my paranoia speaking. Perhaps it is only my experience. I have already lived long enough to know that things circle back on themselves.

I suppose I will need to remain wary. And to plot a new magic to protect myself. I have plenty of time to do both. Until then, I will savor the tales my coins tell.

— The Carver

ACKNOWLEDGEMENTS

NO PROJECT IS EVER COMPLETED in a vacuum. A number of people helped make this anthology the wonderful book it is today. I want to thank Amber Clark for her lovely cover photo and for amusing me with its unofficial title: "How does the nickel cross the road? In a river of blood of course!" And to thank John Ward for his ability to make such similar art pieces look so different. A huge thanks to Marc Ciccarone, my editorial intern, who took direction well and was a joy to work with. Of course, thank you to Brian Hades for seeing the potential in my anthology about a piece of obscure Depression Era art. Finally, a huge thank you to my husband, Jeff, who always listens to my "what if" rambles.

This book is dedicated to those who make art in all its myriad of forms.

—Jennifer Brozak

CONTRIBUTORS

Jennifer Brozek is an award winning editor and author. Winner of the 2009 Australian Shadows Award for best edited publication, Jennifer has edited nine anthologies with more on the way. Author of *In a Gilded Light, The Lady of Seeking in the City of Waiting*, and *Industry Talk: An Insider's Look at Writing RPGs and Editing Anthologies*, she has more than forty-five published short stories, and is the Creative Director of Apocalypse Ink Productions.

Jennifer also is a freelance author for numerous RPG companies. Winner of both the Origins and the ENnie award, her contributions to RPG sourcebooks include *Dragonlance, Colonial Gothic, Shadowrun, Serenity, Savage Worlds*, and White Wolf SAS. Jennifer is also the author of the long running *Battletech* webseries, *The Nellus Academy Incident*.

When she is not writing her heart out, she is gallivanting around the Pacific Northwest in its wonderfully mercurial weather. Jennifer is an active member of SFWA and HWA.

Jason Andrew lives in Seattle, Washington with his wife Lisa. His short fiction has appeared in markets such as *Shine: An Anthology of Optimistic SF, In Situ*, and *Dark Tales of Lost Civilizations*. In 2011, Jason received an honorable mention in Ellen Datlow's List for Best Horror of the Year for his story "Moonlight in Scarlet"."The Value of a Year's Worth of Tears and Sorrow" was inspired during a morning commute through downtown Seattle when the author speculated that there was a hidden city just beneath the surface that he would never know. This story includes a number of interesting local legends such as the Wishing Chair, the Saints, and the Seattle Underground.

Peter M. Ball is a writer from Brisbane, Australia. By day he works as the Digital Content and Community Manager at Queensland Writers Centre, a job that saw him run the inaugural Australian GenreCon in 2012 in addition to providing support to the subscribers of *The Australian Writer's Marketplace*. His short fiction has previously been published in magazines such as *Apex*, *Shimmer*, and Strange Horizons, as well as the *Dreaming Again*, *Interfictions II*, and *Eclipse 4* anthologies. His faerie-noir novella, *Horn*, was published in 2009 by Twelfth Planet Press, and was followed by *Bleed* in 2010.

Brisbane seemed like a magical place when I was in my early twenties and trapped on the Gold Coast. They'd just built the train-line between the two cities, which meant we could sneak up there for a weekend and experience the kinds of stores, clubs, and sub-culture that the Gold Coast didn't really embrace. In many ways Brisbane has lost its luster now that I live there, but *Tithes* is a kind of love-letter to the city I used to visit and the strange things that used to follow me home.

Gary A. Braunbeck is a prolific author who writes mysteries, thrillers, science fiction, fantasy, horror, and mainstream literature. He is the author of 19 books; his fiction has been translated into Japanese, French, Italian, Russian, and German. Nearly 200 of his short stories have appeared in various publications. Some of his most popular stories are mysteries that have appeared in the *Cat Crimes* anthology series.

He was born in Newark, Ohio; this city that serves as the model for the fictitious Cedar Hill in many of his stories. The Cedar Hill stories are collected in *Graveyard People* and *Home Before Dark*. His fiction has received several awards, including the Bram Stoker Award for Superior Achievement in Short Fiction in 2003 for "Duty" and in 2005 for "We Now Pause for Station Identification"; his collection *Destinations Unknown* won a Stoker in 2006. His novella "Kiss of the Mudman" received the International Horror Guild Award for Long Fiction in 2005.

Erik Scott de Bie is a speculative fiction writer whose tastes run from the fantastic to the horrifying and everywhere in between.

He is best known for his work in the Forgotten Realms fantasy setting, where his fifth novel, *Shadowbane: Eye of Justice*, hits the stands in September 2012. His work has appeared in anthologies such as *Close Encounters of the Urban Kind, Human for a Day, Dangers Untold*, and the *When the Hero Comes Home* series. He also moonlights as a game designer for the Dungeons and Dragons and Marvel Heroic Roleplaying games. Erik resides in Seattle, where he is married, and lives with cats and a dog.

Dylan Birtolo currently resides in the great Pacific Northwest where he spends his time as a writer, a gamer, and a professional sword-swinger. His thoughts are filled with shape shifters, mythological demons, and epic battles. He has published a couple of fantasy novels and several short stories in multiple anthologies. He trains with the Seattle Knights, an acting troop that focuses on stage combat, and has performed in live shows, videos, and movies. In addition he teaches the academy for upcoming actor combatants. He has had the honor of jousting, and yes, the armor is real— it weighs over 120 pounds. The true inspiration for his story centers around a character who is only briefly seen at the beginning and end of the tale. What would happen over years as these coins continued to show up and inflict their curse? Surely some characters would become interested in them, either for malignant or honorable purposes.

Nathan Crowder has a problem with authority that likely stems from his Existentialist/librarian father and hippie mother. His discovery of punk music in the early 80s did nothing to help this. "Sins of the Flesh" has a fascinating DNA. It was inspired by a combination of his love of the Minneapolis punk music scene, the loss of the city's public space, and his belief in truth no matter the price. His fiction embraces a certain working-class aesthetic, a search for uncomfortable truths, and a love of popular culture. Nathan is primarily a horror writer, but his defiance of being pigeonholed has led him to write westerns, mysteries, urban fantasy, zombie erotica, sci-fi, and even clown noir.

His short fiction appears across numerous publications and anthologies, including *Close Encounters of the Urban Kind, Cthulhurotica, Rigor Amortis*, and *Rock 'n' Roll is Dead*. In the real world, he haunts the coffeehouses and karaoke bars of Seattle's Greenwood neighborhood.

Richard Dansky. The Central Clancy Writer for Ubisoft/Red Storm Entertainment, Richard Dansky is one of the leading videogame writers working today. An accomplished tabletop RPG designer as well, he's published five novels and writes regularly for Sleeping Hedgehog, Green Man Review, and other publications. Richard lives (and occasionally works) in North Carolina with his wife and a variable number of cats, books, and bottles of single malt scotch. His story, "Justice in Five Cents", is a twist on the traditional "cursed item" narrative, whereby the cursed item gets passed along for a very good — but not entirely obvious — reason.

Mae Empson writes short stories and poetry, often referencing fairy tales, myths, or superstitions. Of note to this story, she was an undergraduate at the University of North Carolina at Chapel Hill, where she spent a great deal of time studying music and practicing on her mother's French horn. While there, she also graduated with honors in English and in Creative Writing, and earned the Robert B. House Memorial Prize in Poetry in 1995.

She enjoyed researching hobo nickels in preparation for this anthology. The hobo nickel in this story is based on the work of a carver called "Apple Cheek" whose carvings do look a bit like Dvořák with the pop-eyes and rounded cheeks and thick beard.

Mae's fiction has also appeared on-line in *The Pedestal Magazine* and *Cabinet des Fees*, and in anthologies from Prime Books, Dagan Books, and Innsmouth Free Press. Mae is a member of the Horror Writers Association, and of HorrorPNW— the Pacific Northwest chapter of HWA.

Kelly Lagor lives in San Diego where she writes, watches old movies, and plays banjo and ukulele in a band. "Something in the Blood" is her homage to a childhood spent watching Roger Corman Poe adaptations, and wandering around the north side of her hometown, Chicago. She is a Submissions Editor at *Apex Magazine*, and a graduate of the Viable Paradise Workshop.

Jay Lake lives in Portland, Oregon, where he works on numerous writing and editing projects. His recent books include *Kalimpura* from Tor and *Love in the Time of Metal and Flesh* from Prime. His short fiction appears regularly in literary and genre markets

229

worldwide. Jay is a winner of the John W. Campbell Award for Best New Writer, and a multiple nominee for the Hugo and World Fantasy Awards.

"Spendthrift" is set in the Pacific theatre of WWII, a time and place that has long interested Jay. He was entertained by the effort in tying that setting to the concept of this anthology.

Nathaniel Lee is a writer living in North Carolina with his wife, child, and obligatory cats. He puts words in order, and sometimes people give him money for them.

"Silver and Copper, Iron and Ash" was written (almost) in a single marathon sitting. Most of that Sunday is kind of a blur to me now, though I do remember shouting a lot at the cats, who both decided that Right Now was a great time to sit on my lap and smack my keyboard. This, for me, was primarily a "striking image" story (as opposed to a deep character exploration or a nailbiter plot). The image of an ominous sleepwalker sniffing in a darkened room had occurred to me several weeks prior, and I'd jotted it down to wait for the right story. When I read the premise of the anthology, I suddenly "saw" the slumped body and "heard" the ringing of the falling coin, and I knew I'd found the place for it.

Martin Livings. Perth-based writer Martin Livings has had over seventy short stories published in a variety of magazines and anthologies, and has been nominated for the Ditmar, Auralis and Australian Shadows awards. His first novel, *Carnies*, was published by Hachette Livre in 2006, and his first short story collection, *Living With the Dead*, was published in 2012 by Dark Prints Press to celebrate twenty years since his first publication.

The events of "In His Name" are partly inspired by Pir Shaliyar, a traditional mid-winter Kurdistani festival. But corrupting that harmless event on the cold streets of post-WWII New York was entirely my own sick idea.

Seanan McGuire is the New York Times bestselling author of two urban fantasy series, and moonlights as Mira Grant, a bestselling science fiction author. Her Rose Marshall stories first appeared in the online publication *The Edge of Propinquity*, and she is delighted to be continuing Rose's adventures. When a hitchhiking ghost meets a Hobo Nickel, nothing good can come of it, and the ghostroads have never been known for mercy. Seanan lives on the West Coast with three large blue cats, a great many creepy dolls, and too many books.

Glenn Rolfe is an author from the haunted woods of New England. He has studied creative writing at Southern New Hampshire University, and continues his education in the world of horror by devouring the novels of Stephen King and Richard Laymon. He, his wife, Meghan, and their two girls currently reside in Augusta, Maine.

Andrew Penn Romine lives in Los Angeles where he works in the visual effects and animation industry. His fiction appears online at *Lightspeed* Magazine and *Crossed Genres* as well as in the Edge/ Absolute XPress anthologies *Broken Time Blues: Fantastic Tales in the Roaring 20s* and *Rigor Amortis* and in *Fungi* from Innsmouth Free Press. He has also contributed articles to *Lightspeed* Magazine and *Fantasy* Magazine. He's a graduate of the 2010 Clarion West workshop.

The desperate voice of the doomed hobo in "Vinegar Pie" coaxed Andrew into the shadows of his jungle camp one night, and he was compelled to sit down and transcribe the man's tale of woe. Many thanks are due to Andrew's wife Carol for suggesting the title and helping him bake a few vinegar pies for "research."

Kelly Swails is a web editor and writer whose work has appeared in several anthologies. When she's not writing she reads, knits, or hangs out with family and friends. There's an internet rumor that she sleeps occasionally, but that has yet to be proven. When presented with the concept for the *Coins of Chaos* anthology, her thoughts turned to death. Then she asked herself "what would be worse than losing a child?" "The Price of Serenity" provides the answer.

Brandie Tarvin. As the editor of Tied-In, the International Association of Media Tie-In Writers (IAMTW) newsletter, Brandie Tarvin has her finger on the pulse of every author who produces fiction with other people's characters. Her first published work, a short story in the *Transformers: Legends* anthology, was based on the popular toy series. Tarvin is now a regular contributor of prose material for the Shadowrun series of role playing games and related fiction. Tarvin writes for the *Blue Kingdoms* fantasy series edited by Jean Rabe and Stephen D. Sullivan and is a freelance author for Catalyst Game Labs. She is working on Latchkeys, a collaborative new YA series, is a member of the Science Fiction and Fantasy Writers Association of America (SFWA), the Horror Writer's Association (HWA), the IAMTW and attended the Viable Paradise writing workshop in 2009. She also works as Publication Coordinator at Musa Publishing's Urania imprint.